**"Look, Ms. Hamilton. If you're not will-
ing to talk to me here, you'll have to
come to the station."**

His body blocked most of the light emanating from
the porch behind him, so she stood in shadows.
Nevertheless, he noticed the auburn shade of her
hair, its soft red hue natural and sexy.

He'd note this characteristic in her profile as a witness. That was his only reason for noticing.

"Okay, I'll come to the station so you can question
me there."

The lady was full of surprises. "Fine. Make it nine
o'clock this morning."

"Fine."

"Meantime, I'll send a tech out here to take your fingerprints for comparison with the crime scene, and
then you can leave."

She stared but said nothing, and he watched as she
walked away. She turned once and glanced back at
him, and then she was gone.

Mitch realized wi... ...that the challenge of
Cara Hamilton ha... ...ore.

Right now, nine

Dear Harlequin Intrigue Reader,

Temperatures are rising this month at Harlequin Intrigue! So whether our mesmerizing men of action are steaming up their love lives or packing heat in high-stakes situations, July's lineup is guaranteed to sizzle!

Back by popular demand is the newest branch of our Confidential series. Meet the heroes of NEW ORLEANS CONFIDENTIAL—tough undercover operatives who will stop at nothing to rid the streets of a crime ring tied to the most dangerous movers and shakers in town. *USA TODAY* bestselling author Rebecca York launches the series with *Undercover Encounter*—a darkly sensual tale about a secret agent who uses every resource at his disposal to get his former flame out alive when she goes deep undercover in the sultry French Quarter.

The highly acclaimed Gayle Wilson returns to the lineup with *Sight Unseen*. In book three of PHOENIX BROTHERHOOD, it's a race against time to prevent a powerful terrorist organization from unleashing unspeakable harm. Prepare to become entangled in *Velvet Ropes* by Patricia Rosemoor—book three in CLUB UNDERCOVER— when a clandestine investigation plunges a couple into danger….

Our sassy inline continuity SHOTGUN SALLYS ends with a bang! You won't want to miss *Lawful Engagement* by Linda O. Johnston. In Cassie Miles's newest Harlequin Intrigue title—*Protecting the Innocent*—a widow trapped in a labyrinth of evil brings out the Achilles' heel in a duplicitous man of mystery.

Delores Fossen's newest thriller is not to be missed. *Veiled Intentions* arouses searing desires when two bickering cops pose as doting fiancés in their pursuit of a deranged sniper!

Enjoy our explosive lineup this month!

Denise O'Sullivan
Senior Editor, Harlequin Intrigue

LAWFUL ENGAGEMENT

LINDA O. JOHNSTON

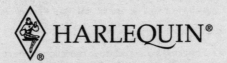

HARLEQUIN®

TORONTO • NEW YORK • LONDON
AMSTERDAM • PARIS • SYDNEY • HAMBURG
STOCKHOLM • ATHENS • TOKYO • MILAN • MADRID
PRAGUE • WARSAW • BUDAPEST • AUCKLAND

Special thanks and acknowledgment are given to Linda O. Johnston for her contribution to the SHOTGUN SALLYS series.

ISBN 0-373-22786-8

LAWFUL ENGAGEMENT

ABOUT THE AUTHOR

Linda O. Johnston's first published fiction appeared in *Ellery Queen's Mystery Magazine* and won the Robert L. Fish Memorial Award for Best First Mystery Short Story of the Year. Now, several published short stories and novels later, Linda is recognized for her outstanding work in the romance genre.

A practicing attorney, Linda juggles her busy schedule between mornings of writing briefs, contracts and other legalese, and afternoons of creating memorable tales of the paranormal, time travel, mystery, contemporary and romantic suspense. Armed with an undergraduate degree in journalism with an advertising emphasis from Pennsylvania State University, Linda began her versatile writing career running a small newspaper, then working in advertising and public relations, later obtaining her JD degree from Duquesne University School of Law in Pittsburgh.

Linda belongs to Sisters in Crime and is actively involved with Romance Writers of America, participating in the Los Angeles, Orange County and Western Pennsylvania chapters. She lives near Universal Studios, Hollywood, with her husband, two sons and two Cavalier King Charles spaniels.

Books by Linda O. Johnston

HARLEQUIN INTRIGUE
592—ALIAS MOMMY
624—MARRIAGE: CLASSIFIED
655—OPERATION: REUNITED
688—TOMMY'S MOM
725—SPECIAL AGENT NANNY
757—GUARDIAN OF HER HEART
786—LAWFUL ENGAGEMENT

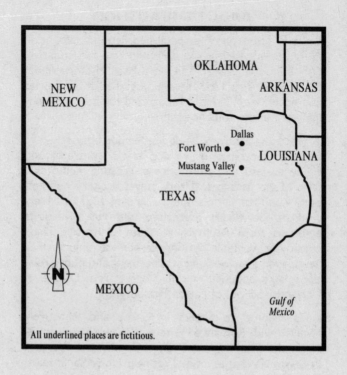

All underlined places are fictitious.

CAST OF CHARACTERS

Cara Hamilton—Certain that Mustang Valley's recent rash of crimes are all related, the crusading reporter is just the writer to expose the connection.

Deputy Mitchell Steele—He's determined to solve Mustang Valley's latest murder—and to prove his father's death two years earlier was not a suicide.

Nancy Wilks—Cara's friend, the office administrator at Lambert & Church, was killed because of something she intended to show to the reporter. What was it…and where is it now?

Donald Church—Does this attorney know something he hasn't disclosed?

Sheriff Ben Wilson—He became sheriff when Mitch's father allegedly committed suicide. Is there a reason why he hates Mitch so much?

Deputy Hurley Zeller—A nasty man in uniform who wants to be sheriff.

Roger Rosales—As the local representative for Ranger Corporation, can he explain why the company's name keeps popping up each time "murder" is mentioned in Mustang Valley?

Beauford Jennings—Cara's boss, and owner of the *Mustang Gazette.*

Della Santoro—The community college professor is Cara's friend and an expert on Shotgun Sally legends.

Kelly McGovern Lansing—This feisty Texan will do whatever it takes to seek justice.

Lindsey Wellington—She promises to help Cara find the truth behind Nancy's death.

Shotgun Sally—The legendary frontierswoman influences the lives of Kelly, Lindsey and Cara in their quest for the truth!

Many, many thanks to the other Shotgun Sallys authors,
Susan Kearney and Ann Voss Peterson,
and of course to Allison Lyons, our editor.

Thanks, also, to Fred—for everything.

Chapter One

Cara Hamilton's heart beat a familiar, thunderous tattoo of anticipation deep inside her chest. She parked at the curb, slung her large purse over her shoulder and exited her small yellow Toyota.

It was nearly one o'clock in the morning. Though most residences along Caddo Street were dark, lights blazed in the first-floor apartment of the three-story converted Victorian in front of her. Cara's friend Nancy Wilks, who lived there, had called half an hour ago. She hadn't said much, only that she had something important to show Cara.

But Cara sensed that, whatever it was, it could be the key to the biggest story of her life.

That was why she felt the familiar rush of excitement. She was on the trail of something newsworthy. And this time it was something *beyond* newsworthy. Something that could blow the blasé citizens of Mustang Valley right out of their couch-potato seats. Make her career.

Only... As she stood outside her car and glanced around the sleeping neighborhood, a sudden, strange chill enveloped Cara. It was northeast Texas in midsummer. Humid and warm, even at night. Too hot to make her feel so cold.

As she shivered nonetheless, her skin prickled.

"It's the news itch," she whispered aloud, determined to shrug off her inexplicable uneasiness. "I've been stung by the tattle bug. Right, Sally?"

As if her idol, Shotgun Sally, the stuff of incredibly inspirational folklore, could respond. But as usual, the silly little device of talking to her, using her legendary language, lifted Cara's spirits.

Not that she'd do so where anyone else could hear.

Cara flinched at the click of her car door closing. The night had been silent except for the crisp chirping of crickets, and their singing halted at the sound. Not even traffic noise from the highway, only a few miles away. And nothing at all from the direction of downtown Mustang Valley.

Cara's own deep and uneven breathing broke the stillness. That and the light tap of her boot heels on the pavement.

The humidity hung heavy in the air, stifling Cara, moistening her bare arms, for she wore a short-sleeved blouse tucked into her long skirt that matched the soft buckskin-colored vest over it. Why didn't the heavens just split into a thunderstorm and get it over with?

She winced as her footsteps grew louder when she walked up the three steps to the wooden porch. So what? She was expected.

There was no reason to hide her presence.

The outside light was on, but shadows gathered beyond the porch rails. Cara rang the doorbell for the first floor apartment, hearing the muffled chime from within. Beside this door was another, which led to the stairway to the upper floors.

Cara waited for a moment, listening. She heard nothing from inside. No reason to get impatient…but she was.

Her odd uneasiness began to loop knots inside her.

She rang the bell again.

Still nothing.

For the heck of it, she tried the doorknob. It turned easily in her hand, and she was able to push the door open. Maybe Nancy just figured Cara would enter when she arrived.

But why hadn't she come to greet her?

Speaking of edgy nerves…hers had begun shrieking at her. Quiet! she insisted, to no avail.

Cara stepped inside and closed the door behind her. "Nancy?" Damn! Her voice shook. "It's Cara," she called more loudly. "I'm here."

Nothing.

The entry was a tiny hallway, painted pale yellow. A small glass hanging fixture bathed it in soft light.

Cara had been here before. To the left was an open, arched doorway into the living room. Ahead was the way to the kitchen, bathroom and the apartment's single bedroom.

"Nancy? Where are you?"

If Cara had felt unnerved before, now she trembled with tension. Tattle bug? Heck, she felt as if an army of ants marched formations along her spine.

"Nancy?" Cara called. She glanced into the living room. Though the lamps on either side of the floral print sofa were lit, the room was empty. She continued down the hall.

The farthest door on the right, the one to the bedroom, was ajar. "Nancy?" Cara's voice rasped, and she cleared her throat. No reason to feel so weird. Nancy was probably in the bathroom with the door closed, the water running so she couldn't hear Cara.

But neither could Cara hear water in the pipes.

She called out once more, "Nancy," as she pushed the bedroom door open. And gasped.

Nancy was there. Wearing a pink top and blue jeans,

she lay on her bed, facedown, her dark hair askew as her head hung over the side.

"What's wrong?" Cara cried as she dashed over to her friend, who remained motionless.

Cara's question was answered in less than a moment, when she turned Nancy over. Her eyes were closed—and there was an ugly, black-rimmed red hole in the middle of her forehead. And so much blood...

USING HER CELL PHONE, Cara had called 911. Help was, she supposed, on the way.

There would be no help for Nancy.

Cara's head spun as she glanced sidelong at the poor, limp body that lay half off the bed, turned back just the way Cara had found her. Before calling, though, she had put two fingers at the side of Nancy's neck. No pulse.

Nancy's skin hadn't been cold. This had only just happened.

No surprise. Nancy's call had only been twenty minutes earlier. Cara had left her home nearly immediately, since Nancy had sounded...well, excited? Scared? Cara wasn't sure now.

Had she guessed what was about to happen to her?

No, Cara thought as tears filled her eyes. *I won't fall apart.*

After all, she wasn't actually here. This hadn't actually happened. Her intense, dedicated friend Nancy. Nancy, the office manager who'd so angrily spilled details of her employer's disgrace to Cara off the record after the scandal broke, wasn't actually dead.

Get real, she instructed her mind. No defense mechanisms for Cara Hamilton. She was a realist. Nerves of steel, despite her earlier folly. A gritty, down-to-earth investigative reporter ready to do whatever it took to get a story, go wherever that story might lead her.

Yeah, but none had ever led her directly to a murder victim before....

Get to work, Hamilton, she commanded herself. Someone could arrive at any moment.

"What was it, Nancy?" she whispered, forcing herself to draw closer to the bed again. "What did you want to show me?" It had been something important. Cara was convinced of it.

She shook so hard as she surveyed the area around Nancy's body that she had to lean on the mattress to keep from falling.

Nancy's sheets were white with pink flowers. She had a handmade quilt on her queen-size bed. Everything was bunched about her. Gently, Cara rifled through the bed clothes but found nothing to explain Nancy's call.

It had to have something to do with the law firm where she had worked. Of course Lambert & Church was in the process of disbanding, after what had happened before.

A siren wailed in the distance. Coming here, Cara was sure. No more time to waste.

Quickly she scanned Nancy's bedroom. It was tidy, as usual, nothing out of place—not even any of the books on her bookshelves. Nothing that didn't belong there.

Cara ran down the hall into the bathroom. Into the kitchen. Into the living room. She looked through the mail on the end table near Nancy's sofa. The newspapers on top of yet more filled bookshelves. Nothing unusual. Nothing to interest a reporter.

Nothing except Nancy's body in the bedroom....

Oh, Lord! It dawned on Cara that the killer could still have been there when she arrived. Could *still* be there.

No, she'd have seen him. Or her. Been attacked, too...

Cut it out, Hamilton. She forced her mind back to what was important. What had Nancy called about?

Another disquieting thought struck Cara. What if the

thing wasn't here because whoever did that to Nancy had taken it?

What if whatever it was had been the reason Nancy had been killed?

Nancy had called Cara to show her.

Cara could be responsible for Nancy's murder.

A loud knock sounded on the front door. "Yes," she called as she hurried in that direction.

"Sheriff's Department," called a muffled male voice. "Someone here called for help."

HIS STETSON IN HIS HAND, Deputy Sheriff Mitchell Steele followed the waif who had met him, wide-eyed, at the door. As she led him down the hall of the old, converted house, her walk was brisk, sure, and the swing of her hips caused her long skirt to sway about her legs. Her curly red hair just skimmed the collar of the white blouse extending from beneath her brown vest. Despite the heat, she wore attractive boots, and a large purse hung from her left shoulder.

She'd introduced herself quickly and glanced at the name badge on his uniform shirt before turning her back and telling him to follow. Cara Hamilton.

He knew that name.

He'd only gotten a whiff of her scent, something that reminded him of a mountain spring, fresh air...

She stopped outside an open door and looked at him again. Her full lower lip, pink without a hint of lipstick, trembled, and her hazel eyes remained huge. "Nancy's in there." Her softly Texan voice was husky but sure.

He glanced inside, took in the scene. He immediately went to the bed and checked the victim for any sign of life.

But the answer was more than clear when he turned her

over. She had been shot by a small-caliber gun. No exit wound.

He was glad when, only a moment later, he heard voices and Cara Hamilton showed a couple of fire department EMTs into the room. They took charge of the victim, and he moved out of their way. But he was certain they could try to revive her from now until tomorrow's sunset with no success.

A shame, he thought. The victim was a young woman. She didn't deserve to die like that.

Sticking his hat under his arm, Mitch pulled his cell phone from his pocket and called the station, quickly telling the dispatcher what he'd found and instructing her to send some deputies to secure the area and a team of forensics technicians, pronto. As he spoke, he scanned the room to determine whether the murder weapon was there and visible. He didn't see it.

And then he looked down at the woman who stood beside him in the doorway. She watched the medics with an expression so fierce that she seemed to be willing them to save the victim's life.

"Ms. Hamilton, I'll need to ask you a few questions."

Her stare, as she looked up, appeared startled, as if she'd forgotten he was there. Was she in shock? How could she not be?

But her expression immediately narrowed. "You're going to catch the SOB who did this, aren't you, Deputy?"

"Yes," he replied in all sincerity. Her question implied that *she* hadn't done it. Maybe she hadn't. But until he knew more, he could not rule her out. "I'll need a statement from you to get started."

She led him down the hall. When she tried to direct him into the living room, he pointed instead toward the front door. "We'll talk outside. There'll be less chance of contaminating the crime scene."

"Fine."

They stood on the porch under its light and away from railings the suspect might have touched. Mitch had already scoped out the porch's wood deck. Despite the humidity, the day had been dry, so there was little likelihood of finding muddy footprints. No, footprints were more likely to be discovered on the ground, but only if the perpetrator stepped off the paved walkway. Had he—she?—walked right up to the front door and been let in by the victim? Or would they find evidence of a break-in—a broken window, a jimmied door, a picked lock?

"So, Ms. Hamilton, I gather you know the victim." He removed a small notebook from a pocket and began to make notes.

"I *knew* her, yes." Her voice was sad despite her ironic tone. "Her name was Nancy Wilks. We've been friends for years."

"Good friends?"

"Not extremely close, but..." Her voice trailed off. "I was here tonight because she called me. She said...she said she was feeling rotten because she had just lost her job, and she wanted me to come over to commiserate."

Cara Hamilton was lying. Mitch did not need the intuition inherited as part of his half-Native-American ancestry to tell him that. He knew it as surely as if she'd proclaimed it in neon lights. He stopped writing and looked at her.

No matter how boldly her mouth lied, her body language didn't. He observed her despondency, her sense of loss, written in the sorrow of her gaze as she met his eyes—without a hint of her verbal guile. She stood with her arms folded, as if hugging herself in comfort after her ordeal of finding the body.

For an insane instant, Mitch wondered what it would feel like to take the small but curvy woman into *his* arms to soothe her grief. He hardened his glare, but her expression remained sorrowfully innocent.

"Right," he said. His job wasn't to contradict her. Or to feel sympathy for her. But if he could catch her in a lie... "So you came over at—" He glanced at his watch. "What time *did* you get here?"

"I don't know exactly," she replied. "I can't have been here more than twenty minutes, though. I...I found her the way you saw her." Her voice broke.

"I see. So then what did you do?"

She described pretty much what he'd anticipated. She'd checked to see if her friend was alive, then called the emergency phone number and waited.

"And what did you do while you waited?"

"Do?" The question seemed to take her aback. "I didn't do anything. I just...waited."

"Mm-hmm," Mitch said noncommittally. "And did you touch anything?"

"No." Her response came too fast.

"If you did, you should mention it, in case your fingerprints are found someplace they shouldn't be."

"I know better than to disturb a crime scene," she lashed back. But there was a defensiveness in her tone that told him that, once again, she was lying.

"I'm sure you do." He regretted his sarcastic tone immediately.

She frowned for an instant, then, almost visibly tucked away her anguish. Her small chin raised, her hazel eyes intense, she asked, "So how will you start to investigate this murder, Deputy Steele?"

"Exactly the way I'm doing it, Ms. Hamilton. By securing the crime scene." He nodded at the white Sheriff's Department sedan that had just pulled up to the curb. A couple of deputies exited and headed toward them. "By

having the scene checked for evidence,'' Mitch continued.
''And by asking questions.''

"I see. And how do you—"

''As I said, *I'm* asking questions.''

''Of course, but—''

He continued as if she had remained silent. ''*Not* you,
though I'm sure it's hard for a reporter with your reputation to let someone else do the interrogating.''

She closed her mouth. The way she regarded him
seemed speculative, but of course he knew who she was.
He figured everyone in Mustang Valley, maybe in the
whole of northeastern Texas, knew of investigative reporter Cara Hamilton and her incisive articles in the *Mustang Gazette*.

Why was she really here? To visit a friend, or to research a story? Maybe, but it was awfully late for either.

To commit murder?

He doubted that but couldn't rule it out. He'd have the
techs check her for gun residue, just in case.

The patrol deputies reached them—a couple of guys
he'd worked with often. A couple of good ones, fortunately, who didn't challenge his authority. The department
was small enough that everyone took on a variety of du-
ties. And small enough that Mitch knew which fellow
officers hated his guts.

He quickly filled these guys in, and they headed off to
start the log of who entered the crime scene and to cordon
it off with yellow tape. Not a moment too soon. The
neighbors had gotten wind that something was up and
were trickling from nearby homes. A couple appeared in
another doorway of the victim's house—the upstairs ten-
ants? They might be valuable witnesses. A deputy approached them.

Mitch turned back toward Cara Hamilton, only to see

the twitch of her skirt as she headed once more through the door to Nancy's apartment.

Damn. He hurried after her, grabbed her arm. "Stay out here," he demanded.

She started, then looked from the fingertips that still vised her slender, warm upper arm, back to his face.

"I'm sure I don't have to remind you again that this is a crime scene, Ms. Hamilton."

"Of course not, and that's exactly why I have to—"

"You have to stay here, out of the way."

Some guys, Mitch figured, would melt into an ugly little puddle of ooze under the fiery glare she turned on him. He merely glared back.

"I've got press credentials with me, Deputy Steele." She pointed to the oversize bag over her shoulder. "You don't want to be accused of violating the First Amendment of the United States Constitution, do you?"

"And I'm sure you don't want to be arrested for obstruction of justice," he said without missing a beat.

"I have no intention of obstructing anything," she said smoothly. "I want you to solve this case. Fast. And I'll even help you." The sound of her melodic voice was as gentle as the evening breeze, caressing his ears, his soul.

Abruptly, to shatter the spell she seemed determined to weave about him, he said, "You'll help by answering my questions and by staying out of the way. You'll be invited to any press conferences just like other media representatives, and—"

"I'm not just like the other media people, Deputy," she countered harshly.

What had happened to the sorrowing, sympathetic young woman of a few minutes ago? She was all business now. He believed her. She wasn't like other media people. Though he knew there were a lot of reporters as abrasive, stubborn, irritating and challenging, few probably wrapped up those repulsive characteristics in as beautiful a package.

But so what if Cara Hamilton was a good-looking woman, with guts and strength to boot? She was still a witness. Maybe a suspect.

Most likely, though, she had just found the murdered body of a friend. Sure, she'd been shocked and fragile when Mitch had first arrived, but she had not fallen apart. Now she was asserting herself, doing her job. As Mitch was doing his.

If she weren't trying so hard to get in his way, he might admire her.

"Let's go back over what happened from the moment you heard from Ms. Wilks this evening, Ms. Hamilton. The forensics technicians should be here shortly, and they'll need to get your prints for comparison purposes, plus do more testing to eliminate you as a suspect." Maybe. "And then—"

"Your father, Martin Steele, was the former sheriff of Mustang County, wasn't he?"

Mitch froze. He knew what was coming next from Cara Hamilton, crime-scene witness—and ace reporter. "Yes," he replied curtly. "Now tell me, where were you when Ms. Wilks—"

"Why did your father kill himself, Deputy Steele?"

Chapter Two

As the look in Deputy Mitch Steele's eyes, a shade of leonine gold beneath straight black brows, shifted from vaguely suspicious to blank, Cara could have kicked herself.

She had ruined any sliver of hope that he would cooperate as she tried to find out what had happened to Nancy.

And she *would* do everything necessary to find the person who had killed her friend. Not only for her story, but for herself.

Of course the story she was working on would definitely merit attention, for it went far beyond Nancy's murder. Maybe even Pulitzer material, for it involved—

"Excuse me, Ms. Hamilton," Mitch said, looking over her shoulder. She glanced in that direction and saw that a van with the Sheriff's Department logo had pulled up Caddo Street and was now double parked beneath a streetlight in front of Nancy's house. The crime-scene technicians, she figured. A good excuse for him to avoid her.

To avoid her question—the one she would take back in an instant, if she could.

"Cara," she said quickly.

His attention returned to her momentarily as his gaze turned quizzical.

"My name is Cara," she said, inviting him to use it. Maybe that small intimacy would make him forget what she'd asked, even though she wouldn't forget it. Because despite regretting that she blurted it due to the consequences it would cause, she still wanted an answer.

"Right. Cara."

She knew his first name was Mitch, not from his name badge, but she remembered it from news stories about his father. He didn't invite her to use it and he walked away, toward where the technicians removed gear from their van.

Cara watched his confident stride. Most men looked tall to her because she was only five foot one. But Mitch Steele *was* tall, at least six feet. He held his head high, his broad shoulders thrown back beneath his khaki uniform shirt, as if in challenge to any bad guys who happened to be watching.

In challenge to the world. Cara knew a little of Mitch Steele's background, and she was aware that the world had challenged *him*—or at least his family. She'd no doubt that Mitch, still working for the Sheriff's Department, had to live every day under the stigma that surrounded his deceased father.

Sheriff Martin Steele was enmeshed in a scandal a couple of years ago—one much bigger than the earlier grumblings of nepotism when he'd hired his son. Before his involvement in the bribery plot was proven or disproved, he committed suicide.

He wouldn't have done that had he been innocent—would he? And yet his arguments, arguments reported in the *Mustang Gazette* and other media, had made sense.

Too bad Cara hadn't worked on that story. Back then she had still been listening to her boss, Beauford Jennings, when he gave her assignments. That had been before Beau had made it clear that to him, too, nepotism trumped merit. And ethics. His nephew Jerry, Cara's casual boy-friend at the time, had stolen her firsthand, undercover research to write his own article on how local liquor stores, including one owned by a county commissioner, sold alcohol to kids known to be minors. Jerry broke the story and ended the commissioner's career. That move catapulted Jerry out of Mustang Valley and into the world of big-city news.

Beau's only regret was that Jerry was gone.

After that Cara didn't ask for Beau's opinion. She donned disguises and slung hash in local eateries for her story about restaurants' cleanliness standards. She'd received applause after her article and surreptitious pictures got a popular place closed down by the local board of health—pictures showing the owner grin as one of his wait staff spat into the food of a patron who'd criticized the service last time he'd eaten there. That was when Beau had finally promoted her out of the copy room to reporter. He'd hinted of further promotions, too.

Score one for our side, Cara had thought. Her idol, the legendary Shotgun Sally, had reputedly once worn flouncing skirts and gone undercover as a dance hall girl to write a story on how it felt to be a fallen woman. She, too, had trounced all over those who failed to take her seriously. At least for her first big story, Cara had only had to put on a lacy apron over a short dress. Oh, and glasses and a wig.

Since her experience with Jerry, though, Cara hated the idea of sharing information with anyone. She'd made it clear to Beau that she would follow her own leads, write her own stories.

Beau had stopped underestimating her, at least when it suited him, but others hadn't. Maybe it was because she was a woman, maybe because she looked so young. Though she used it to her advantage, she detested it.

Almost as much as she hated anyone to interfere with her getting her story. She'd allowed it once, but never again.

And now, she had even more impetus to get the story. She sighed and glanced back toward Nancy's house. Her friend had been murdered. Maybe even because *she'd* been on the way....

Cara swallowed hard as she forced her gaze back toward the dimly lit street.

Mitch turned and preceded the techs back up the walk toward Nancy's house—and where Cara stood. She half expected him to brush by her. Instead he stopped.

So did her breathing, for an instant, while she tried to figure out what to say to fix things between them.

"So, Deputy, any more questions for me? I definitely want to cooperate so you can solve this murder." Assuming the Sheriff's Department *did* solve this one.

Was it her imagination, or did the blankness in his gaze soften just a bit? "I'm sure you do. And, yes, I'll have more questions for you, though not right now."

"Good. Then I'll just follow these people and take pictures while they work." She reached way down into her bag, past the notebook, cell phone and personal digital assistant, to extract her digital camera. "That way, when you catch the perpetrator, I'll be able to describe the entire process."

Mitch Steele was one handsome deputy even when he scowled. If Cara recalled his father's story correctly, Mitch's mother was Native American, which would help explain the blue-black richness of his hair, the strong slant to his nose, the sharpness of his cheekbones and other features. That scowl of his only emphasized the well-honed planes of his face.

But when he let the corner of his mouth curve up in a

half grin that way, Cara was sure he drove every woman in her right mind wild with lust.

She was in her right mind....

"No," he said, bringing that creative imagination of hers back to reality.

"Pardon?"

"Ms.... Cara, I appreciate your cooperation. But you do not have my permission to get in the way."

"I'll stay out of the way. I promise."

"Mm-hmm." Though his murmur sounded affirmative, she was sure she was losing his attention, for he had turned to talk to one of the techs.

"If you let me follow them, I'll tell you something I don't think you know about Nancy," she blurted out.

Damn! When was she going to stop speaking before she'd thought things through? She wasn't always so adept at sticking her foot in her mouth. Something about this deputy was spurring her to foolishness.

But she had definitely regained his attention, for suddenly those piercing golden eyes were staring hard into her face. "If you have some knowledge about Ms. Wilks that's relevant to this case, Cara, you'd better spill it. Now."

MITCH WATCHED as the lovely Ms. Cara Hamilton backpedaled. It would have been amusing if he hadn't been certain that whatever she was hiding could be of significance in solving the murder of Nancy Wilks.

"You misunderstood." The wide-eyed innocence in her luminous gaze didn't convince him one bit. "I meant I don't think you know how rotten Nancy felt that her job was disappearing so fast. She'd liked working at Lambert & Church. You know, the law firm where Paul Lambert was a partner? The guy who killed himself in jail after his murder of a local rancher was exposed?"

"Of course I know of it." But Mitch hadn't been directly involved in the case, despite its high profile. Maybe *because* it was so high profile, for though he had the seniority and authority to supervise on the most critical cases, Sheriff Ben Wilson made sure Mitch had other responsibilities that kept him busy. Like reorganizing the deputies on patrol so those who worked hardest got more to say about choosing their shifts.

Just like he'd been swamped with putting together the latest program to keep kids off drugs during the investigation of the murder prior to the one involving Lambert, the first murder the town had seen in two years. Most people claimed it was even longer than that. High profile? Heck, that one had been the *highest* profile, since the mayor himself had turned out to be the killer. And the victim had been a lawyer at the same firm, Lambert & Church.

The same place where the latest victim had worked. Was there a connection among the three killings? Hell, yes. There had to be. Mustang Valley wasn't exactly a hotbed of crime. And with that same law firm at the center of all three... Mitch would follow that connection and see where it led.

Unlike the other killings, solving this case was *his*. And once he put it all together, he'd insist on the recognition he deserved. For once. No matter how much it galled others.

Although, partial invisibility would help with his personal, highly frustrating, agenda. So would following Sheriff Wilson's orders—more or less.

Still, good thing Ben Wilson hadn't thought that putting Mitch on the night shift for a while would lead to something big. Like being the first at a murder scene. And that gave him the advantage in staying in charge.

This time, his self-imposed patience—so much against his driven nature—would pay off.

"Now, if you'll excuse me, Deputy—" Cara Hamilton's lilting voice interrupted his thoughts. In the shadowed light from the nearby streetlamp, she watched his face with what appeared to be total concentration. Almost as if she were trying to read his mind.

A disconcerting idea.

"Sorry, Cara. We're not through. I still want to know exactly what you're hiding."

He had to hand it to her. The woman was good. Her innocent smile hardly wavered. "Not a thing. But if anything comes to me, I'll be sure to let you know, Mitch. Okay?"

His mouth opened as he instinctively started to correct her. It might be all right for him to use *her* first name, but if she used his, he risked losing his appearance of authority. And distance. And everything that would give him an edge over this civilian.

No matter how much he'd liked the way she'd said it.

But before he could say anything, she'd turned and headed for the house. Again.

"Hey." He hurried after her, swinging around so that she nearly walked straight into him. She looked up with that same guileless expression he was coming to recognize. The expression that lied as easily as her mouth. Guileless? Heck, the woman was an expert at deception. And nosy as all get-out. In his face, and in his way.

"Look, Ms. Hamilton. If you're not willing to talk to me here, you'll have to come to the station."

His body blocked most of the light emanating from the porch behind him, so she stood in shadows. He could nevertheless see how her forehead crinkled as she mulled this over. He observed the arch to eyebrows, which, despite the dimness, seemed a similar shade of auburn as her hair. Its soft red hue must be natural, then. Interesting.

He'd note it in her profile as a witness and potential suspect. That was his only reason for noticing.

"Okay," she said.

"What?" She'd confused him.

"Okay, I'll come to the station so you can question me there."

The lady was full of surprises. "Fine. Make it—" He glanced at his watch. He'd have to be here for a long while, till the crime-scene investigation was well under-way. "—nine o'clock this morning."

"Fine."

"Meantime, I'll send one of the techs out here to check you out."

"To get my fingerprints so you can eliminate me as a suspect." She confirmed what he'd told her before, her tone a little sarcastic, as if she didn't believe he thought the forensics exam would clear her.

Maybe it wouldn't, though right now his main reasons for sticking her on his suspect list—her limited coopera-tion and her being at the victim's at one heck of a bad time for a social call—weren't exactly proof of her guilt.

"That's right. And to check to make sure you don't have any gunpowder residue on you, too. That kind of thing." Or any blood, though he saw none on her.

She stared but said nothing. He allowed her, this time, to walk away. As he watched her, she glanced at the house once more and then, assessingly, back at him. He shook his head.

With a look of annoyance, she headed toward the side-walk, her long skirt swaying again with her determined stride. Was she going to leave before the techs checked her out? He held his breath, ready to go after her, until she turned again, crossed her arms and stood there, obviously impatient.

He realized with surprise, and irritation with himself, that the challenge of Cara Hamilton had whetted his appetite for more.

Right now nine o'clock seemed very far away.

UNLIKE THE MAJOR metropolitan area of Dallas/Ft. Worth to the northeast, the population of Mustang Valley wasn't very large. Neither was the population of the whole of Mustang County, which was why the Sheriff's Department had jurisdiction even in town.

As a result the station funded by the taxpayers was compact, too. Only ten years old, it looked more like an architect's vision than a functional law enforcement command center, all glass and steel and vulnerability—if any terrorist, or even petty crook, thought it worth the effort to attack.

But its small size was compact, too. Which was why Mitch was able to keep his ears open to comings and goings at the front desk even as he sat in the nearby computer room. He'd begun entering his initial report on the Nancy Wilks murder investigation into one of the aging, outdated machines.

It was nearly nine o'clock. Would Cara Hamilton actually come, or would he have to look for her? If she came, would she be on time?

Mitch heard the clump of heavy footsteps on the wood floor. More than one set. Definitely not Cara.

"Is Steele in?" demanded the voice of his boss, Sheriff Ben Wilson.

"Yeah," replied the deputy on duty. He must have gestured toward the room where Mitch sat, for in a moment Wilson and his favorite senior underling, Deputy Hurley Zeller, entered.

Wilson, in his fifties, tall and rangy in his loose khaki uniform, had the leathery, tough skin of a much older varmint. He'd never made any attempt to hide his disdain of Mitch or his rage that he'd inherited the son of the disgraced former sheriff and didn't have any reason to fire his ass and oust him from the department. He probably even held it against Mitch that his dad had become sheriff first.

Ben glared at Mitch with narrowed brown eyes. The odor of cigar smoke clung to Zeller and him. "I just came from the crime scene on Caddo Street. The Wilks murder."

Mitch nodded. "I'm just finishing my initial report."

"Got it solved yet?" Hurley Zeller sneered.

Wilson's flunky Zeller, nearly as wide as he was tall, was a smart-mouthed son of a bitch who smiled a lot, particularly while emitting his nastiest utterances. And Zeller could be damned nasty at times. He was around thirty-five, older than Mitch's twenty-nine, but acted as if he still was a hot-blooded teenage kid more often than not. But he did a superior job of kissing up to the sheriff, who bought it.

"I'm working on it," Mitch replied mildly to Zeller's jibe.

"The deputies there said you have a suspect already," Wilson said. "That reporter bitch Cara Hamilton was caught right there red-handed."

"She was there," Mitch agreed, sticking his hands behind his back so his boss wouldn't see that he'd clenched them into fists. The guy was jumping to conclusions. No need for him to accuse Cara Hamilton...yet. "The weapon wasn't found, though. Hamilton wouldn't have had time to ditch the gun."

"Maybe." Zeller stepped closer to Mitch. "Or maybe you just missed it." He turned to Wilson. "How about putting me in charge of the case, boss? I won't miss any big clues."

"The way you don't miss the target at shooting practice?" Mitch stuck an expression on his face that he intended to be as innocent as any of Cara's. Not that he could make himself look as young and sweet. But Mitch had learned well the art of acting, particularly since joining the Mustang County Sheriff's Department. From his intentionally placid demeanor, no one here would guess how tightly he was coiled inside, prepared to spring in an instant if he let himself.

Mitch hadn't thought Zeller's small brown eyes could narrow any more, but he scrunched them into something he probably thought looked menacing. Instead, he appeared like an ape with gas. "I always pass the tests. And I'm sure you'd feel better if they let you use a bow and arrow."

Mitch again flexed his fists behind his back. Most guys around here were at least subtler in their cracks about his half-Native-American ancestry. He forced himself, as always, not to respond, knowing that ignoring Zeller was more of an insult than trading barbs. If it were not for his own quest, more important to him than anything else, he'd have decked Zeller long ago.

Facing Ben Wilson with more calm than he felt, Mitch said, "Here's what we know so far about the Wilks murder." He gave a rundown. It wasn't a lot. The coroner's report hadn't come in yet, but he described the apparent cause of death: a bullet to the head. "No sign of a weapon at her home, so we won't have its description till we get more from the coroner. No sign of forced entry. The neighbors interviewed so far noticed nothing out of the ordinary, so the weapon's noise must have been suppressed. The reporter, Cara Hamilton, said she was there because the victim called her to chat about losing her job.''

"You bought that?" Wilson's voice was edged with sarcasm.

"No. In fact, she's due here now for further interrogation."

"Fine. I'll sit in."

Mitch opened his mouth to protest, then shut it. He knew how to conduct a good witness interview. But having Ben there would ensure he wouldn't get second-guessed later.

Just then, in the next room, he heard the soft, determined voice he'd been listening for. "My name is Cara Hamilton. I'm here to see Deputy Steele."

CARA HADN'T THOUGHT she'd feel so unnerved by being the subject of an official interrogation. This was a first. In her line of work, it was unlikely to be the last.

But she enjoyed situations so much better when *she* was the one asking questions.

Mitch had come into the station's reception area almost immediately after she'd arrived. He showed her down a short hallway into a moderate-size room that resembled a company's conference room, with a big, scuffed wood table in the center.

What had she expected—a jail cell with a wired chair in the center where she'd be strapped in?

Not that the chair he showed her to was comfortable—physically or emotionally. She had the seat of honor at the head of the table. Not quite wired...

Mitch sat beside her. He looked tired, with the shadow of a dark beard emerging and circles beneath his golden eyes. Bedroom eyes—sexy, yes, but even more a sign of exhaustion. She doubted he'd gotten any sleep that night.

Of course, neither had she. She'd gone home, written

a story about the murder on her computer and e-mailed it to the *Gazette,* requesting a photographer to follow up since her digital shots weren't professional. Then she'd showered, changed and lain in bed, her eyes wide open.

Nancy had called her. Nancy had been murdered....

As Cara's former fiancé Andrew McGovern had been, only a few months ago. They hadn't been together in a long time, but his death had still hit her surprisingly hard.

She'd called her parents at six-thirty this morning so they'd hear the news from Cara about Nancy, and about Cara finding her—not from the radio, TV or someone else. They still lived in the house in Mustang Valley where she'd grown up. Always overprotective, her mother had been proud when Cara had joined the editorial staff of the *Mustang Gazette,* but when she'd insisted on becoming a hard-hitting investigative reporter—

"Ms. Hamilton, this is Sheriff Wilson," Mitch said. "He'll be joining us this morning."

"We've met." Forbidding her nose from wrinkling despite the smoke smell hovering around the sheriff, Cara shook his hand. She had tried interviewing him for stories now and then, but he'd always been condescending, overbearing and snide, a combination that always set her teeth on edge. Right now he regarded her as if prepared to place her under arrest. "Good to see you again, Sheriff," she lied. As pleased as she'd be to run into her worst enemy, whoever that was. Of course, her list of enemies was expanding, thanks to her revelation in print of all sorts of nasties committed by the subjects of her stories.

She wasn't sure, though, which was her *worst* one.

She accepted a cup of coffee, then exchanged pleasantries about the weather with the sheriff until Mitch Steele interrupted. "So, Ms. Hamilton, let's start at the beginning for Sheriff Wilson's benefit. You were a friend of Ms. Wilks?"

"Yes. Not close…" The way she was with her dearest friends in the world, Kelly McGovern—Kelly Lansing now—and Lindsey Wellington. "But we got together for lunch often, exchanged birthday cards, that kind of thing. She even sent me a postcard from Orlando when she was on vacation a few months ago." Cara stopped abruptly, thinking of how excited Nancy had been to get away. And now she'd never—

"Okay, let's get to what happened last night," Mitch said. "You received a phone call from Ms. Wilks about when?"

Putting her grieving aside for the moment, Cara went through the story again, not changing any of it. As far as they were concerned, Nancy had called because she was depressed about losing her job and needed someone to talk to.

No way would Cara mention that Nancy had something important to show her. Not until Cara knew what it was.

Obstruction of justice? Maybe, though she hoped not. Mostly she was trying to protect her source. Though that source was now dead.

Cara's mouth worked on automatic as she continued describing her arrival, what she had found.

Her mind continued to spin. Maybe Nancy's reputation had been on the line, and that was why she'd called Cara. Despite her apparent efficiency and dedication, had she done something shady at the law firm and been ready to 'fess up? Did she have evidence she'd intended to show Cara?

Cara had to know. She had to write the truth about the Nancy Wilks's murder.

And about the others.

"Ms. Hamilton?" Mitch Steele's deep, irritated voice broke into her thoughts.

"Yes?"

"Tell us again what you did between the time you called 911 and when the authorities arrived."

Conducted my own quick, fruitless search. "I tried to do something for Nancy, but I could tell she was gone." She tried to sound matter-of-fact, but had to swallow suddenly. Damn him. She wanted to stay remote, objective, observe it all like a good reporter. But when she was asked questions that made her relive how she'd found Nancy, would she always want to cry?

"Right," Mitch said. "And did you touch anything?"

Had they found her fingerprints? That could be explained. She'd been at Nancy's apartment before, though not recently.

"Well, I touched Nancy, and her bedclothes. And of course the doorknob when I came in, and the door to her room, I think."

"Ms. Hamilton, I don't think you're being entirely forthcoming here," the sheriff drawled softly from behind Mitch.

"Pardon?"

"We've reason to believe that Ms. Wilks called you for a different reason. That you came to her home in a panic and killed her, and that you searched the place, then called for help. What did you find, and where did you put the gun?"

Cara felt the color drain from her face. She glanced at Mitch. Did he think she killed Nancy, too? She couldn't read his expression, though the way his mouth was set, she thought he was angry. At her?

No. She was suddenly sure that Mitch was mad at the sheriff for going on a fishing expedition.

Relief warred with anger. Mitch Steele, the deputy at the scene, might not have ruled her out, but she doubted he considered her a viable suspect. Yet he wasn't going to contradict his boss.

She, on the other hand, could do just that. And more. For the main reason she had agreed so easily to come in for questioning was that she'd hoped to get some questions of her own answered.

She looked over Mitch's wide shoulder toward Sheriff Ben Wilson. He regarded her with what appeared to be impassive curiosity.

She'd get him to show more emotion or she'd eat her favorite notepad—which she still carried in her purse.

Coolly she stared back at the man who'd just accused her of murder. "Sorry, Sheriff. You'll have to do better than that. Nancy called me, I came, and I found her body. Period. I can't be a real suspect in her murder, and you know it. Did your technicians find any gun residue on me? Any other reason to suspect me?" She didn't wait for an answer. "Look. Nancy was depressed about losing her job at the law firm. You know, Lambert & Church? Where one of the lawyers, Andrew McGovern—" Her fiancé years ago. She swallowed and continued, "Andrew McGovern was murdered by our esteemed former mayor, Frank Daniels. A friend of mine, Andrew's sister, Kelly, solved that one."

"Now, wait a minute." The sheriff was on his feet. "You're under a misunderstanding there."

"I don't think so." Cara glanced at Mitch, whose dark eyebrows were raised. Was he laughing at her, or with her? She continued, "Then there was the murder of rancher Jeb Rawlins. He was killed by Paul Lambert, and that case was solved by a new associate at the firm, Lindsey Wellington, who's also my friend. She's now engaged to Mr. Rawlins's nephew, who'd been wrongfully accused of the killing. There seem to be a lot of false allegations around here, instead of crime solving, don't you think?"

"You're out of line, Ms. Hamilton." Fury turned the

sheriff's face flaming red. Should she feel afraid? Maybe, but she didn't.

Instead, she finished with the question that she'd come here with. "Suppose you tell me, Sheriff Wilson, what the connection is among the three murders. There has to be one. They all involve Lambert & Church. And why is it that your department failed to solve the first two killings? Can we be sure you'll solve this one, or should everyone in town who had any connection with Lambert & Church be afraid for their lives?"

Chapter Three

Since Ben Wilson had become sheriff, Mitch had stirred up his ire a lot, mostly unintentionally. He'd always stifled his impulses and pulled back to avoid jeopardizing his own covert and frustrating investigation. As a result, he'd never seen Ben's leathery face as scarlet as it was now.

Damn, but he liked it!

Ben's mouth was open, as if to expel the air pumped out by his heavy breathing. Leaning toward Cara across the conference table, he sputtered, "Ms. Hamilton, if you even so much as hint in your paper that this department is doing less than a fine job, I'll—" He broke off as he obviously searched in vain for something dire enough to threaten her with.

She rose and stood behind her chair, hands resting on its back. Mitch noticed that her nails were short and unpolished, businesslike. The hands of a woman who didn't pamper herself.

"I report the facts, Sheriff Wilson," she said. "That's all." Her smile was so sweet that she might have been eating cherries. But there was an intensity in her glare, a tilt to her chin, all evidence that Cara Hamilton wasn't intimidated.

Mitch wanted to grab the sassy reporter and kiss those grinning lips. Like other urges, though, he kept this one to himself. Cara was standing up to the irritating, heavy-handed Ben Wilson as Mitch would have done, given a choice. And Mitch was enjoying every moment of it.

"Well, just watch your *facts*, missy," Ben hissed. "You'd better make good and sure they're true, or I'll sue you and your paper for slander. You tell that to your editor, Mr. Beauford Jennings, hear? In fact, I think I'll give Beau a call myself a little later, set him straight."

Cara's smile faded. "Beau doesn't buckle under threats, Sheriff, and neither do I." But the hint of uneasiness in her expression suggested Ben had scored a hit. "Now, if you gentlemen will excuse me, I have research to do."

"I'm not through with you, Ms. Hamilton." Ben walked around the table till he faced down Cara. Mitch nearly smiled when she did not step back.

"I've told you all I know, Sheriff. Now, go do your job and find out who killed Nancy." The sureness in her tone wavered a bit at the last. "She was my friend." Cara finally dropped her gaze, and Mitch figured she didn't want the sheriff to see any sign of weakness, like tears.

They might not move Ben Wilson, but Mitch had an urge to soothe the brash, yet altogether human, reporter. Instead, he stayed out of it.

"That act won't convince me you didn't kill her," Ben growled. "In fact, I *will* go do my job, like you said. I'll conduct a nice, thorough background check on you, interview everyone you've ever known, make sure Beau knows how close we're observing you. You'll be so busy watching your own behind that you won't have time to write lies about anyone. You can go write about weddings and funerals like a good little girl."

"Not on your life," Cara retorted, raising her head once more to glare up into the sheriff's looming face. Ben's scowl could have etched steel, and Mitch could all but see the steam rise in Cara. "And I told you not to threaten me."

Time for Mitch to break this up before something irreparable happened. Maybe Cara belonged in jail, though he doubted it. But if she did, it shouldn't be for irritating the sheriff. "Okay, Ms. Hamilton. We get the picture, and I think you do, too. You can go now, but we'll be in touch. I'm sure we'll have more questions."

She turned her glare on him and opened her mouth as if to fling him an angry retort. Before she said anything, though, the door to the interrogation room opened and Hurley Zeller burst in. "How we doing here? Boss, there's an important call for you." He waved a portable phone handset. "Want me to continue the interrogation?"

"No, it's over," Ben said.

As he turned away from Cara and took the phone, Mitch said, "Allow me to show you out, Ms. Hamilton."

"No need," she said quickly, but Mitch nevertheless led her around Ben and Hurley, who eavesdropped on his boss's conversation.

The call must not have been that important, for it only took Ben a few seconds. Or maybe it had just been Hurley's excuse to interrupt.

"Don't go far, Steele," Ben called as Cara stepped in front of Mitch into the reception area. "We need to talk."

"In a second, chief." Mitch took a few more steps so Ben couldn't see him, then bent slightly, inhaling Cara's fresh scent once more. "Watch your step," he whispered into Cara's ear, then turned and headed back.

In the interrogation room, Ben and Hurley were engaged in a private discussion, heads together, oblivious to his return. He froze in the doorway, straining to hear.

"The bitch'll ruin the election," Hurley grumbled. "We've gotta—"

"Okay, Steele," Ben interrupted, raising his head

abruptly as he apparently noticed Mitch. "You're evidently tight with Ms. Hamilton, so here's what I want. You talk to her, make sure she understands we're all working hard here. We're focused on this latest murder and we'll bring the perpetrator to justice. Like she figured, she's not our top suspect, but we won't let her off the hook. Not yet. Tell her I'll grant her an interview sometime when we're not all so riled up, okay? Better yet, I'll talk to her boss, Beau, tell her that. Just keep an eye on her."

Frustration and fury shot through Mitch so fiercely that they burned like lightning bolts. He'd just been given his latest little assignment to keep him busy while someone else conducted the investigation.

Not that spending more time with Cara Hamilton would be a painful pastime, though a guy had to consider every word around her. But he wasn't about to baby-sit while this investigation was bungled like the others. For she'd been right on target. Outsiders had solved the last murders, instead of the Sheriff's Department, who should have.

And that could be of major significance to Mitch and his own quest. At least one person in the department had to have been involved in his dad's murder but had been cagey enough to prevent Mitch from gleaning all but the most circumstantial evidence for two long and frustrating years. The cover-up was deep. That could mean it came from the top.

And...election? What election were they talking about?

Mitch thought fast. "Sure, chief. Promising to talk to her is a fine way to get on Ms. Hamilton's good side so she'll spill what she knows. It'll help me run the investigation of the Wilks murder."

"Don't worry about that," Ben said, one hand in the

air as if to halt contradiction by Mitch. "Hurley'll take over."

Mitch would have given anything to be able to punch the smirk off Deputy Zeller's ugly face, but he didn't. He stood still. He also stood his ground. Sure, he remained here because of his own investigation, but that didn't mean he'd turned his back on his law enforcement career. "Not a good idea," he said with more calmness than he felt. "I was there first and got a good walk-through of the crime scene even before the techs arrived. I have a sense of what was there, the neighbors' reactions, a lot of insight—"

"Yeah, like you can just call up a vision and solve the murder." Hurley's tone was derisive.

"Maybe some of my ancestors could have done just that," Mitch replied, forcing the words out mildly. He knew better than to respond to harassment revolving around his Native American blood. Despite being charged with upholding the law, the Mustang County Sheriff and his department were unconcerned about protecting anyone from discrimination based on ancestry, origin or anything else. But Mitch wasn't about to point that out. He was after something much bigger than whistle-blowing about harassment.

Keeping the flames of his temper on low, he continued, "Managing Ms. Hamilton will be a priority, but I want to head the investigation. Of course, I'll have to solve it fast or risk her writing a story that claims I don't know what the hell I'm doing." Would Ben be smart enough to bite on that not-so-subtle bait? For what Mitch had left unsaid was that he would wind up as the public scapegoat if the department failed, once again, to solve the murder.

On the other hand, he hadn't been on the other investigations. *He* hadn't been the one who'd blown them.

And he didn't intend to fail on this one, any more than proving what had happened to his father.

"Okay, go ahead," Ben said finally. "Hurley'll be your backup. You need any help, you go to him."

Right, Mitch thought. Just like I'd go to a rattlesnake for first aid.

"Yeah." Hurley sneered again. "I'll help you, Steele."

Mitch gave a quick, purposely inexpert salute. "I'd better get back to work, then."

As he exited the room, he saw that Cara had not yet left. She leaned over the reception desk, an alluring smile on her face as she spoke in undertones to the young deputy seated there. He was clearly in over his head. His face, bright red, wore a stupid grin. The phone was ringing, but he made no move to answer.

Cara obviously wanted something from the deputy. Since she was in the information business, Mitch could guess what it was.

"Going to answer that?" Mitch drawled. The deputy's eyes widened at being caught flirting. He grabbed for the phone.

Cara's charming smile melted as she looked at Mitch. "I thought you'd leave as fast as you could," he said.

"So did I." Cara headed toward the exit at last. Mitch walked beside her. "So are you still in charge of the case?"

"How—" He blinked. Could she have heard his conversation while standing out here flirting? Or was this just a diversion so he wouldn't try to extract what the deputy had disclosed to her?

"How did I guess you might not be?" She gave an enticing little laugh. "Research. Intuition. A combination. But you took charge at the crime scene, and my initial checking on the Sheriff's Department shows you've never been put at the head of any investigation more exciting than a bungled burglary. You've cracked major cases when someone else was in charge, though. My suspicion is it's not lack of skill that keeps you from getting the responsibility.''

''Could be.'' Mitch was amazed at her perceptiveness, though realized he shouldn't have been. This was one smart woman. As he'd already figured, he'd have to watch himself.

''So,'' she said as they stood on the concrete landing right outside the door. ''Are you still in charge?''

''Yeah,'' he said. ''I am.''

''Good. I'll be at the coffee shop of the Lone Star Lodge at noon today for lunch.'' The Lone Star Lodge was a seedy motel on the outskirts of town with a greasy spoon eatery attached. Not a place anyone who cared about respectability would head for. That meant it was a good place to go and not be seen.

''I've a proposal for you,'' she continued. ''Care to listen?''

Her smile was so wily and irresistible that he had an unexpected urge to run his fingers through the curly red hair that gave her the contradictory appearance of imp and angel all at once. Kiss those beguilingly clever lips.

She was daring him. He knew it. But he also knew she might have information he needed. And so he'd play along—so smoothly that she'd imagine she was in control.

''Sure,'' he said. ''I'll meet you there.''

BEFORE CARA HEADED for the Lone Star Lodge and her meeting with Mitch Steele, she had work to do.

Though the idea of going to a lodge with that delicious hunk of a deputy, a place with rooms for overnight or hourly stays, a place with beds...well, it certainly made her think of more than cooperating with him on a news story.

Her legendary idol Shotgun Sally, star investigative reporter of her time, was reputed to have had a lawman lover....

You've a murder case to look into, she reminded herself brusquely. *You might be the reason Nancy died.* That notion punished her for her incorrigible ideas. So did sliding into her car, which was stiflingly hot from sitting under the summer Texas sun.

She'd flirted with the desk deputy at the sheriff's station but learned nothing. Maybe she was foolish in using everything at her disposal, including feminine wiles, to get what she wanted.

Maybe not.

After all, Shotgun Sally always said, "Folks'll talk a lot plainer to a female who acts dumb and keeps her ears open while she yammers than one who looks too smart and keeps quiet."

Cara had a lot to say to Deputy Mitchell Steele. It might even involve telling him what he wanted to know. But only if he would reciprocate.

For now, though, she headed for the offices of the *Mustang Gazette,* in a big, old building on Main Street.

Though she dreaded it, first thing she did was visit her boss's office. Beauford Jennings was, unfortunately, in. His nose was buried in the front page of their latest edition. Other Texas papers were stacked on his desk.

"Hi, Beau." Cara slung her purse over the arm of a chair and sat down across from him. "I've some stuff to tell you."

"Anything new on the Wilks story?" Beau put down the paper and regarded Cara as if she were a sheet of newsprint he was trying to read. He squinted beneath glasses perched on the end of his pink-tipped nose.

Beauford Jennings, sixty-two years old, had inherited the *Gazette* when he was in his forties. He prided himself on being an old-time newspaper man, complete with wrinkled white shirt, suspenders and an honest-to-goodness antique manual typewriter buried under the mounds of paperwork always heaped on his desk.

He kept in close touch with his nephew, Jerry. Followed Jerry's career as he climbed each rung of his ladder to success on the *Dallas News*. And undoubtedly, despite all Beau had promised Cara, hoped that someday Jerry would return to run the *Mustang Gazette*.

"I'm working on it," she replied to his question.

"Handle this one carefully. In fact I may just take over. You did a good job reporting on those other murders, but you weren't as close to the victims then." She didn't bother to remind him that she once had been close to Andrew. "I think I'll—"

No way! "You've heard from our esteemed sheriff?" Cara interrupted. This one was hers. It wasn't just a story. As in the killings of Andrew McGovern and Jeb Rawlins, it could involve deep-down-and-dirty investigative reporting. This time she was in the thick of it, since she had found Nancy's body. She could handle the story. She would handle it.

"You bet I've heard from Sheriff Wilson." Beau removed his glasses and squeezed the bridge of his nose. "He's awful touchy about this. Said he'd sue the pants off me if I dared to criticize his department's handling of the case. He said you and he have already had words, too. Maybe someone else with more objectivity would be better on this one."

"I'm damned objective, Beau, and you can't say otherwise." Cara picked up the *Gazette* from where he'd laid it and pointed to her article. "There's not a thing wrong with this."

The story she'd e-mailed soon after leaving Nancy's last night appeared on the front page: a straightforward report on the murder, interviews with neighbors that she'd obtained after the techs took samples from her, and who to contact at the Mustang County Sheriff's Department with information that could lead to the killer. Vanilla stuff. No controversy. A damn fine job of reporting.

"No, it's a good story, Cara. But—"

"Promise you'll let me stay on it, Beau."

"Only if you—"

"And promise that this will be *the* one. If I can break the story about who killed Nancy, and tie it to the other Mustang Valley murders—"

"What do you mean?" Beau stood behind his desk. Concern and confusion etched wrinkles on a high forehead that was already well pleated.

"The Andrew McGovern and Jebediah Rawlins killings both had something to do with the law firm Lambert & Church."

"You're stretching things, Cara. Just because the first victim worked there and the murderer in the second case was a partner—"

"The third also worked there. And there's more. The first two killings also had something to do with land that one of the firm's main clients, Ranger Corporation, has been buying. I don't know yet how that fits in with Nancy's death, but I've a hunch it does." Could whatever Nancy had wanted to show Cara been the link? "Promise me, Beau. This could be Pulitzer material. If I break the case, you'll promote me this time to editor in chief."

"Sure, Cara, but—"

"Promise me. Or this time I *will* pull a Jerry and leave."

"Your family's here in town, Cara," Beau said. "You grew up here. And—"

"Same went for Jerry. He's gone. I'm here…for now. Promise me."

Beau's deep sigh of resignation was probably audible even over the hum of the high-tech printing presses on another floor of the building. "Well, okay. But—"

"Thanks, Beau." Cara grabbed her purse and ran.

CARA WAS ALREADY SEATED in one of the old-fashioned high-backed booths at the Lone Star Lodge coffee shop when Mitch arrived. It was a good place to go if one wanted to be out of the way. Not that he'd truly be anonymous in this dump; his uniform garnered glances from the few patrons.

He shook some of the dampness off his Stetson, for it was drizzling outside, unusual at this time of the year.

The only restaurant employee in sight was a plump, aproned waitress who leaned over the counter talking to one of the customers. Mitch joined Cara before the waitress could show him to a table.

Cara had fastened her curls back with combs, maybe because of the rain. As much as Mitch liked her earlier wayward, untamed look, he found this one becoming, too. The oval shape of her face, the loveliness of its soft features, were framed rather than overpowered by her attention-snatching red hair. Of course, noticing details was just part of his job.

She glanced at her watch as he slid onto the cracked vinyl seat, setting his hat down beside him. "Not bad," she said. "Are you always this prompt?"

"Are you always early?" he countered.

"Depends on who I'm meeting." Her saucy grin nearly made his socks slide down his ankles.

She was flirting! Not that he trusted it. Especially when she leaned toward him, enough that her blue knit top pulled taut across her breasts.

Some men, he expected, would babble anything that came to their mouths after a tantalizing view like that, for their minds, and the rest of their bodies, would be occupied elsewhere.

Not him. He was adept at forcing his attention where it belonged, not succumbing to distractions. "You want to talk cooperation?" Crossing his arms, he leaned back till his shoulders met the stiff wood of the booth and stared into her sparkling hazel eyes, not where her posture invited him to look.

"Absolutely." She leaned back and crossed her own arms.

"Then let's get serious." Not that he hadn't thought seriously of taking her up on her unspoken promise. What if he'd kissed those now-pouting lips right there, in front of the lackadaisical waitress and the patrons who, till now, had paid Cara and him scant attention? Maybe she'd let down her guard if she thought she'd succeeded in distracting him.

"Okay." She grinned. "Just testing. I've practiced all sorts of ways of getting people to talk to me. Men seem to prefer that one."

"I'll bet."

The waitress took their order: burger and fries for both, cola for Mitch.

"Coffee for me," Cara said. "Black. Oh, and bring me an extra pickle, please." When the waitress walked away, she told Mitch, "I considered a salad but doubted I'd feel safe that the ingredients were handled as they should be in this place."

"I read your exposé of how some restaurants treat food," Mitch said.

"Really?" Her face lit up. This time it appeared genuine.

He nodded. "Very enlightening."

"That's what I want to do." She leaned forward again, a serious expression on her face. Her top was no longer taut against her curves, but Mitch noticed them, anyway. "I want to enlighten people. I need to report the truth, Mitch. About Nancy's death and the others, too, if I can prove the connection. Will you help me?"

"Only if you help me." He gritted his teeth but kept his mouth closed. Though he had grown up far from his mother's family, she had imparted to him the Native American lore she'd grown up with—much of it involving the natural world that was once theirs in the land now known as the United States. As a result, Mitch suspected that his maternal ancestors might call him, at this moment, as foolish as a clod-headed coyote cheated out of its food by a crafty fox.

But he had a feeling that, acceptable procedure or not, cooperating in a limited way with the persuasive, single-minded Cara Hamilton would buy him a greater likelihood of solving the Wilks murder faster than pulling rank on her as a law enforcement professional. Having things made public too fast could ruin his chance to get this case solved right. Of course, she wasn't the only reporter he might need to deal with. But for now she was closest to the situation.

"Of course I'll help." But she spoke too quickly for Mitch to believe her.

"You'll share information?" he demanded.

"If you will."

"Some things I have to keep confidential to do my job. I won't tell you about a piece of evidence and have it blabbed in a story if keeping it quiet would help convict a suspect."

He didn't like this new stoniness in her expression. What was she thinking?

"Understood," she finally said. "But if I hear of something and tell you about it, I expect reciprocity. You'll share as much as you can. Tell me it's off the record, if you have to, as long as you don't overdo it. And let me know when I can put it on the record.''

Was this becoming a deal with the cagey fox who would hide the food and starve the rival coyote? Maybe. But working with her, in limited cooperation, would be a hell of a lot better than working totally against her.

But before agreeing to anything, he decided to test her. ''Fine, as far as it goes. But I want to know one thing first. What were you hiding from me before when I questioned you? Why did you really go to Nancy Wilks's house so late last night?''

She hesitated, as if deciding whether to show him the cards she held before he revealed any of his own. She finally nodded. ''Nancy did call me. She said she had something to show me.''

''Like?''

Cara shook her head, and the curls held back from her face shimmied enticingly. ''I wish I knew. And, yes, I told you a fib. I wandered around her place looking for it after I saw her…her body but didn't find a thing.''

''I see. What do you think it was?''

Her shrug appeared frustrated, and her reply was interrupted by the waitress's arrival with their drinks. When the woman left again, Cara said, ''Something from the law firm, maybe. I've no idea what, but it was important enough that she wanted me to come over at one in the morning. Unless your crime-scene guys found something I didn't, I suspect the killer took it.'' She drew in her breath. ''I also suspect it could be why she was killed.'' She closed her eyes, and when she opened them again they shimmered with tears. ''If I'd gotten there sooner—''

''Then you could have been killed, too,'' Mitch said bluntly.

Cara blinked. Her soft lips parted as if she was about

to protest, but she didn't. Mitch guessed what he'd said hadn't escaped her notice.

Plates with burgers and fries—and two pickles for Cara—were placed in front of them by the waitress, who slapped their check down, too, mumbled something about enjoying their meals and hurried away.

"Was there anything at the crime scene that points toward a suspect?" Cara asked as she lifted the top bun from her burger and inspected it. Apparently nothing looked wrong, for she put it back together and took a healthy bite.

When her eyes returned to watch him, they were narrowed and suspicious, as if expecting him to lie the way she had. Or maybe to bolt.

"Nothing yet." Mitch also started to eat.

"You'll let me know?" Cara urged.

"What I can."

"But you've got to…" There was a worried note in her voice, but she seemed to visibly cast it away. "Good enough," she finished with a sigh. "For now." Her momentary silence as she stared at the wooden booth over his shoulder made Mitch wonder what she was thinking. Then she gave a small nod, as if she'd answered her own internal question, and said, "I'm going to go at it from the other angle. This murder has to be related somehow to Andrew McGovern's and Jebediah Rawlins's murders."

"Their murders were solved," Mitch reminded her. "Two separate killers. Our former mayor did Andrew in, and Paul Lambert killed Rawlins."

Cara nodded. "But there's that law firm connection. And maybe something to do with its client, Ranger Corporation. I'm considering a political connection, too, since Mayor Daniels was involved in the first murder."

Political… That reminded Mitch of the snatch of conversation he'd heard between Sheriff Ben Wilson and Deputy Hurley Zeller: that Cara's snooping might ruin the election. He'd mulled it over. Why would they care? The only thing he could figure was that Ben was thinking of running for mayor. The top county commissioner had taken the position temporarily after the former mayor's disgrace and death, and had made it clear he didn't want to stay there. If Ben won the next mayoral election, it would leave the sheriff's position open. Zeller and Mitch were the most likely candidates, but Mitch knew who Ben Wilson would back. And it wouldn't be him.

Could Ben win? What kind of mayor would he make? Heaven help Mustang Valley!

"Mitch?" Cara was staring at him. "Did you think of something important?"

Important to him, not this case. "Not really."

"You promised to share, damn it." She rose and grabbed her big purse, reaching into it for her wallet.

"Sit down," Mitch urged. "I *am* going to share what I can. That's what I can promise, no more." He didn't like promising even that. Solitude and secrecy were as vital as breathing to him.

Cara suddenly looked young and vulnerable again, almost the way she had when he'd come across her at the crime scene.

Something had hurt her.

And he had no business feeling as if he wanted to slug the hell out of whoever, or whatever, it was.

"Cara, tell me what the problem is."

She stared at him, then slid back into the booth. "Nothing. But if we're going to work together, then we're *both* going to work together. Understood?"

"As long as you understand that I can't tell you everything," he repeated.

She stared, then held out her hand over the table. He

did the same and shook. Her hand was small in his. Touching her warm, vibrant skin, even in so businesslike a gesture, made his temperature rise.

He released her and took a quick, cooling sip of his cola. When he looked up, she was still studying him, as if determining whether she could trust him.

Obviously their deal, such as it was, was important to her.

To him, too. He needed an alliance of sorts with her, some degree of control over this determined reporter.

He'd made himself learn the appearance of teamwork at the Sheriff's Department, though trust was as foreign a language to him as the cawing of crows. Especially with the way he was often treated as an outsider. Was that due to his father's bad judgment in hiring him and for taking bribes? Or was it due to Mitch's own heritage?

Or to his preference for keeping his own counsel?

Probably a combination, though he was certain that no one in the department knew he was continuing his own investigation. After two long, frustrating years there were times he wondered if he was still investigating, since new leads were all but nonexistent. But he was patient. He made himself exude patience, as if he were a runner and calmness was his sweat.

It didn't hurt that he had encouragement from his contact at the state attorney general's office.

Now he'd have to make sure Cara and he didn't work at cross-purposes. Otherwise, she could blow this new murder investigation, intentionally or by accident.

"Let's talk strategy," he finally said. "How do you plan to research your story?"

"Well," Cara said slowly, as if making up her mind whether to speak. Then her voice took on its usual determination. "I'm going to call my friend Lindsey Wellington. She's at Bart Rawlins's ranch. They were the ones who figured out Paul Lambert killed Bart's uncle Jeb, then tried to frame Bart for it. She was an associate at the law firm, so she's out of work. Which is fine with her for now. Bart and she are going to be married. Maybe she can shed some light on what Nancy wanted to show me.''

"Good idea. You'll let me know what she says?''

Cara nodded. "And I'm planning to meet with the Ranger Corporation's Mustang Valley representative to get his perspective on the killings.''

That direction could lead to quicksand. "Be careful,'' Mitch warned. "I've heard the guy—Rosales—is up in arms about the allegations against his company. The talk at the department is to tread carefully there, not make unsubstantiated claims.''

"I won't allege anything I can't back up. I'll report the facts. They're public, anyway. Our dear former mayor killed Andrew McGovern to hide his conflict of interest because of his investment in Ranger Corporation. By the way, in the spirit of sharing information with you, I was once engaged to Andrew.''

That jolted Mitch. "Sorry,'' he murmured.

"It was a long time ago.'' Yet it still drew shadows in the depths of her soft hazel eyes. "And Paul Lambert,'' she continued more strongly, "killed a rancher to try to get control of his property so it could be sold to Paul's client, Ranger Corporation.''

"Looks that way in both cases,'' Mitch acknowledged, "but no evidence we found pointed to Ranger's direct involvement in the killings. They'd apparently just come to town to buy property for some development. We couldn't hang anything on them showing they solicited either the mayor's investment or their lawyer's eagerness to make the property they wanted available.''

"But you looked?''

"The guys on those cases did,'' Mitch said. He gave

her a rundown of the unclassified stuff he knew—and that elicited a big smile from her.

If information got her to smile like that, he wondered what else he could tell her... *Don't be an ass, Steele,* he cautioned himself. Cara Hamilton was a reporter. A very good reporter.

"Too bad we can't question either Mayor Daniels or Paul Lambert about a connection," Cara said when he was done. While trying to escape after being found out, the mayor had crashed his car into a tree and died. Lambert had committed suicide in his cell. "Do you think Lambert's partner, Donald Church, would know anything?"

"If so, I doubt he'd tell you. He's a lawyer. He won't violate attorney-client privilege and talk about the firm's client, Ranger Corporation—particularly if it might somehow link him to all that's gone on, or at least make him look like a fool. Far as I know, he still intends to practice law here, though the former Lambert & Church firm is down the toilet."

"I can't prove that whatever Nancy wanted to show me had anything to do with Ranger, anyway," Cara acknowledged. "But I'll talk to Church to see what his position is. And to see what else I can learn. Could be something else was wrong at the law firm that prompted the murders—including Nancy's."

"Maybe," Mitch agreed. "But don't jump to conclusions."

"Of course not." She smiled at him. "And now that I've shared my next moves with you, how about sharing yours with me?"

The idea of their sharing moves... Had she intended the double entendre? She'd shown she wasn't above flirting to get what she wanted. Intentional or not, the thought heated him to near boiling. He found that damned disturbing. ''I'll check in to see what the crime-scene guys learned,'' he said coolly.

''You'll let me know the results?''

''What I can.'' Which wouldn't be much. His primary responsibility was to the people of this county, to bring down the perpetrator. Hers was to get a good story.

She studied him again, then said, ''Mitch, do you...'' Her voice tapered off. ''Okay, let me just be blunt,'' she finally said. ''I wasn't kidding before when I talked to Sheriff Wilson, Mitch. It seems odd that the County Sheriff's Department didn't solve the first two murders.''

''It'll solve the third.'' He would see to it.

''You don't think that the...well, inability to solve the others was intentional, do you?''

''No.'' He inserted false conviction into his gaze. There *was* something Cara didn't know, but he was not about to enlighten her.

There had been a fourth murder that had had something to do with the Lambert & Church law firm. The connection seemed indirect, but it related to a scandal.

The scandal that had destroyed Mitch's father. And had, apparently, led to his suicide.

But Mitch was sure his father had been murdered.

And now he was in charge of investigating Nancy Wilks's death. He'd be able to dig more into Lambert & Church and its clients without being second-guessed by his boss. This could even be the break he needed.

And working with Cara Hamilton could provide the additional cover he required. He'd use her, if necessary. And this time, nothing—not Cara or anyone else—would keep Mitch from solving his father's murder, too.

Chapter Four

Cara sat in her Toyota, windows down to try to dispel some of the damp heat. She watched as Mitch pulled out of the nearly empty, rutted parking lot of the shabby restaurant in his white sedan marked with the Mustang County Sheriff's Department shield.

An official car. A car that displayed his authority. If it wasn't such a symbol, though, it would be too ordinary to suit Mitchell Steele. Despite how mild mannered he appeared, she didn't buy it. He belonged in some huge, powerful sport utility vehicle that he could command over the rugged terrain of Mustang County beyond town. Or maybe on a big hog of a motorcycle.

Something a man who was all male would pick.

Despite his apparent aloofness, Cara had seen something in the depths of Mitch's eyes suggesting that he was very, very human. Very masculinely human. She'd never met a guy with so much sex appeal.

While engaged in a neutral business chat with him, her mind had kept turning to the seedy Lone Star Lodge and all its nearby beds. Wondering how he would be between the sheets. No, on top of them. They would be too hot together for any kind of covers over their entwined bodies.

Nothing beat a lawman lover....

Get out of my mind, Shotgun Sally, Cara thought, laughing aloud. But only for a moment.

She'd made a deal with Mitch Steele. A devil's bargain to share information with him.

He was to share information with her, too.

Right. The way Jerry Jennings had when he'd stolen her research and run with it, leaped on it as a springboard for his own flourishing career. He'd used it. Used *her.*

Just as Mitch Steele was apt to do if she unearthed anything juicy.

She slammed her hand against the steering wheel. It wasn't as if she had a choice about dealing with Mitch. Not if she wanted any cooperation from the Sheriff's Department.

She would live up to her end of the bargain, and she would make damned sure Mitch didn't take advantage of her. Or stand in the way of a really good story.

It's only a sin to blunder now and again if you don't learn a gosh-darned good lesson from it. Another favorite Sally-ism. One Cara would take to heart now. "Thanks, Sally," she murmured into the thick, sweltering air.

Idly Cara glanced around. The one-story, sprawling inn looked sun weathered, in need of a good coat of paint. It was the kind of place that rented rooms by the hour. Apparently, Mustang County's lovers weren't very lusty that afternoon. Just three other vehicles besides Cara's remained in the parking lot, two cars by the restaurant and a pickup truck near the sign that indicated where the inn's registration was.

The landscaping around the place looked as sparse as the patrons, just the rolling, scrub-covered terrain that comprised a lot of Mustang County.

Cara reached into her oversize purse, past her notebook and into the bottom where her cell phone usually hid. When she found it, she used its internal directory to find the phone number for the Four Aces, Bart Rawlins's ranch.

She waited as the phone rang once, twice, three times, blotting her lightly perspiring face with a tissue from her bag. Could she be interrupting Bart and Lindsey in some prenuptial recreational activities?

Once again she laughed at herself. She had to get her mind out of the bedroom, notwithstanding the pact she had struck with the sexy Mitch. They *would* work together. Even if he didn't intend to. She'd simply get enough tantalizing stuff to tease him with so he'd share with her, too—

"Hello?" It was a woman's voice. Out of breath.

"Lindsey? It's Cara. Am I interrupting anything?"

A brief hesitation. "No. We were just outside, on the way to the pasture when I heard the phone. I ran back."

"I see." Cara inserted a teasing note of incredulity into her voice.

"Never mind," Lindsey said firmly, then laughed.

Cara could picture her friend, with her slender build that shouted of all the workouts she did, gleaming brown hair and brilliant green eyes. A lawyer, from a family of eastern lawyers. She'd come to Mustang Valley to prove her own worth as an attorney and had gotten more than she'd bargained for. Her first case had been a murder defense, and she'd won. Had she ever! For not only had she gotten her client off by finding the real killer, she'd fallen in love with him. Bart Rawlins and she would be getting married soon.

"If this is a bad time, I'll call back," Cara said. "I need to talk to you, though, about Lambert & Church."

"And Nancy Wilks." Lindsey's voice sounded strained. "I heard the news, of course. And that you found her. I was going to call you later to make sure you were all right."

Cara leaned back in her car seat, swallowing hard as she recalled the sight of Nancy the night before. "I'm okay."

"Of course you are," Lindsey said. "Cara, I'm so sorry. Do you want me to come back to town to be with you? Or you could come to the ranch."

And become the third person on a near honeymoon? "Thanks, anyway, but I'll stay here. I'm working on the story. Lindsey, I was there because Nancy called me. She said she had something to show me. Do you have any idea what it might be?"

Cara trusted Lindsey with this information, for though the former associate at the Lambert firm was a relative newcomer to town, Lindsey had quickly become a close friend of Cara's and her other dearest friend, Kelly McGovern. Kelly, who'd helped to solve the murder of her brother, Andrew, was now off on her own honeymoon with Wade Lansing, of all people. She'd recently married Wade, who'd been Andrew's best friend and the owner of the wildest tavern in Mustang Valley.

Cara figured that a shared goal, fraught with mystery and danger, was a powerful aphrodisiac, for she'd never imagined Kelly and Wade as a couple. But now she realized they were perfect for each other.

"I wish I knew what Nancy had in mind," Lindsey replied to Cara's question. "Shotgun Sally always said things happen in threes, and now I believe it."

That was one thing Cara, Lindsey and Kelly had in common: all were fascinated by the many stories of the celebrated Shotgun Sally. Her legend was filled with escapades that were sometimes contradictory but always amazing and enthralling. Cara figured that the inconsistencies were, in fact, consistent. Sally was, after all, an early investigative reporter. She took on many different guises to get her stories, as Cara was willing to do.

"First Andrew McGovern, then Jeb Rawlins and now Nancy."

Lindsey continued. "All dead. Do they know who killed Nancy?"

"No, but I intend to figure out not only who did it, but how the three murders are related."

"You think they are?" Lindsey asked. "I mean, I know about the law firm connection, and that Ranger Corporation's name cropped up in both of the first cases, but the killers can't be the same. The mayor and Paul Lambert are dead, so neither could have had anything to do with Nancy's death. And there's no question that they were the respective murderers."

"On the surface, I don't see the firm's connection, either." Cara agreed with the assessment previously jumped on by Mitch, too. "But if there's something hidden, I intend to find out."

"Just be careful," Lindsey cautioned. "And let me know if there's anything I can do."

"There is one thing," Cara said.

"What?"

"Go back to Bart. Give him a great big kiss and… whatever."

Lindsey laughed and hung up.

As Cara turned on her engine and pulled out of the parking lot, she noticed that the pickup truck left at the same time.

Strange. She hadn't seen anyone exit the inn.

"I'M GLAD TO MEET YOU, Ms. Hamilton," said Roger Rosales, Manager of Regional Development for Ranger Corporation.

Cara smiled as they shook hands. His grip was firm, his return smile practiced. Except for his tan summerweight business suit and beige tie, Roger wasn't what

Cara expected. He looked even younger than Cara's twenty-seven years, with beaming brown eyes and hair the shade of café au lait.

He looked like someone's younger brother, playing at being in charge. But Cara knew better than to underestimate anyone.

Just like she had no intention of misconstruing her uneasy alliance with the sexy Deputy Steele.

"Please sit down." Roger motioned toward a wooden chair upholstered in a soft plaid that matched the heavy draperies in his richly appointed office. The Ranger Corporation's presence in Mustang Valley wasn't very large, but Mustang Valley wasn't very large, either. The compact office suite, composed of this room and the reception area, was located in the most prestigious building in downtown—an old, stately edifice, whose granite exterior had been well maintained for over a century.

It had probably even been there in Shotgun Sally's time.

"Thanks for seeing me, Roger," Cara said. "I'm working on an article about big companies headquartered elsewhere that do business in Mustang County. There are a surprising number and—"

"I read in your paper, heard on the news, that you were the one who found poor Nancy Wilks last night," he said, interrupting, his smile sympathetic now as he leaned toward her over a desk that appeared to be highly polished mahogany.

Good thing Cara had already determined not to underestimate this sweet-appearing young man. *A polecat who'd painted his white stripe black.* That's what Shotgun Sally would call him.

"That's right," Cara said with a shiver. "I did find Nancy."

"Terrible thing." He shook his head. "There've been

a lot of killings lately in this area. That's made Ranger Corporation start rethinking whether or not to locate a development here.''

''Really? What kind of development is Ranger considering, Roger?'' Cara was determined to take control of the interview. She enjoyed verbal sparring, but on her own terms.

''Oh, that's confidential,'' he said. ''Especially since we've been treated so badly in the media. If anyone learned what we hoped to accomplish here, it might get trashed even before we could show how much it would help this area's economy.''

Cara was beginning to loathe the boyish grin that hid this man's cunning depths. He was turning her interview into his own lobbying effort.

''Did Mayor Daniels know Ranger's plans?'' she asked.

''If so, the information did not come from me.''

''So you weren't aware that Mayor Daniels's investment in Ranger Corporation could be considered a conflict of interest?''

Roger shrugged. ''Stock in Ranger Corporation is not traded on the major markets, but it's not that closely held. We don't teach ethics to the people who own shares.''

''And the fact that your attorney, Paul Lambert, murdered a rancher to try to make his land available for Ranger Corporation—you weren't involved in his ethics, either?''

For the first time, Roger's eyes narrowed. He no longer looked so young or guileless. In fact, he appeared ticked. *Good!* Cara thought.

''Look, Cara. I know you're a good reporter. I've read some of your stuff. I assume you could prove your allegations. But don't imagine you can pin anything on Ranger. We had nothing to do with what Mayor Daniels did in Andrew McGovern's murder. Nor did we solicit the Jeb Rawlins's murder, whether or not it was committed by Paul Lambert—who, by the way, was innocent until proven guilty, so now we'll never know, since he took his own life. And if you decide to print an article with allegations against Ranger, the company will take any steps necessary to protect its reputation, including suing for defamation.''

Cara's ire was raised. The man was threatening her— or at least her paper. And that meant her career could suffer. And her career was everything to her.

She might not be easily cowed by the likes of Roger Rosales, but her boss Beau Jennings would be.

''Did I say I intended to make false claims?'' she demanded. ''I believe truth is always a defense in that kind of lawsuit.''

Roger put his smile back on his face. This time it looked more like a sneer. ''Prove Ranger's involvement. I'll bet you came here hoping I'd admit a connection not only to those ugly crimes, but to poor Ms. Wilks's murder, too.''

The thought had crossed Cara's mind. ''Is there a connection, Roger?'' she asked sweetly.

''This meeting is over.'' He rose. ''Thank you for coming.''

''You're very welcome,'' she said sardonically, also standing. She took a few steps toward the door, then turned back. ''Oh, and don't get too comfortable thinking we've resolved anything. I'm interested in anything that affects Mustang Valley, and my research on Ranger Corporation is nowhere near complete. If I find evidence to tie Ranger to anything shady—well, keep reading the papers, Roger. You might see something enlightening.''

The menace in his glare seared her. Though she'd refused to feel intimidated by his promise to sue the *Gazette,* she again resolved not to take this man too lightly.

He had something to hide. She was sure of it.

This was a conversation she would share with Mitch, including the threats, explicit and implicit. He'd probably find them interesting. Maybe they'd give him extra impetus to seek a link between Nancy's murder and Ranger Corporation.

Head high, she strode out to the reception area.

By late afternoon, Mitch could hardly keep his eyes open.

To remain alert, he rose and stretched, his arms spanning into the next guy's allotted space in the cramped deputy administration room. He was senior enough that he'd been assigned a corner, and it was crowded with boxes of paperwork. Glancing at his watch, he realized he'd spent the past two hours on his barely comfortable chair at his gouged wooden desk.

The deputy admin room smelled of the spicy Mexican lunches favored by the officers who inhabited it. By now most had abandoned their rabbit warren of desks and were out in the field on their various assignments.

Not Mitch. After briefly revisiting the Nancy Wilks murder scene earlier to check its status, he'd come in to go over reports and talk on the phone with the Dallas labs where evidence had been sent for analysis. Mustang County was too small to afford state-of-the-art equipment, and Mitch would allow for no less to be used in this investigation.

Deputy Stephanie Greglets walked in, followed by Deputy Hurley Zeller. Stephanie was a tall woman who was recruited into the Mustang County Sheriff's Department just after Mitch joined, with little prior experience beyond police academy training. Hurley kept panting after her, but Mitch was glad to see her constantly put the crude man in his place. It helped that she practiced martial arts and was far tougher than her harasser.

"How's the investigation going, Mitch?"

"Nothing conclusive yet," he said, "but—" His cell phone rang. He reached into the pocket beneath his badge and extracted it. "Hello?"

"Mitch? Cara. Have a minute?"

"Yeah. Hang on." Mitch saw Hurley studying him. Whatever Cara wanted to say, he didn't want Zeller listening in.

"That your new girlfriend, the murder suspect?" Hurley's guffaw followed Mitch as he headed for the stubby but brightly lit hall.

"Yes, Cara?" He leaned on the gray wall beside the building's rear exit.

"I talked to Lindsey Wellington. No help there. And then I visited Roger Rosales. I'm sure he knows something, Mitch."

"Like what?"

"He was playing games with me. He tried to tell me how to do my job, and—"

"How's the redheaded babe?" Hurley Zeller stood in front of Mitch, smirking, gut stretching the khaki of his uniform above his belt. "You gettin' any?"

"I'll call you back." Mitch snapped his phone shut. Damn. He hadn't wanted to be so abrupt with Cara, especially when she'd actually called to share something—though she hadn't gotten to the meat of it. "You want something, Zeller?"

"I wouldn't mind a little of what you're getting." His wide grin showed the yellowed teeth of a frequent smoker. "How good is she?"

Mitch controlled his urge to erase Hurley's face, invoking the serenity of his native ancestors as he did a lot recently. "If you mean Ms. Hamilton, she's agreed to cooperate with the Sheriff's Department in the investigation."

"She's got no choice. The preliminary lab report says your Ms. Hamilton's prints were all over the Wilks murder scene."

Mitch refused to show surprise. Not at the fingerprints, but because Hurley had seen the findings. "Of course they were. She found the body. And what were *you* doing with the lab report?" It was on Mitch's desk. He'd been working on it.

"I asked the lab for extra copies of everything. That way I'll be up to speed when you ask for my help."

Yeah, and Mitch would do that when he took up snowboarding in hell. "I'd better tell Ben you need something to do. Since you're messing around in my case, you've obviously got too much time on your hands." Mitch looked at the big paws resting on the sides of Hurley's protruding waist. "You know, my car needs a good washing. Why don't you take care of that while I work on the department matters I'm assigned?"

"Like screwing Ms. Hamilton?"

"Go—" Mitch began, then shut up as Stephanie Greglets joined them in the hallway.

"Hurley, the chief's looking for you," she said.

"See ya, Steele," Hurley said, grinning again at Mitch.

Mitch sighed as he forced his anger down. No use responding to a jerk like Hurley. But he personified what so many others here expressed more by what they didn't say than what they did say. Good thing Mitch worked best alone. He despised anyone looking over his shoulder. And the few times anyone had offered to work with him, their reasons had been obvious. They wanted the credit. Or they wanted him to take the fall if something went wrong. He was, after all, his father's son.

"Don't let Hurley get to you," Stephanie said.

He looked at her. She wore her dark hair in a cap that was almost masculine, though her soft facial contours and long lashes were definitely female. A pretty lady. Not his type, though.

His type... Cara Hamilton's cute and sexy face popped into his mind, and he forced it right back out again.

"Right," he said to Stephanie, and turned away.

"Actually, Ben didn't send for him," Stephanie said. "I needed to talk to you."

Mitch turned back. "Yeah?"

"I figured you'd want to know that not only Hurley, but Ben, too, is getting copies of the lab reports. And he's intercepted the phone records you asked for."

"Damn. Thanks, Stephanie." He stopped for a moment, looked at her. Why would she tell him?

As if responding to his unasked question, she said, "Like I've said, I want to help you in this case. It's a murder. High profile. I was kept off the other murder investigations because I'm a woman, though no one here would ever admit to that kind of discrimination. I've seen the prejudices against you, too—your background, your dad. Maybe we can help each other. And if I can be on the team that solves this latest murder, it can't hurt my career, right?"

What she said made sense. But Mitch was too leery to bite. "Right," he replied anyway. "We'll talk later." Now, he wanted to talk to the sheriff about some phone records.

The sheriff wanted to see him, too. Ben Wilson sat at his large desk. Behind him hung an autographed photo of the governor of Texas with the flags of Texas and the United States flanking it. The office was nearly the size of the whole deputy admin room.

Fortunately, Hurley wasn't there.

"Sit down, Mitch," Ben said. Mitch took one of the low wooden chairs facing the desk. Its rounded back hit him just above the kidneys. "I've just gotten a nasty call from Roger Rosales, local rep of Ranger Corporation. Seems that Ms. Cara Hamilton has been harassing him. Threatening him."

Damn. Mitch wished he'd gotten Cara's version of the conversation before this confrontation. "I need to talk to her anyway, get clarification of part of her statement. I'll find out what happened."

"You do that," Ben said.

"By the way, I understand you received some phone records I requested—calls to and from the murder victim Nancy Wilks."

"You heard it wrong. The records I got are from the Lambert law firm. They were already collected for what would have been the prosecution of Paul Lambert in the Rawlins murder."

"I need to see them. Some might have been Ms. Wilks's."

"Later. Meantime, I'm counting on you to get Ms. Hamilton off Ranger Corporation's case. Threaten her, call Beau Jennings about her, whatever. We've enough important matters around here that we don't need to throw that reporter in jail for acting malicious, you know?"

"Yeah, I know," Mitch said grimly. It was time he got the details of Cara's conversation with Roger Rosales.

He signed out for the day so he'd be on his own time, not that he was done working on the murder. He'd go chat with Cara. With no interruptions.

Reaching his car, he slipped inside and called her on her cell phone.

"Cara, I need to continue the conversation we started earlier," he said when he reached her. "Where are you?"

"Just getting out of my car across from Nancy's. I'm

going to—'' She ended with a quick intake of breath. ''No!'' she screamed.

Mitch heard a shriek of brakes before a noise like metal slamming metal. And then nothing.

Chapter Five

Stunned, Cara lay across the hood of her car, her legs dangling over the front, her dark-blue denim skirt hiked up.

All those self-defense lessons she'd taken for years and she hadn't been able to use them—not against machinery and metal.

Fortunately, she'd had the presence of mind to leap up on the hood when the pickup came barreling down Caddo Street straight toward her. At least the idiot driving it hadn't ploughed into her car. He had just scraped its side.

But he wouldn't have been able to keep going then, would he? This hit-and-run had seemed intentional.

"Are you all right?" Cara recognized Mrs. Bea Carrow, who stared at her in concern from the sidewalk. The middle-aged lady was one of Nancy Wilks's upstairs neighbors Cara had interviewed yesterday morning.

"Sure," Cara said. Or tried to say. Adrenaline still pumped through her so hard that she continued to gasp for breath. She slid off the hood, though she remained leaning against her car for support. Her legs wobbled as if made of elastic. She pulled her skirt down. "Did you see what happened?"

Bea shook her head. Not a strand of her blue compact

hairdo moved out of place. "No, but I saw the truck speed down the street."

"I saw it," said a teenager on a bicycle. Under his bright-blue-and-red helmet, the boy was wide-eyed and appeared nearly as shaken as Cara felt. "He looked like he was going to hit you."

"Yeah." Cara became aware of a pain in both arms and along the side of one leg. Her whole body would turn black and blue. "Did you get a good look at the driver?" When the kid shook his head, she asked, "How about his license number? Did you see it?"

"No," the boy said.

Since he appeared ready to cry, Cara said, "That's okay. No harm done." Except that he got away. For now.

"Can I drive you to the hospital?" Bea asked.

"No, thanks. I'll catch my breath, then I'll be fine."

"If you're sure—"

Cara nodded, though she wasn't sure at all.

At least she had the presence of mind to remind Bea who she was, introduce herself to the boy, Tommy Dalford, and hand him her card. "I'm working on a story about poor Nancy's death for the *Gazette*. I'm sure this was just an accident, but…" She got promises from both of them to let her know if they remembered anything important about the speeding, menacing truck.

When Bea and Tommy left, Cara shakily headed back to the street—though she looked carefully to make sure the guy wasn't plowing toward her again.

She ruefully surveyed the long scrape along the side of her poor little yellow Toyota. Not bad enough to turn into her insurance company and get hit with a big rate increase, but it would take a bite from her budget to fix. And she certainly wasn't going to live with it that way.

At least she was going to *live*….

The sound of a motor startled her. She hurried back to

the curb and watched as the vehicle screeched to a stop beside her car. It was a white sheriff's department sedan. Mitch Steele leaped out without his hat, slamming the door. His uniform was crisp and clean—unlike Cara's rumpled clothing.

"Cara! What happened? Are you all right?"

Only then did she recall she'd been in the middle of a phone call with him. That showed how shaken she was. Vaulting out of the way of a speeding truck could be the only reason she would forget she'd been speaking to the sexy deputy with whom she had to weigh every word.

"I'm okay," she said, ignoring the wobbliness in her voice and hoping he would, too. She scanned the ground for her phone till she found it against the curb in a couple of smashed pieces.

"You don't look okay." Mitch's strong hands grasped her arms, holding her steady—sort of. Irritably she realized her body still trembled as much as her voice. She looked up defiantly into his face. His golden eyes studied her as if she were a fragile vase that had been slammed against a wall.

Fragile? Her? Still, the idea that Mitch worried about her felt surprisingly good. "I appreciate your concern, but—"

"Now tell me what the hell happened."

So much for his considering her delicate. "A truck. I saw it earlier today after we left the Lone Star Lodge, and—"

"You saw it before?"

"I think so. It pulled out after me, though I didn't see anyone get into it."

"Can you describe it? Did you get a license number?"

"Yes and no." She blinked as he went out of focus, then back again. "Mitch, I'm sorry, but could you take me home? We'll talk there, but I really need to sit down."

MITCH KNEW WHERE CARA LIVED. It was in her witness statement in the Wilks murder. He was aware of the new Mustang Valley apartment complex that attracted singles and young marrieds—nicely landscaped grounds, amenities including swimming pool and spa and apartments that were small but well equipped. The kind of place for someone too busy to worry about maintenance or repair.

Not the kind of place Mitch liked, but he was glad Cara lived there because it had a security system.

He accompanied her to her apartment and found reasons to like it even more. Cara had decorated it to look as vibrant as she was. Beneath the sloped ceilings, bright splashes of color in handmade wall hangings, braided rugs and chair throws contrasted with bright white walls and starkly shaped wooden furniture.

She walked in ahead of him, then collapsed onto her sofa and pulled off her low-topped western boots. She hiked her feet up under her, tucking them beneath her long blue skirt. ''You know,'' she said, ''there aren't many times I'd say this, but if I could live the last day over, I think I'd take a trip.''

''Where to?'' He figured she'd choose a big, bustling city full of news.

Instead, she said, ''A rafting tour of the Grand Canyon. Or just camp out in the mountains somewhere.''

Both sounded inviting to Mitch. But he wasn't here to daydream with this attractive woman who kept surprising him. And he certainly wasn't here to daydream *about* her. Still, when she stretched her legs out and leaned sideways, her curly red hair contrasting with the deep-green afghan tossed carelessly over the back of the couch, he imagined sitting beside her, taking her into his arms. Holding her. Touching her—

Back off, damn it. If he let her under his skin, she'd only distract him more. And letting someone, especially someone outspoken and likely to call attention to herself—and him—get close to him, was a big mistake.

"I suppose you want to know if I have any idea who tried to run me over," she said sleepily, blinking at him.

"Do you?"

"No. I doubt it was Roger Rosales, since I saw the truck before I met with him. Unless it was a different old blue pickup. And unless he killed Nancy and was following me because he knew I was on my way to her place at the time, and—"

"Okay, point taken. I've already radioed in for the patrol units to watch for a blue pickup with a scraped side. Now, fill me in on your conversation with Rosales." He pulled his small pad from his pocket and took notes, though nothing Cara said shed light on the Wilks murder. Nor did it amount to her threatening the guy, as Rosales had claimed to Sheriff Wilson.

When she was through, Mitch relayed what Ben Wilson had insisted he tell her. "I'm here to warn you not to bother Rosales."

He nearly laughed at the fierce expression that shadowed her face. "*He's* the one making threats," she exploded. "Against freedom of speech, the right of the public to know. Just like that damned Sheriff Wayne back in Shotgun Sally's time."

"Shotgun Sally? What does a fictional—"

"She was real!" Cara's anger a moment earlier seemed like a minor irritation compared with her riled demeanor now. Her soft red eyebrows were hooked into furious lines and her full lips parted as if prepared to battle the slightest contradiction. "Don't you know the story of Shotgun Sally and her fight with Sheriff Wayne?"

"Not exactly," Mitch admitted. He'd never paid much attention to legends, except for those about his mother's people that she'd related to him when he was young. And he never considered them anything but stories created to explain otherwise inexplicable things to a complex but unsophisticated people.

Cara's former sleepiness seemed to have evaporated. Her anger, too, for it gave way to enthusiasm as she spoke. "Sally really lived, Mitch. And all the stories told about her—well, most were probably real, even though they seemed to contradict each other because the whole time, she was an undercover investigative reporter for the *Mustang Gazette*. It was a tiny paper then, before newspapers were even started in Dallas or Ft. Worth, but it had a fairly large circulation considering the number of people who lived around here. And the best of Sally's stories was about her clash with Sheriff Wayne. Wayne was the head of the local sheriff's department, and that made him Deputy Zachary Gale's boss. Zachary was Sally's lawman lover."

Lawman lover. The words ignited Mitch's fantasies, and not about Shotgun Sally. Not while he had his eyes trained on the vivacious Cara Hamilton....

Yeah, and the last time he'd gotten involved with a woman for anything beyond a casual roll in the hay he'd learned the hard way that Ellen had been more interested in learning if Native American men did things differently in the bedroom from ordinary men. That had been just before the scandal with Mitch's dad broke. When it did, Ellen left, but not before making it clear to Mitch that he wasn't so exciting after all.

And Mitch was sure Cara wouldn't settle for anything casual. She'd throw herself into a relationship with the same zeal she had for everything else.

Tantalizing...but not for Mitch.

He forced his attention back to her story. It was long and convoluted, and involved the legendary Sally's quest to find her sister, Sarah's, murderer. "Sheriff Wayne claimed to be heartbroken, since he'd been courting Sarah. He tried to pin Sarah's murder on Sally and was loud and outspoken about it. That forced Zachary to appear to go after Sally, accusing her, too—not that he believed it. It was only a ploy so Zachary could keep his job and help her, too.

"Sally hated the way Sheriff Wayne used his authority to try to shut down the *Gazette* for printing slurs about him—even though they were true. Her editor supported her but kept warning her to back off. For a while she hid out on her family land but couldn't do much investigating from there. Eventually she disguised herself as a ranch hand and went to work at a neighboring spread owned by a rich tenderfoot from the east, Clarence McJanuary.

"Sally kept sending news stories back to her editor at the *Gazette,* making innuendos about the sheriff and even Zachary, so no one would know they were working together. And her editor, despite all the arm twisting, kept printing them, bless him.

"Sally suspected Sheriff Wayne was the murderer—until she found evidence that *she* was the intended victim.

"She kept digging and ostensibly feuding with Zachary until she actually was shot by the bad guy, good old Clarence McJanuary. He was after the land owned by Sally's family and figured he'd never be able to steal it as long as she was in the public eye as a crusading newspaper reporter. He'd intended to kill her, not her sister. Sally caught him, and by doing so she meted out the Texas law of the West on her own terms."

"Interesting story." Mitch was surprised that he meant it. "I'd heard some of it before."

"When?"

"I went to high school in Glenside." Glenside was a town only a few miles from Mustang Valley. It wasn't a time, though, that he wanted to talk about. He and his parents had moved there when he was a junior, and it had been a tough time for a quiet kid who'd wanted to fit in. He'd learned his lesson well—by fighting everyone who called him or his Native American mother names. Finally he'd fit in by being left alone. Just the way he wanted.

Cara's expression became contemplative as she looked at him, but she seemed to think better of asking what was on his mind. She finished her story. "Like other Sally legends, this one has multiple endings. One says she died from her wound, though I hate to think that. The one I like best says she just retired from reporting—at least under her own name—and Zachary and she married and lived happily ever after on her family's land, after Mc-January was convicted of killing her sister and hanged."

"And you think this story was true?" Mitch shouldn't have goaded her, but he was coming to like the way she looked when her most belligerent streak took over. In fact, he was coming to like the way she looked no matter what was on her mind.

"Of course it was." Cara seemed ready to argue further, until she yawned into her hand.

"There's nothing else you can tell me about that truck or your interview with Rosales?"

"No," she said. And that meant it was time for him to leave.

As much as he had an urge to stay.

It wasn't the most professional thing for a deputy sheriff to do with a crime victim, potentially hostile witness and reluctant ally, but he bent down and kissed Cara's warm, smooth cheek. He was as taken aback by the gesture as Cara's amazed look suggested she was.

"Lock the door behind me," he said gruffly, "and get a good night's sleep." He left the apartment, shutting the door firmly after him.

DRAT! CARA THOUGHT. If she'd been wider awake, she'd have reached up and given Deputy Sheriff Mitch Steele a *real* kiss.

Yeah, and lost any ability of getting the Sheriff's Department to cooperate with her story research. She'd have run Mitch off as fast as if she'd proposed marriage to him.

Now, where the heck had that come from?

Angry with herself for her thoughts, and for flirting with Mitch while knowing he wasn't the kind of man to succumb to feminine wiles and disgorge the information she wanted, she stood and did as he'd ordered—locked the door.

She still felt sleepy, but wired, too, after her death-defying experience. Despite her soreness all over, she went to the small desk in the corner of her kitchen and turned on the computer, intending to make notes.

Her answering machine light was blinking, so she listened to messages. All could wait to be answered except the one from her parents. They'd called to follow up about Nancy's death and how she was handling it. She didn't enlighten them about her latest misadventure. After assuring them she was all right, she decided to return one more.

"Hi, Della? This is Cara Hamilton."

"Cara? How are you? I'm so glad you called back. I read your article in the paper this morning. You found poor Nancy—how awful!"

Della Santoro had become a friend of Cara's several years ago, when Cara was researching Shotgun Sally for fun, and not for an article. Back then, Della had recently joined the faculty of Mustang Valley Community College as an instructor of literature. Her specialty was the genesis of local legends and how they changed with time. She'd already known a lot about Shotgun Sally, and had been willing to exchange information with Cara and her friends, who were also Sally aficionados.

"I've had better experiences than finding a friend in that condition," Cara admitted to Della.

"Do you know yet what happened? Who did it?"

"No, but I'm working on it. I've written about what happened, of course, but unearthing the murderer will make a heck of a story."

"Like the time Shotgun Sally found her sister, Sarah's, body and turned the experience into a series of articles for her paper," Della said, turning on her professorial voice.

Picturing her in her mind, Cara thought Della really looked like a professor, her dark hair always pulled away from her face with a clip or in a bun, and silver-rimmed glasses she wore perched on her nose. She lived near the community college campus.

"The truth behind that situation has been fairly obscure," Della droned on, "but at first Sally was accused of killing her sister."

Ignoring the repetition of just having told Mitch the story, Cara responded, "Until she proved she had been the intended victim and was attacked..." Cara's voice trailed off before she could say, "Like me." It *wasn't* like her. There was a world of difference between McJanuary's Colt .45 and her attacker's miserable old truck. She didn't even intend to do a story on the hit-and-run...yet. It wasn't really newsworthy, for she hadn't been hurt. But if she found out who did it, and if it was tied in to her investigation of Nancy's murder...

"Right," Della said. "That made quite a story. Of course it's nothing like what happened to Nancy." She hesitated. "Is it? I mean, why did you really go there in the middle of the night?"

"I've been asking myself that all day," Cara said.

"Anyway, let's get together soon. I want to spend some time with you discussing Sally." And escaping from the nasty things going on around her.

"Anytime," Della said.

As soon as she hung up, Cara took a long, muscle-soothing shower, put antiseptic on her scrapes, then climbed into bed. She fell asleep quickly, despite the way her thoughts swirled around Nancy Wilks, a battered blue pickup truck...and the too-brief touch of Mitch Steele's lips.

THE NEXT MORNING, before leaving the house he'd rented because it wasn't far from department headquarters, Mitch made his weekly call to Tim Bender, an assistant attorney general for the State of Texas. While a rookie at the Dallas Police Department, Mitch had testified in a case for Tim and they'd become friends. More important, they'd developed a mutual respect. Tim was the only person Mitch told of his quest to learn the truth about his father's death. Tim had promised the attorney general's support if Mitch found evidence of murder and who the culprit was.

"What's with that new murder?" Tim asked when Mitch identified himself. Mitch filled him in, including the involvement of a reporter for the *Gazette,* without describing his uneasy alliance with Cara. "Any tie to your father's case?" He'd asked the same thing about the other recent murders in Mustang Valley, and Mitch had had to admit he didn't know...yet.

"The law firm connection seems more complex with each new matter," Mitch said. "I'm going to review the department's cold case files again from a year or so before my father's death to see if I can find anything helpful."

It would be the latest of Mitch's ongoing, frustrating efforts. When his dad's death was shrugged off as suicide, Mitch took on the single-minded, surreptitious mission of proving otherwise, collecting the sparse evidence by himself and sending it to Tim for analysis. There'd been nearly no physical evidence, so Mitch had, with Tim's assistance, researched Juniper Holdings, the outfit from which his father had been accused of accepting bribes. Its principals were some attorneys from the East whose backgrounds were spotless. The company had folded shortly after the scandal.

Mitch had also examined the backgrounds of nearly everyone in the Sheriff's Department. Some results were interesting, but nothing pointed to anyone as the potential murderer. Mitch's bet was on Ben Wilson, who, as a deputy, had vied with Martin Steele for the position of sheriff and lost. On Martin's death, he had finally gotten the job he wanted.

Good theory, but Mitch was still seeking evidence to prove or disprove it. Because he had to conduct the investigation clandestinely on his own, time had passed with nothing to show for it but frustration. At least Tim still went along with him.

"I'll focus on matters that involve Lambert & Church," Mitch told him now.

"Good luck," Tim said, "and keep me informed." It was his standard closing to their conversations. After nearly two years, Tim had probably stopped believing there was anything in the death of Martin Steele besides the suicide of a small-county sheriff caught accepting bribes, but Mitch was grateful he never said so.

A short while later, at department headquarters, Mitch visited the dispatcher on the current shift. He reiterated his communication with the deputy on duty last night: all units were to watch for a blue pickup with damage to the right side. He'd call the body shops in Mustang County later, though there weren't many, and the suspect was more likely to have driven the vehicle to the anonymity of Dallas/Ft. Worth for repairs. Or, if it was stolen, just abandoned it.

The deputy administration room was crowded that morning, everyone having checked in but not yet gone out on assignments. Mitch exchanged the usual greetings, pleasant and superficial, unlike the normal garbage handed out by Hurley Zeller, who fortunately wasn't there yet.

When he got to his desk, Mitch reached for the phone. He'd leave a message at the *Gazette* for Cara to call when she got in. If she was sleeping in after her multiple ordeals of the day before, he didn't want to wake her at home. And she no longer had a working cell phone.

"Cara Hamilton." Her familiar impatient voice drew a smile from him.

"Cara, it's Mitch." He kept his voice low so no one could eavesdrop. Darn. If he'd known she was there, he'd have called outside on his mobile phone. "Why are you there so early?"

"Why did you call if you didn't expect me to be here?"

He smiled to himself as he explained his reasoning.

"Thanks for not wanting to wake me," she said. "I always get up early, even when I go to bed exhausted. I don't want to let the day get started without being part of it."

No, he was sure a woman as vibrant and tenacious as Cara would figure she was missing something.

"So…" she prompted.

He shook his head a little at her characteristic impatience. "Cara, I was thinking last night about yesterday's attack on you." He'd thought of little else, stupid when he had a murder to solve. Yet, if he could save a life, that was more important than justice on behalf of a dead woman. Would his mother's people believe Nancy Wilks's spirit could not rest until she was avenged?

Maybe, although they were just as likely to honor her imminent return to Mother Earth.

Whatever, he had two crimes to solve, probably by the same suspect.

"I need a list of everyone you've done stories on recently who was...let's say a little displeased about what you said," he told Cara.

Her laugh was musical. "That means a list of *everyone* I've written about."

Mitch believed it. Cara's admitted mission was to expose wrongs. She'd written a lot of articles, mostly describing things the subjects probably didn't want their closest friends to know, let alone the entire population of Mustang County.

"Then, give me a list of all your subjects." He gritted his teeth inwardly at all the time he was looking at. He would have to interview all potential enemies she identified.

Maybe he could get a junior deputy to help. Stephanie Greglets? But he trusted no one, not even Stephanie, to do the detail work without revealing it to Ben Wilson. And that would put Hurley Zeller in the loop, thanks to his closeness to Ben. Hurley would do anything to solve this murder himself. Mitch wouldn't put it past him to sabotage the case rather than allow Mitch to get credit for solving it.

"Okay," Cara said. "I'll put a list together. Want me to mail it?"

"No, I'll pick it up later," he said. "We'll grab lunch, discuss the next moves in your investigation."

Lunch? He didn't want to date the woman, just keep track of where her nosiness led and keep her out of trouble while making sure he got the information on the case she came up with.

"Sure. See you later, Mitch." And then she was gone.

He quickly cast aside his feeling of pleasure that he *was* going to see her later.

CARA HUMMED as she went through the *Gazette's* morgue.

At least Beau had managed to get the old issues microfilmed, though most modern papers now had everything computerized and indexed. And the *Gazette's* filming, such as it was, was way behind. That meant she had to go through individual issues for months back.

She sat in a filthy extra room, her hands blackened with ink leaching from the newsprint as she thumbed through paper after paper. Her body still hurt from the way she'd slammed it onto her car hood, and a scrape on her arm still stung.

So why was she humming?

She had a lot of work to do. Mitch Steele had just added to it. *Thanks, Mitch.*

As her humming grew even more cheerful, she stopped it. *Mitch.* She was meeting the handsome, arrogant devil of a deputy later. She'd be sharing information with him.

Would he share any with her?

Not voluntarily, she was sure. "If you want something from me, Deputy Steele," she muttered aloud, "you'll have to cough up information of your own."

Smiling grimly at the page she had just turned, she stopped. There it was—part of what she was searching for.

The article reported the accidental death of Mayor Frank Daniels, in a car accident as he was fleeing capture—an event reminiscent of a Shotgun Sally legend, though that hadn't made this story, of course. Beauford Jennings himself had the byline. It had been too important for him to trust to any reporter on his staff, or so he'd said. Even though Cara was a better writer.

Cara took the paper to the photocopier in the corner of

the room. Fortunately, though it jammed a lot, it was up-to-date, so she was able to zoom in on the article and shrink it to letter size. The copy's print was small, but her eyesight was perfect.

After tucking the copy into a folder, she read the article. The background of the mayor's untimely—or perhaps very timely—death was included. He'd all but admitted to murdering Andrew McGovern, an attorney at the firm of Lambert & Church.

Cara's sigh was long and deep. "Oh, Andrew," she murmured sadly. She knew now it was better that they'd mutually broken things off. They'd dated in high school, then gotten engaged when he returned after law school. He'd been sweet but stuffy, and marriage to him could have been stifling. But she had loved him. And still mourned for him, even if he hadn't been the right man for her.

Maybe there *was* no right man for her. Mr. Right would have to support her in her career. Be someone with whom she could share things. Someone she could trust.

Unlike Andrew. Unlike the devious thief Jerry Jennings. And unlike Mitch Steele.

Her unladylike snort reverberated through the storeroom. How the heck had Mitch insinuated himself into that reverie? "Back to work, Cara."

Of course, she couldn't resist looking up one more topic: Mitch's father. He had been accused of accepting bribes from an outfit called Juniper Holdings, which quickly went belly-up after getting caught at it. Juniper had wanted to do business without the requisite Mustang County authorizations and allegedly hired Mitch's father to pave the way. After being caught, Sheriff Martin Steele had shot himself. Poor Mitch.

Sighing heavily, Cara refocused her attention on the material she needed to construct her story. When she re-

turned to her small office an hour later, she'd found most
of what she'd been searching for: references to Ranger
Corporation in articles about the murders of Andrew and
rancher Jeb Rawlins.

Ranger Corporation had been trying to buy land owned
by Andrew's girlfriend's family—the West Ranch. Jeb
Rawlins's ranch, the Bar JR, and his nephew Bart's, the
Four Aces, adjoined that property. Ranger had been foiled
in its attempt to buy the Rawlins land, thanks to Cara's
friend Lindsey Wellington and her new fiancé Bart Rawlins. Lindsey was living at the Four Aces now with Bart.
Cara had never been to the ranch but knew where it was,
west of town. Lindsey had invited her to visit, but she
hadn't had time yet.

Had Ranger Corporation succeeded in buying the West
Ranch? That would be public record. Cara would visit the
County Recorder's Office very soon.

She didn't know if Ranger Corporation's interest in local land was significant in Nancy's murder. But until she
knew what Nancy had wanted to show her, anything creating a common tie between the other two murders was
worth further investigation.

The most obvious tie was the law firm, Lambert &
Church. Under the cloud of the two—and now three—
killings, it was in the process of disbanding. That was why
Nancy, the office manager, had lost her job. Cara couldn't
talk to Paul Lambert, the now-deceased partner. But she
would interview his former partner, Donald Church.

At the moment she couldn't tie Nancy to Ranger Corporation, despite her desire to find something against that
nasty piece of work Roger Rosales. At least not yet. She'd
keep digging.

And if the person in the truck who'd tried to run her
over was trying to get her to back off?

Not even getting shot had stopped Shotgun Sally.

"And you won't stop me, either," Cara asserted, then turned to her computer to start compiling the list Mitch wanted.

Chapter Six

"Thanks, Mrs. Carrow." Mitch said goodbye to Nancy Wilks's middle-aged upstairs neighbor and headed down the steps and along the paved path to the street.

Well, hot damn.

The wrinkled lady with the shellac-stiff blue hairdo had been most hospitable, giving Mitch a cup of tea, vanilla wafers, and a firsthand account of having seen Cara nearly creamed by that elusive blue truck that no one had located yet. The description made Mitch's teeth clench and his resolve harden. He'd get the bastard that tried to run her down.

Mrs. Carrow had also given Mitch a tidbit that just might let him work on this case without any headache from his worst detractor in the department, even if it wouldn't solve anything for him. Or would it?

As he got into his sedan, he glanced at his watch. Damn! He was going to be late meeting Cara.

Taking tacit liberties allowed to peace officers, he ignored the speed limit as he sped the few blocks to downtown Mustang Valley. He spotted Cara's banged-up Toyota on the street right outside the Mustang Grill. She hadn't left yet.

This must be his day. Something else had gone right.

Only problem was, downtown was busy at lunchtime. He couldn't even find an illegal space to park in.

He circled the block.

If he believed in the lore of half his heritage, Mother Earth might be teaching him a lesson.

Mitch had never resolved his feelings about his mother's people, but neither had she. The daughter of mixed ancestry, though one hundred percent Native American, she had descended mostly from Choctaws and Chickasaws, which themselves might have been one tribe once, according to their legends. But they had definitely mixed in Sunshine Steele's background, along with several other unrelated Plains Indian tribes.

Mitch's mother, seeing no future in her heritage, had shunned it, working as a bookkeeper and marrying into the white culture. Yet she'd still told Mitch spiritual tales, possibly hybrids of those from her parents' people, about the almighty sun, the morals taught from nature's ways, the peoples' one god, the community of all men and women, the concept that the land was not to be owned by the few but to be shared by all.

But the tale she'd told most was how fortunate Mitch was to have half-white heritage. Yet when his father allegedly killed himself, she ran back to Oklahoma and now lived in a community with other Native Americans, near where she had grown up. Heartbreak had apparently resulted in insight: she didn't like the white man's ways nearly as much as she'd imagined.

Mitch hadn't been orphaned, but he was as close to it as a man could be who still had a parent.

His father's death, his mother's defection, his one-time girlfriend's dose of cold water... He had long ago resigned himself to being part of nothing and no one. Getting along well with people was necessary to his job and his own hidden agenda, but being alone was the way of things.

He finally found a spot and pulled in. "Thanks, Mother Earth," he muttered ironically.

As he strode around the block to the restaurant, he considered how he could use the information Mrs. Carrow had told him. And swore to himself he'd keep it from the lovely, inquisitive woman he was about to join for lunch.

Cara sat alone at a table along a wall. It was covered with a red-checked cloth, and matching napkins were at both place settings. Every table was filled, and the restaurant reverberated with conversation. An aroma of grilled meat tantalized Mitch. He hadn't realized he was hungry. He sat down opposite Cara.

"You've blown your record, Steele. You're late."

"Yeah. Sorry."

"So what were you working on this morning? Any leads in Nancy's murder?" Her hazel eyes sparkled with anticipation. She wore a vest again, this time over a soft top in a shade of pale green that emphasized the startlingly red color of her curls. Her hair wasn't pulled back, so it formed a becoming cascade over her smooth forehead and cheeks.

"No," he said. He said it decisively, but her gaze narrowed, as if she saw he wasn't being entirely truthful. But what he'd learned was most likely outside the case.

"Tell me," she said. The delightful openness to her expression had shuttered over. She regarded him as if he was a pile of unappetizing table scraps.

The cheery waitress came over with water glasses and a description of the day's specials. Cara chose a salad— she must have trusted in the Mustang Grill's cleanliness. Mitch ordered a roast beef sandwich, and the waitress left them alone again.

"Look, Mitch." Cara leaned toward him, her hands

clasped on the table. "I've been doing some checking. What I have doesn't amount to much yet, but I won't even let you know what I'm looking into if you don't level with me."

"What makes you think I'm not?"

Her sideways glance looked shrewd. "Are you?"

"What I learned probably has nothing to do with Nancy's murder."

"Probably?" She leaned back, crossing her arms.

He didn't like the way her sudden remoteness felt like an elbow to his gut. But neither did he intend to give in to her. "How are you feeling today?" he asked. "Sore?"

No response.

"No luck finding that truck yet, but—"

"Cut it out, Steele. Maybe this wasn't such a good idea."

She lifted the wide strap of her large purse from the back of her chair. "I'll have the waitress pack mine to go." She pulled out her wallet.

Damn. If she left half-cocked, she'd continue to bulldoze her way through this case and mess up any chance he had to solve it. And maybe get herself killed, too, in the process.

"Tell me what you looked into this morning, Cara, and I'll let you know what I can."

She studied him suspiciously, but at least she paused. "You first."

Two urges warred inside him: one to tell her to take a hike and the other to kiss her silly. He settled on a third. "All right. Sit down." He'd tell her what he could.

The waitress came with their food. When she left, Mitch took a bite of his sandwich. It was tasty—until he looked across the table at Cara's insistent glare.

"So?" she prompted.

"This is off the record, Cara. And it probably has no

bearing on the case. If I'm wrong and it leads to an arrest, then you can use it in a story. Okay?''

Her head was cocked, and her moist lips were parted. He'd hooked her curiosity, and he liked how she wore it.

"Okay. Tell me."

"Nancy's upstairs neighbor described a man Nancy was dating. It sounded like someone I know." He didn't tell her who.

Cara's head shook admonishingly. "I could have told you that. Mrs. Carrow was there yesterday when I was nearly run down by the truck and I told her to call if she thought of anything related to Nancy. She phoned before I came to meet you and described a guy who hung out with Nancy, a uniformed sheriff's deputy. It's Hurley Zeller, isn't it, Mitch?''

OF COURSE it was Hurley Zeller. Cara knew it despite Mitch's sudden blank expression. He was good at not giving his thoughts away. Except that she saw a tiny pulse throbbing at his temple.

He was peeved.

Too bad. If he'd leveled with her in the first place, she wouldn't have played games either.

"Truce," she said. She tugged her purse off the back of her chair where she'd stowed it again and pulled out the list she'd put together. "Here are all the people I could think of who hate me because of things I revealed about them in my stories."

Shotgun Sally had reputedly done that once, too—after she'd realized *she* had been the target when her sister was murdered. She had vowed revenge, stopped at nothing, goaded each of her enemies all over again. She'd even nearly lost Zachary, her lawman lover.

"Are you going to show that to me?" Mitch asked.

Only then did Cara realize she was still holding the list…and staring at the very sexy Mitch Steele.

Lawman lover… *You wish, Hamilton!*

"Oh, sure." She passed him the page.

Mitch whistled. "You *have* been busy."

"There could be more," she said defensively, "but I only had an hour to work on it."

"I mean, you've been busy ticking people off."

"'Flushing out their sins like an old hound dog, and makin' 'em sorrier than a scared quail with a broke wing.'"

Mitch's dark brows rose and his mouth quirked. "A quaint analogy."

Cara felt herself flush under his amusement. "Shotgun Sally used to say it," she muttered.

"You're not trying to be like her, are you? I mean, the story you told me is an example. Most of what's been said about her had to have been exaggerated over time."

Cara wasn't about to argue with Mitch about her idol's exploits. "Do you want to talk about my list, or don't you?"

"Sure." How could he put so much amusement in one word?

Cara glared and snatched back the piece of paper. "If you want my opinion, there are only four or five angry enough about what I wrote to consider getting back at me."

"And they are…?" He sounded all business again.

Cara rattled off a few names. "The worst was Jackson Felmington, a real sleaze bucket, though I treated him as fairly as possible in my story. He's a car dealer, the kind who gives the whole group a bad name. He sells demo models as new, and that's probably the mildest of his shoddy practices. I wrote about him a few months ago. He was hopping mad, threatened to sue the *Gazette* and me and everyone Beau and I ever knew. And if that didn't scare us enough, he mentioned some mob contacts he just happened to have.''

''I remember that story and the follow-up by the Consumer Affairs Section of the state's Department of Transportation. I gather he gave a big mea culpa, paid a hefty fine and promised to be a good boy. Have you heard anything from him since?''

Cara shook her head. ''I figured he'd keep a low profile, let things die down and get back to his sordid business.''

''Could be. Anyone else?''

''Well...there's Shem O'Hallihan.''

''Oh, right. The building contractor. Premium prices for second-rate materials, wasn't it?''

''Yes, but since what he used was legal, he was never arrested, though some civil lawsuits are pending against him.''

''And he threatened you?''

''Not overtly, though it's a good thing I don't own my own place. Otherwise, it just might collapse around me someday from some subtle sabotage.''

''And none of this bothered you?''

''I had a job to do, and I did it. Like you.'' She half expected an argument, that what he did was much more important.

Instead he grinned. It wasn't an expression she'd seen often on Mitch's usually solemn face. It suited him. A lot.

''You're really something, Cara Hamilton.''

She felt a flush rise up her face. She didn't like it. She hated feeling embarrassed. ''Yeah. Well...thanks. I guess.''

His hearty laugh surrounded her. Something else new...and nice. People at neighboring tables looked over and smiled as if his pleasure was contagious. Cara found herself smiling, too.

But then he regained his usual seriousness and waved the paper. "You haven't heard from any of these people recently? You have no reason to suspect anyone more than the others as the driver of the truck yesterday?"

"No," she said.

"Okay."

And that was it. For the rest of their meal, they didn't talk any more about the people who might want to hurt her, about Nancy or even about Sally. They chatted about Mustang County and where else they'd been and other superficial but, thankfully, uncontroversial topics.

Rather, Cara talked. And asked questions that Mitch answered succinctly, followed by many of his own. She had the impression that he purposely avoided mastery of the art of conversation, instead preferring to listen. And he changed the subject quickly when she asked about his father.

Still, when they had finished, when Cara tried—to no avail—to split the bill, she realized that this had felt suspiciously like a date with Deputy Mitch Steele.

Suspiciously being the key word.

When they walked out, Cara stopped by the restaurant door on the busy Main Street sidewalk. "No further leads in the case to share, Mitch? Anything at all I can put in the paper?"

"Not yet. And what I told you before is off the record."

"About Deputy Zeller? Sure," she grumbled.

HER PROMISE DID NOT, however, prevent her from telling her boss, even if she couldn't mention it in the paper. Yet.

She sat in Beau's office. "We can't print anything about it yet," she said. "But I'll follow up. Do you suppose Hurley Zeller dating Nancy Wilks could explain why the Sheriff's Department didn't solve the first two killings?"

Beau's frown carved enough tucks in his brow that he looked twenty years older than his sixty-two years. "How?"

"Well, Nancy worked for Lambert & Church. And the law firm had a connection to both those murders."

"And? You need more than something as tenuous as that to make accusations, or even hint at something deceitful."

Cara sighed. "I know. But it's something else worth following up on."

"Why not?" Beau agreed. "But after that truck incident yesterday, watch your step, Cara. Don't make any more enemies."

That sounded like something Mitch would say. She didn't like it from either man.

Even if they were right.

MITCH USUALLY AVOIDED Deputy Hurley Zeller as if he smelled bad. Which he did sometimes. Always, if Mitch counted his attitude.

Today, though, he needed to talk to Zeller…first thing. If Mrs. Carrow had told both Cara and him about Nancy's dating habits, they were unlikely to be the only ones, despite Mitch's request that she not repeat it until he'd had a chance to look into it. And though Cara had agreed to keep it off the record, she wouldn't forget about it, either. She would dig to see how deep this relationship went.

Not that Mitch gave a damn if Zeller got any bad publicity that was coming to him. But it would do the department no good to ignore or whitewash the liaison.

As a result Mitch crossed the deputy administration room, from his corner to the opposite one occupied by Zeller.

Zeller, seated behind a desk littered with papers and old coffee cups, apparently recognized the rareness of the occurrence. A puzzled expression came over his face till he pasted on one of his simian smiles. "Need help, Steele? Crying uncle on the Wilks investigation already?"

"No, but under the circumstances I'd have expected you to shed a few tears, crocodile or not, over our latest victim."

Hurley's smile vanished. "What do you mean?"

"How long were you dating Nancy Wilks?"

The color disappeared from the hefty man's face, immediately replaced by a flush so red that Mitch half expected to see blood seep from his pores. Was the guy about to have a stroke?

"Who told you that?" There was a hint of Zeller's usual bluster in his voice, as if he was about to deny it.

"One of Nancy's neighbors. You'll see it in my report."

Hurley's gaze dropped. "I only took her out a couple of times," he muttered. "I met her at the law firm during our investigation of Paul Lambert, and she and I hit it off. But I figured it wasn't a good idea for me to be seeing her after we took Lambert into custody, especially after he offed himself. It might look bad."

"And I don't suppose she made a fuss about your dumping her, so you had to shut her up to keep your little conflict of interest from becoming public." Mitch was stretching things, but he wanted to see Zeller's reaction.

It was pretty much as he'd expected. Zeller half rose, fists clenched at his beefy sides that bulged out of his uniform trousers. "No way, Steele. You're not gonna solve your sloppy investigation of Nancy's case by pinning her murder on me."

Mitch tensed, half expecting Hurley to take a swing at him. But before he could reply, Sheriff Ben Wilson appeared in the door of the admin room.

"Steele. Zeller. My office. Now."

BEN WASTED NO TIME once Mitch was seated beside Hurley, across the desk from their superior. "I just got a heads up about an article that'll appear in the next *Gazette,* Hurley, and it involves you."

An article in the *Gazette?* Mitch's blood began to simmer as he continued to listen.

In his buddy Ben's presence, the usual confident bluster returned to Zeller's voice. "Yeah? What's that?"

"Were you dating our vic, Nancy Wilks?"

Mitch glanced over at Hurley and saw rage in his tiny eyes. If glares were lasers, Mitch figured he'd have been fried.

Hurley shrugged. Obviously he hadn't told Ben yet.

Though Hurley neither confirmed nor denied the allegation, Ben kept talking. "I just got a call from Beau Jennings at the *Gazette.* He said he just came across some information confirmed by eyewitnesses that'll appear in a story in tomorrow's edition, but first he wanted my statement on whether I was aware one of my deputies had a relationship with the victim." He glared at Hurley, but when his gaze landed on Mitch, it was downright hostile. "I don't suppose you know how Beau happened to hear this nasty rumor, do you, Steele?"

He could guess. It was a good thing the beautiful, vivacious, untrustworthy reporter Cara Hamilton wasn't present. He wasn't sure what he might have done to her.

He knew one thing he wouldn't do with her. Not again.

He knew better than to hand anyone information pertinent to a case. Of course, Cara had learned this tidbit independently. But she'd promised to keep it off the record, at least for now.

And what had she done? She'd immediately told her boss—who just happened to be the owner and editor of the newspaper. As if she could avoid her promise through such a slimy technicality.

Well, she had cooked her own goose in this investigation. From now on Mitch would insist that she share everything she learned. Otherwise he would haul her in for obstruction of justice.

And he would be damned if he would trust her again.

Chapter Seven

Cara nearly choked on toast at her breakfast table the next morning when she scanned that day's first edition of the *Gazette*—delivered, of course, to her doorstep.

"Damn it, Beau," she shouted into her empty kitchen, over the drone of news from a Ft. Worth station that she kept low on her TV each morning. She pounded her small table so it sidled along the hardwood floor. He knew how she felt about someone stealing her research for a story. She'd made it more than clear when Jerry did it, though she'd had to swallow some of her fury then, since the guy had been her boss's nephew.

And this time it was her boss who'd done it. Probably thought he made it right by adding eyewitness backup and giving her some of the credit. Instead he might have made it worse.

Her dim-witted boss was going to ruin everything she'd tried to accomplish by her uneasy alliance with Mitch.

The follow-up articles on Nancy's murder dominated the front section, practically filling the first page. News of the murder had been picked up by all the local Ft. Worth and Dallas TV stations. Probably their local papers, too. One *Gazette* article was actually hers, written late yesterday after further interviews she'd conducted: a couple of columns of human interest about Nancy's childhood in

Mustang Valley, her grieving family, her bewildered and irate friends, the funeral arrangements.

The other article had started out as hers, with on-the-record information about how the investigation was going so far. Not that she'd checked every fact with Mitch, but she'd been careful to keep things general: yes, the Sheriff's Department was doing its job, and evidence was still being collected and assessed. No, there were no suspects in custody yet. Nothing about her attack by a truck, as there wasn't anything to tell. There was nothing controversial in the article. Mitch would have blessed it as she'd written it, she was sure.

Only, her version wasn't what made it into the paper. No byline, at least, but Beau had credited both himself and her at the end. And in it he'd added that item she'd imparted to him off the record: part of the investigation centered around one of the Sheriff's Department's own—a deputy who'd dated the victim. No names named, but a hint of a big exposé in the offing.

Mitch would be furious.

Cara had already showered and dressed for the day in one of her favorite outfits—long skirt, blue this time, with a soft yellow blouse, a many-pocketed beige vest and her low-topped boots. She made sure she had all necessary paraphernalia in her purse. New tapes for her handheld recorder? Check. Enough paper in her notebook? Check. Usually she grabbed her cell phone from its charging cradle. Today, she just made a mental note to arrange for a new one.

Cara drove to the newspaper office first, rehearsing in her mind her impending confrontation with Beau. She felt deflated but unsurprised he wasn't there yet. Hadn't even called in, an intern told her. *Chicken!* Cara thought.

Her phone light blinked in her office, signifying a message. From Mitch, the last person she wanted to talk to?

Of course. "Call me, Cara." His curt tone confirmed he was royally peeved. She decided to wait, let him cool down before she called.

Plus, it'd be a lot better to have something to bribe him with before trying to convince him not to terminate their pact. Telling him she'd done nothing wrong, that it was Beau who'd spilled the beans, wouldn't cut it. But if she had some juicy new information to dangle before his gorgeous golden eyes...

She sat at her desk, munching on the malted milk balls she always kept in a glass jar and making notes on her game plan to follow up on the story of Nancy Wilks and the other murders: who to interview, in what order, what other research was needed.

It wasn't the only story she was working on, of course—just the most important. She dashed off an article she'd already researched on the second car accident in three weeks at a busy and dangerous local intersection. Then, as she got ready to call to set up interviews regarding Nancy's murder, her phone rang.

She didn't recognize the number on caller ID. Was Mitch so eager to chew her out he wasn't waiting for her return call? Wincing in advance, she lifted the receiver. "Cara Hamilton here." She forced her usual confidence into her tone. No use starting out wimpily with him.

"Hi, Cara. It's Della. Are you free for lunch today?"

She shouldn't be, with a list as long as the one she'd jotted down plus the other stories nipping at her heels. But a nice, quiet meal with someone who wouldn't give her a hard time sounded perfect. "Sure. When and where?"

They made plans, and Cara entered the time and place on her personal digital assistant.

Then she called to set up her first interview of the day.

"Lambert & Church," answered a female voice.

"Hi, this is Cara Hamilton of the *Mustang Gazette*." Unless undercover on an assignment, Cara preferred being upfront. "Who's this?"

A long pause. "I'm sorry, but we have nothing to say to the media." The droned words sounded scripted. Probably were.

"I understand. I'm sure it's been difficult for you. For me, too. I don't know if you're aware of it, but I'm the one who…who found poor Nancy." Cara had meant to pretend to get choked up, only it wasn't pretense. She swallowed. "It was terrible. I was wondering…" She let her voice drift off.

"Yes?" The woman sounded compassionate this time.

"I'm working on the human interest angle." It wasn't a lie since she was doing that and the hard news, too. "I'd like to talk to Mr. Church about Nancy, how she was hired by the firm, how she'll be missed, that kind of thing."

"Oh. Well…I'm sorry, Ms. Hamilton, but he's not here this morning. I know he's not talking to media people who've called, but maybe you—"

"Will he be back this afternoon, say around two-thirty, for me to call back?"

"I think so."

"Then I'll try again later. Thank you so much…. I'm sorry, what did you say your name was?"

"Wanda."

"Thanks, Wanda." Cara gently hung up. She didn't know Wanda but would check her out before showing up on the firm's doorstep that afternoon. She wouldn't wait to schedule an appointment, since she was determined to get an interview with Donald Church. And whatever she learned could provide tidbits to tease Mitch with.

The phone rang again. Without thinking, Cara lifted the receiver. "Cara Hamilton here," she said.

"Deputy Steele here."

Damn. Speak of the devil. And she hadn't prepared herself. But just the resonant sound of his voice, even when it was so chilly, spiraled ribbons of warmth through her body. "Hi," she said brightly.

"We need to talk, Cara," he said.

"Absolutely, but not right now. I have to dash off for an interview." Only partly a lie—she did have to dash off to avoid this discussion, and she hoped for several interviews, sometime today. "But I have some interesting stuff to share with you later, Mitch. So in the meantime, consider what you can let me in on."

"That's exactly why—" She heard the explosion in his voice.

"Talk to you soon." She winced as she hung up.

And she prayed that, as she filled up the nearly empty jar on her desk with malted milk balls, she would have something interesting enough, later on, to convince him not to hang up on *her* in the future.

CARA SAT AT THE TABLE in the Mustang Grill for the second time in two days. Once again she inhaled the delicious scent of charring meat, stared around the room at crowded tables covered with checkered tablecloths. She liked the place, though usually didn't eat there this often. But it was the restaurant where Della Santoro and she traditionally met to talk about Shotgun Sally.

So here she was again, at the same place where she'd had such a pleasant lunch with Mitch Steele yesterday while they formed their alliance. The alliance that would probably self-destruct, thanks to Beau Jennings.

"Are you okay, Cara?" Della's voice projected like the professor she was in the noisy dining room. As always, her dark hair was pulled starkly from her face, emphasizing its nearly rectangular shape, her chin being small and blunt. As she leaned over the table, her concerned frown exaggerated the contrast between her thin, dark brows and her pale complexion. Worry darkened her gray eyes.

"Sure," Cara said. "I'm fine."

"But your finding poor Nancy that way. I know it was a couple of days ago now, but it must still feel awful."

Cara shut her eyes for a moment. "Yeah. It was pretty bad. And I can't even try to put it behind me since I'm still working on the story."

The research was frustrating. Her attempts that morning to set up interviews had been pretty fruitless. The most productive call she'd made was to Lindsey Wellington, at the Four Aces Ranch. From her, Cara learned that Wanda, the receptionist who'd answered the Lambert firm phone, was a relatively recent hire and one of the few people remaining till the doors were closed.

To make sure the morning wasn't a waste, Cara went to the County Recorder's office to look up Ranger Corporation's land holdings. She'd found some interesting things, but not as much as she'd hoped to.

Not enough to impress Mitch Steele and shore up their tenuous collaboration.

"Can't the *Gazette* put someone else on the story?" Della reached for the rosé she had ordered with one of her pampered hands. Cara knew she spent hours in nail salons, and her slender fingers were tipped with perfectly manicured pink nails that matched the shade of lipstick marking her wineglass.

"I'm sure any reporter would be glad for a hand in this story," Cara said. "Even Beau is putting his own two cents' worth in." Darn him. And he'd been avoiding her, so she hadn't even been able to chew him out about it yet. "But this one is mine."

"Are you sure you can be objective?" Della leaned back while her steak sandwich was placed in front of her. Cara had ordered the same thing that day, forgoing her usual salad. If she had to eat in the same place, at least she didn't have to eat the same thing.

"As objective as Shotgun Sally," Cara responded to Della as soon as the waitress was gone once more.

"Well, she wasn't very objective," Della said. "Especially after she found her poor, slain sister. But even other times, when she went undercover to do her exposés of dance halls and—"

This was what Cara had intended. The subject was changed to one she delighted in delving into, especially with Della: Sally and her delicious escapades. Real escapades embellished by time.

There weren't many women like Sally, though there'd been a few. Nellie Bly, for example, whose name was actually Elizabeth Cochran. She'd been a crusading newspaper reporter on the *Pittsburgh Dispatch* and Pulitzer's *New York World* in the late 1800s, had dressed like a seamstress to do her story on the outrageous conditions in the garment industry. She'd even gone around the world in eighty days to match the Jules Verne story.

Sally had done all her crusading here, in northeast Texas. That was why her legends were local.

And Cara had come to love every one of them. Especially the ones that said Sally had a lawman lover....

But not like *that* one. With a start, Cara realized that, as she was lulled practically into a hypnotic state listening to Della pontificate on a favorite Sally story, she'd been staring toward the restaurant door—and Sheriff Ben Wilson had just walked in. His eyes locked with hers, and she was dismayed when he stalked through the crowded tables right toward her. His short-sleeved khaki uniform was rumpled. And he looked angry.

"Ms. Hamilton." He didn't even acknowledge she was with someone else. "Your car's going to be towed in about—'' he glanced at his bony wrist and the outsize watch that clung to it ''—two minutes.''

She looked at her own watch. ''Thanks for the warning, Sheriff, but I've got another half hour on the meter.''

''Not anymore. That part of the street has been marked as a temporary no-parking zone.''

''That part of the street, or just my parking space?''

She didn't like the cadaverously thin man's evil grin. ''It don't matter.''

''Does this have something to do with the article in the *Gazette* this morning?'' she asked. ''If it does, talk to Beau Jennings. He—''

''I'm talking to you. Like I talked to your new boy-friend Deputy Steele about opening his mouth around nosy reporters.''

Uh-oh. Talk about alliances splitting apart. The idea of having Mitch so angry that he'd never even talk to her again, let alone share information, splashed sorrow through her. But she refused to let that happen because of extraneous stuff.

She turned from the sheriff long enough to take a sip of water. Fortunately, she hadn't joined Della in a glass of wine. She needed her head clear.

As she drank, she caught Della's worried expression and tossed her a brief, reassuring smile—wishing she *felt* reassured, too. Then she looked back up at the angry man near the table—but not before she noticed fascinated stares of restaurant patrons aimed at them.

''If you're mad about the reference in the paper to the possibility that one of your deputies dated Nancy Wilks, Sheriff, I learned that information from a source I won't reveal, not from anyone in your department. But does the deputy's relationship with Ms. Wilks have anything to do with that matter I mentioned when I was in your offices day before yesterday?''

She would be discreet, since slinging as-yet-unproved accusations at the sheriff wasn't a good idea. Mostly, though, she intended to do an exclusive story on why the Sheriff's Department slipped up in the first two murder investigations as soon as she knew, and could substantiate, the answer. No sense really riling Ben Wilson sooner than necessary.

Her discretion apparently made no difference to him, though. He grabbed her arm. "Come with me, Ms. Hamilton."

She raised her eyebrows and smiled sweetly, though her heart raced. "Are you arresting me, Sheriff?" She tried to draw her arm away. He only squeezed tighter, hurting her.

"No, he's not," said a familiar, deep and very welcome voice from behind him.

As the sheriff pivoted to see who dared to contradict him, he released her. Behind him, Cara glimpsed Mitch.

"Your car was being towed, Ms. Hamilton," Mitch said. "Sheriff Wilson was just being kind enough to warn you."

"No!" Cara stood and grabbed her purse off her chair. "He's the one who set it up."

"Don't press your luck," Mitch told her. "I told the tow truck driver to come back in an hour. I trust you'll be done by then. If not, he'll move your car for you."

Cara could only imagine the furious glare that Ben Wilson must have sent Mitch's way. Mitch's handsome face stayed impassive, but something flashed in his deep-golden eyes.

"I don't recall assigning you to traffic control, Steele," Ben hissed. "But maybe that's where you'll be from now on."

Oh, shoot. Bad enough for her to lose Mitch's confidence, but she didn't want to be the cause of him getting demoted, too.

She gently tapped Ben Wilson on the shoulder. "Sheriff, I'm sorry. I'll go move my car. And as to the other thing—"

He turned to look at her, his complexion red with anger. "I told you before to watch your step, Ms. Hamilton. I won't warn you again." He again pivoted and began making his way through the restaurant.

Cara half expected Mitch to trail placatingly in his wake. Instead, the good-looking lawman bent down. "Like I said on the phone before, Ms. Hamilton, we need to talk." His tone brooked no contradiction. Fine. She wanted to talk to him, too. But not here or now.

"Sure. Later this afternoon. And if I can do anything to help smooth things over for you with the sheriff, then—"

"You've done enough." With a final warning glare, he turned and headed for the door.

Cara didn't realize she'd been holding her breath until it came out in a deep, frustrated sigh.

"What was that all about?" Della asked.

She deserved an explanation. After all, her lunch had been spoiled by a big, ugly, embarrassing scene. "I've been trying to cooperate with the Sheriff's Department as I do my research about Nancy's death, but it hasn't been easy."

"I'm not so sure about that." Della must have restored her lipstick, for her mouth was a soft shade of pink as it widened in a smile.

"What do you mean?"

"That Deputy Steele is very easy...on the eyes."

Cara laughed. "I can't argue with that. It's his abrasive personality that makes things tough."

"Maybe." Della's expression looked speculative, turning serious. "I really think you should reconsider doing this story, Cara. It seems dangerous. And to have even the sheriff against you—"

"I'll be fine." To change the subject again, Cara returned to the topic they'd met to discuss. "Let's get back to Sally. I've never been sure where her family's land was. You know, where she hid out while being stalked after her sister was killed in her place? Before she went undercover on McJanuary's ranch?" It *was* of interest to her. But the only reason she'd thought of it now was her foray through county records that morning.

Della's face resumed its pinched, professorial look as she pondered the question. "I don't actually know, but I'll look it up and tell you what I find."

That turned into the segue that Cara had hoped for; once again they were back to dissecting Sally tales.

Even though her own thoughts swirled. What was she going to do about the sheriff's anger? She wouldn't stop trying to figure out what Deputy Hurley Zeller dating Nancy Wilks had to do with her murder or the others— if there even was a connection. But how on earth could she get back into Mitch's good graces? She needed his cooperation if she wanted her story to be perfect.

And she couldn't help wondering if, deep down inside, there were other reasons she wanted Mitch not to despise her. Della was right. Mitch *was* very easy on the eyes.

"And of course," Della was saying, "Sally couldn't trust anyone after her sister was killed. Not even her lawman lover."

Chapter Eight

Back in her office, later that afternoon after a stop at the county recorder's office, Cara was excited to find she'd received an e-mail from Kelly McGovern Lansing—though why one of her dearest friends was sending e-mails from her Hawaiian honeymoon escaped Cara. "I saw in the news about you finding Nancy Wilks," the message read. "Are you okay?"

"Fine," Cara responded. "I'll give you details about what's going on with me if you'll do the same." Cara pictured her tall, aristocratic, blond friend's amused reaction. After all she and her new husband, Wade, had gone through in solving the murder of Kelly's brother, Andrew, they had really needed this time alone. Cara ended her e-mail. "Hope you're having fun." Grinning wickedly, she pushed the send button. And paused.

Fun? Right about now, she wondered what the word meant.

With a sigh she studied both lists she'd started to compile in separate computer files. One was a to-do list of steps to make sure her research on all the murders, including Andrew's, was comprehensive enough. The more she thought about what to look into, the more detailed it grew, like a flowchart used for computer programs:

If X says one thing, then interview Y. If X refuses to talk, then…

What complicated matters further was that she intended to share her information with Mitch. He was still mad at her for sharing the info about Deputy Zeller with Beau. Maybe he was right. She'd told Beau not to run with it, but she couldn't control what her boss did with the news. She'd finally caught Beau in his office, when she'd first come in. She had begun to scold him, but he'd pulled rank on her. Made it clear he would pull her off the story altogether if she gave him too hard a time about his editorial decisions. She'd had to back off—for now.

But she couldn't back off from sharing with Mitch. In fact, asking for his help would be a deliberate attempt to smooth over their bumpy relationship.

Relationship? Hah! Didn't she just wish…?

No. Just because she found him to be one heck of a hunk didn't mean the ill-tempered, single-minded deputy could be equated with Shotgun Sally's lawman lover. No matter how tempting the idea.

Still, just the act of sharing her thoughts would, she hoped, demonstrate her sincerity. Maybe get them back on the right track. But that would come later. For now she would focus on the other list: her would-be enemies— people to eliminate from suspicion in the attack on her yesterday. Then she could put this inventory aside and commit her concentration to the other, more important matters.

Reaching for the phone amid the clutter on her desk, she called O'Hallihan Contracting. Unfortunately, Shem O'Hallihan, owner and chief director of substandard building materials, wasn't there. Whoever answered the phone claimed he'd been out of town all week.

That seemed to eliminate him as a suspect in trying to run Cara down, but *seemed* was the operative word. She wanted to talk to him, confirm where he was at the critical time. And to read from his expression and body language whether he'd hired someone else to do the dirty work.

That would have to wait until he officially returned to town. Cara gave her name and asked to have Mr. O'Hallihan return her call—not that she expected him to do so. Hanging up, she made detailed notes of questions and suspicions in her computer file.

Then it was time for further calls. A couple more people she'd slurred by telling the truth in recent exposés were unavailable, too. She had little success in learning when they'd be around.

To her surprise, she reached her fourth subject, Jackson Felmington, right away. More surprising was that the odometer-adjusting car dealer had heard of her own misadventure. "I wondered when I'd hear from you, Ms. Hamilton." He spoke as smoothly as…well, a used-car salesman.

"Really? Why is that?"

"A little bird told me you almost had a nasty accident. Something about your stepping in front of a truck that was just minding its own business going down the street. But it missed and you're still alive. I was so pleased to hear that." His tone didn't hint at the sarcasm Cara knew was behind his words.

Shocked, she hesitated before asking, "And just what little bird told you that?"

"Sorry, Ms. Hamilton, but I never reveal my sources. Just like you. But if I were you, I'd watch my step and not get too close to the street anymore. Come to think of it, maybe you shouldn't even go out in public."

She stared at his name on the computer screen, picturing the all-American middle-aged man with gray-streaked ginger hair and an ever-present crocodile smile.

Cara figured he hired all the muscle-bound mechanics he needed to keep his company and its inventory running economically. Too economically, since he got top, new-car prices for automobiles that had been run into the ground.

Might one of his mechanics, who obviously knew their way around vehicles like old blue pickup trucks, been hired to run her down?

"Thanks for the good wishes. And exactly why did you think that incident would mean you'd hear from me?"

"You've accused me of every other nasty thing you could think of, in print. I figured you'd try to pin that on me, too."

"Should I?"

A silence. Then, "Just try it, you bit—"

Shuddering at his suddenly malicious tone, Cara interrupted. "Oh, I will, if I can find any evidence it was you," she said sweetly. "Tell that anonymous little bird, if it's not you, that I've every intention of learning who it is and exactly how he or she happened to know the details of my 'accident.'"

As she hung up, she realized that she'd reached the end of her list without meeting the goal she'd set for herself. In fact, she hadn't eliminated any suspects from her first list.

One of the people she'd called might have been the person who'd tried to run her down yesterday. She'd put her money on Jackson Felmington, if he hadn't made it seem too obvious.

THOUGH HER CONVERSATION with Felmington had shaken Cara, it did not stop her from carrying out the next action she'd planned for that afternoon.

Not that Deputy Mitch Steele would approve of this direction any more than the last, but, hey, for now they were enemies, not allies.

Down the street from the *Gazette,* she entered the well-lighted yet somberly professional reception area of Lambert & Church, as confidently as if it were still a viable law firm and she was a potential client. Except that she could see, by boxes piled in every corner, that it wasn't "business as usual" at the Lambert firm.

"May I help you?" The woman behind the desk looked young and harried. Maybe this was Wanda, whom Cara had spoken with earlier.

"Yes, thanks. I have an appointment with Donald Church."

The receptionist's eyes widened, and she glanced down at her desk. "I…I'm sorry, Ms.… Er, I don't show any appointments for Mr. Church right now. He didn't—"

"Oh, that's okay, Wanda," Cara said, taking a chance. "I'll just go in." The puzzlement on the girl's face widened her eyes. Apparently, Cara had guessed right, though the receptionist didn't know who she was. All the better.

Cara inhaled. Despite whatever methods had been used to try to eliminate the odor of smoke from the ruined office annex, they hadn't succeeded. That was where Andrew had been murdered, his body torched in an attempt by Mayor Frank Daniels to hide the murder.

Poor Andrew…

Steeling herself, Cara breezed past the reception desk, skirting around stacks of cartons, and headed left when she reached the hall. Since the receptionist didn't try to correct her, she assumed she'd gone the right way. She hadn't been in Donald Church's office for some time.

Fortunately, the attorneys' names were listed on plates beside their doors. Cara made a surreptitious thumbs-up when she passed by the office that had been her friend Lindsey Wellington's, who'd come and gone from the firm in a short time. It had been Andrew's office when he'd first started working here, back when they'd been engaged. Cara hurried past, trying to ignore those old memories.

Where was Nancy Wilks's office? She'd been office manager, so she might just have sat in a cubicle somewhere, or had an inner, windowless room of her own. Had the crime-scene techs checked the space for clues into Nancy's murder? Cara would have to ask Mitch...if they were still speaking to each other.

Cara started when someone exited an office right in front of her. And then she smiled. It was Donald Church.

"Mr. Church," came Wanda's voice from behind her. "I'm sorry but I didn't know you had an appointment with this lady."

Perplexity creased Donald Church's round face. "I didn't schedule any appointments today, Ms...." His eyes opened wide as he recognized her.

When Andrew had just started working here, she'd come around a lot to meet him for lunch. She'd met Paul Lambert, Donald Church and the rest of the staff, though it was before Lindsey was hired.

"You're Cara Hamilton, aren't you?" Church asked.

Cara nodded. "I'm sorry I didn't call to set something up, Mr. Church, but I really need to speak with you. It's about Nancy Wilks." And the other murders, though she would lead him into that gently.

"Oh, yes." He sounded sympathetic. "I heard you found poor Nancy, didn't you?"

Cara nodded.

"I'm not sure how I can help, but come in. We'll talk. Finding her must have been terrible. Would you like some coffee?"

"Sure."

Church told Wanda to bring two cups and led Cara into his office. It was large, and as cluttered with boxes as the reception room. He took a carton off a chair facing the desk and motioned Cara to sit.

Donald Church wasn't much taller than Cara, and he was rather plump. He looked older than his partner Paul Lambert had, though that might just have been because

Lambert kept in better shape. Cara remembered Church as being a jovial sort, but his round face was sober now.

"Such a shame about Nancy," he began. "The Sheriff's Department has been here, and I've answered what questions I can, but there's not much I could tell them."

"Do you know anyone who might have wanted to kill Nancy?" Cara asked.

He stared, eyes narrowing. "You're not just here because you want sympathy about finding her, are you? Are you doing one of your vicious newspaper stories? Did you come here expecting me to point a finger at someone and accuse them of murder? Or, worse yet, to confess my own guilt?"

He definitely wasn't the man she recalled, who'd had a good sense of humor and liked to crack jokes. Of course, nothing about Nancy's death was a joking matter. Or Church's partner's murder of another person and subsequent suicide. Or the firm's relationship to the murder committed by the mayor. All in just a matter of months.

"No, sir, I didn't," she said. "But you're right about my working on an article about Nancy. She was my friend, and if I can help figure out who killed her, I will. But I want facts, not innuendoes. And I'm not accusing you or anyone else."

He didn't look mollified, but after Wanda had brought coffee and left again, he said, "Look, Cara. I understand your wanting to help find Nancy's killer. I want justice for her, too. But I have no idea who did it. And right now, this firm is in shambles. *I'm* in shambles. I don't know where to go from here." There was a catch in his voice as he leaned over his desk, his hands holding the sides of his round, balding head. When he looked back at Cara he said, "Go ahead and ask questions. But don't expect any helpful responses. And I'll answer some even before you ask. No, I don't know who killed Nancy. And no, though I'd been partners with Paul Lambert for years, friends with him for longer than that, I'd no idea what he was up to. Is there a connection between what he was doing and Nancy's death? Or Andrew's for that matter? Oh, I can see how the firm must look to everyone outside. And I must seem a fool or worse to be here and not know anything about it. But I don't.''

DEAD ENDS. That was all Cara had achieved that day.

She sat back in her own desk chair at the *Gazette* and stared once more at the computer screen.

Oh, and suspicions, of course. She didn't want to believe Donald Church knew more than he'd said, but could he have been that ignorant of Andrew's discovery of the mayor's conflict of interest in investing in Ranger Corporation? Could he not have known his own partner and friend Paul was capable of committing murder for his own benefit, and a client's?

Ranger Corporation.

She spent the next hour online, following information she'd gleaned—as well as a hunch. ''Her reporter's nose was aglow with questions,'' Shotgun Sally would have said. No stings from the ''tattle bug,'' though, or prickling with the ''news itch.'' And no wonder. Far from getting the dope for a really good story, when she was done hunting, she had even more questions.

Impulsively she lifted the phone receiver, glanced at her computer notes and punched in the phone number on her screen.

''Roger Rosales.''

''Hi, Roger.'' Cara identified herself, though she figured by his silence that he'd recognized her voice. ''I was checking through County Recorder files and saw that some property west of town recently changed hands. I don't mean the West Ranch that Ranger Corporation bought from Andrew McGovern's girlfriend a few months ago. And not the property Ranger tried to acquire from

Bart's uncle Jeb before he was murdered, or Bart's land, either, of course, but land adjoining them. The new deeds I found weren't in Ranger's name.''

"So why are you calling, Ms. Hamilton?" He sounded as though he was speaking through tightly clenched teeth.

"I'm getting to that. The thing is, I didn't recognize the names of the companies who own those properties now. They aren't local, and I've checked state records, too, and found them confusing—limited liability companies with partnerships as their members, and limited partnerships as partners, that kind of thing. I hardly found the names of any people anywhere, and those I did ferret out appeared to be lawyers in the East somewhere, probably representing unnamed clients. So I figure I'd just come right out and ask—is Ranger Corporation affiliated in any way with Eastern Mustang Property Acquisition or Texas Mustang Valley Sites?''

"Sorry, Ms. Hamilton, but I have another call coming in." And then he was gone. He hadn't denied anything, but he hadn't admitted anything, either.

That wouldn't stop Cara from hunting for connections. In fact, she intended to ask for help. She had one heck of a resource whose own sources could undoubtedly cut through the crap and get to the heart of who owned what. And how Ranger was snugly involved in it all.

Except that her resource was one of her biggest problems. She would have to face him head-on. And the very idea of being face-to-face with this particular problem gave her warm jitters.

That big, six-foot, good-looking, ornery problem could be helpful, if he chose to. Just as easily, he could stand right in the way of her biggest story ever.

With a sigh and a smile, she grabbed her purse from the back of her chair and headed off to find Deputy Mitch Steele.

"YOU PROMISE you'll be out of here soon?" The man facing Mitch on the Caddo Street sidewalk was nearly a foot shorter than him, but his unpleasant nature made him seem large enough to tempt Mitch to knock him down a few pegs.

The effort wasn't worth increasing the sweat lightly beading on Mitch's brow in the humid summer heat. "We'll be gone when the forensics technicians say they're done collecting evidence."

His measured response did nothing to temper the anger on John Ayres's wizened face. "Look, Deputy. I'm already going to lose a lot of money thanks to the crime committed on my property. I'll have to scrub that apartment and repaint, and there'll still be a stigma on it. The least you can do is make sure I can start working on it right away."

The least you *can do,* Mitch thought, *is have compassion for your murdered tenant.* John Ayres owned the property where Nancy Wilks had rented the first-floor apartment. "I assure you we want to finish here and catch the suspect as soon as possible, Mr. Ayres."

"Not good enough." His jaw jutted farther, a tempting target.

Mitch's knuckles itched. Despite how he'd carefully schooled himself in patience, he wasn't sure how long he could keep his cool with this jerk. Ayres thought he owned this property? Hell, as far as Mitch was concerned, his mother's people had the right idea. The earth belonged to everyone. That meant the people of Mustang Valley would all have an interest in this Caddo Street apartment building.

He wondered what Mr. Ayres would say to that.

Not that it mattered. The deed was in Ayres's name. Under Texas law, it *was* all his, and Mitch knew he couldn't argue with that.

A car pulled up on the street beside them—a scratched yellow Toyota. Cara's.

The corner of his mouth twitched, as if it had a will of its own. He'd no intention of smiling just because the frustratingly single-minded woman had somehow tracked him down. He hadn't suggested where to meet, though he'd agreed with her earlier to get together and talk.

Why wasn't he surprised she'd found him?

Her car door slammed. In moments she approached along the sidewalk. A huge smile lit her face. "Hi, Mitch." Her huge purse was slung over her shoulder. She wore the same outfit she'd had on earlier: blue skirt, yellow blouse and vest. "I thought you might be here." She looked pointedly at John Ayres, then held out her hand. "I'm Cara Hamilton."

Ayres didn't look charmed as he gave a quick shake. "John Ayres," he muttered.

"Oh, you're—you were—Nancy's landlord, weren't you?"

The old man nodded as Cara reached into her bag for something. She extracted a pocket recorder.

"How did you feel, Mr. Ayres, when you heard that poor Ms. Wilks had been killed right in her own apartment?"

"You're that reporter," Ayres accused.

"That's right. Now—"

With a scowl at Mitch that he turned back on Cara, Ayres stomped away.

"Guess he didn't want to give you an interview," Mitch said.

"Guess not, but that's okay. I didn't want to talk to him, anyway. But you looked like you needed rescuing."

Startled, Mitch looked down at Cara. Her auburn brows were raised, and her expression suggested apology.

"Truce?" she asked.

Mitch didn't want to let go of his anger with her so

easily. Maybe her only sin—telling her boss that Deputy Hurley Zeller dated the victim Nancy Wilks—wasn't a big one, but the repercussions of her indiscretion hadn't been pleasant.

Worse, she might have added yet another impediment to Mitch's own covert investigation. Bad enough he was disliked because of his heritage: one side Native American, the other scandal-ridden, allegedly corrupt sheriff. But he'd been around long enough to become part of the furniture—like a well-planted bug. People didn't watch their mouths so much around him anymore.

Not that he'd heard anything that led to solid evidence about his father's murder. Yet. At times frustration nearly got the best of him. But then he'd remind himself that he had supposedly learned patience, in different ways, from both sides of his heritage.

But Cara's intrusion into his plans had caused the sheriff and others to recall their distrust of him. It couldn't be allowed to continue.

She'd asked for a truce. He was still considering it, and not with much favor.

A troubled look shadowed her hazel eyes and she looked away from his, causing him a sudden fit of withdrawal. Not that he was addicted to sharing gazes with Cara. But that suddenly haunted expression made him want to touch her.

"Look, Mitch," she said in a low voice. "I'm really sorry about what happened. I know what it's like to have something you share with someone misused. I shouldn't have trusted Beau."

Her apology knocked him for a loop. He hadn't expected it. Was it genuine? It certainly sounded that way, but speaking of learning not to trust someone…

As she lifted her gaze back to his, the clouds racing across the Texas sky seemed to have suddenly gone off the radar. Or had Mother Earth just decided to allow the sun to shine?

"Can we go somewhere to talk?" Cara said. "I want to tell you what I learned today. I've got some possible leads, but I need help with them."

Ah. That was the reason for the apology. Mitch's cynicism kicked back in. No matter how appealing this woman was, he had to keep at the forefront of his mind that she had an ulterior motive. He wanted to solve the Nancy Wilks murder, as he did all murders—for justice; Cara Hamilton wanted to for the sake of her story.

"What, Mitch?" Her gaze was searching, as if she wanted to extract his thoughts from his mind.

"Nothing." He immediately regretted his abruptness, seeing a look of pain shoot across her face.

Man, was she a good actress. And yet... He wanted to believe in her sincerity. In their partnership.

That just might be because he had an urge every time he was around her to strip off her clothes, very slowly, and lay her down...

Maybe she could read his thoughts, for though she didn't look away, he thought he saw his desire mirrored in her eyes. He *knew* he wasn't imagining her faint flush.

And there they stood, on the sidewalk of a residential street, right outside a murder victim's house.

"Let's take a walk," he told her.

"Okay." Her agreement came quickly, as if she, too, recognized this was the wrong place, the wrong time.

The wrong people, too, he and she. And they always would be.

He measured his stride to hers as they headed down the sidewalk. He wasn't surprised that, despite her petite size, she walked with the same determination that she seemed to throw into everything. He barely had to slow his usual pace at all.

"Tell me what you learned today," he said.

She described her visit to the Lambert & Church offices, her uneasy interview of Donald Church. One of the other deputies had already interrogated the law firm partner, but Mitch intended to have a go at him, too. Soon.

When Cara told Mitch about the calls she'd made to people on her plausible enemies list, those she'd ticked off by her articles, *he* was ticked off, too. "Didn't I tell you not to do that? If one was the person who tried to run you over, letting them know you suspect them may only rile them further."

They'd stopped walking. She folded her arms and tilted her head back, ready to do battle with him. Her mouth was set stubbornly. As her soft red curls slid backward, he resisted the urge to brush them back into place.

Why did he find such belligerence appealing? Or was it because he'd begun to want this woman so much that whatever she did sent sparks through him that put his entire body on notice?

"Next time, will you clear it with me first?" He couched his order in a request. "Maybe we can talk to them together."

"Sure." He ignored Cara's skeptical expression that belied her positive response and resumed their walk down the sidewalk.

She kept up, continuing her rundown of what she'd done that day. She described her research in the County Recorder's Office. "And then I called Roger Rosales."

When Mitch tried to stop this time to chew her out, she took his arm and towed him along. Every nerve ending in his body seemed suddenly to have rushed to where she held him. To his surprise, he laid his free hand over hers. It must have surprised her, too, for she looked startled as their gazes met. Her smile stoked his juices even more.

He didn't scold her. He didn't let go of her, either, even as she got to the point. She wanted something from him. That was why she was sharing again.

Of course.

"Can you use your sources to find out what relationship Eastern Mustang Property Acquisition or Texas Mustang Valley Sites might have with Ranger Corporation?"

"Possibly," he replied, making a mental note of the company names. If they did have a connection with Ranger—

"And you'll share the information with me?"

"Possibly," he repeated.

She planted herself suddenly in front of him, glaring up with flashing eyes that were dark with anger. "Not good enough, Mitch. If we're partners—"

"We aren't partners," he told her, irked that she still didn't get it. "Me, deputy." He pointed toward himself. "You, civilian." He pointed toward her.

She grabbed his finger. Hard. As if she hoped to break it.

That would look great to the others in the department—a job-related injury given to him by a gorgeous but angry waif he'd just as soon have kissed as pointed at. He stared at her pouting, enticing lips, even as she used them to swear at him.

"Damn it, Mitch. We have a deal. I may be a civilian, but I'm one with a need to know. And information of my own. And—"

"And one who was nearly run over by someone aware of your 'need to know' and what you do with it."

"But I told you what you asked today, shared all the information I got. It's only fair that you reciprocate."

"I've already told you I will—as much as I can without compromising my case."

"But—"

"Isn't it clear to you yet that what you're doing is dangerous, Cara? I need to spend my time tracking down Nancy's killer, not holding your hand." He gently pried his finger away from her grasp. "And making sure you don't get hurt."

"You're not my keeper or my watchdog, Mitch."

"No, just your 'partner,' right?"

"Only to the extent *you* say so. That's not good enough." Before he could stop her, Cara had stalked off. In a moment she was back in her car. She scowled at him as she drove away.

It felt as if she had stared daggers at him. Why else did her anger make him feel as though she'd pierced his soul?

What's more, why did he have the feeling that she'd thrust herself into harm's way, just to pay him back?

AFTER TAKING TIME to get herself a new cell phone, Cara returned to her office at the *Gazette*. She looked around for Beau, mostly so she could avoid him rather than talk to him. She wanted to transcribe her notes of the day onto her computer.

She wanted to mull over more carefully the way she was dealing with Mitch. Why did they seem to irritate each other the way fingernails on blackboards screeched at a listener's nerves? And that was without even trying.

What she would prefer trying with Mitch was positive reinforcement. If he scratched her back, she would scratch his.

The sudden imagery of two naked bodies, breasts to chest, hugging each other so they could use their nails on each other's backs… It was almost too erotic for her to contemplate. At least while standing up in the realism of her own messy office.

So she sat down at her desk. And noticed the light blinking, signifying she had a message.

The voice, when she played it, was not familiar. She couldn't even tell if it was a high male tenor or a low female alto. "Hello, Ms. Hamilton," it said. "I hear you are looking for answers about Ranger Corporation. I have a few. If you want to hear them, meet me at five o'clock this evening at the Mustang Valley High School jogging track.''

Cara glanced at her watch. Four forty-five. She would have just enough time to get there, if she hurried.

Unwise to set up a meeting with an anonymous source? Maybe. But the track was public. And she'd be careful.

She tried hard not to break any speed limits on her way from Main Street to the Mustang Valley Municipal Park. The high school was right next door. She parked and ran from her car, through the grove of trees toward the chain-link fence surrounding the school's familiar athletic area. She'd been on the track team herself when she'd been at MVHS. It seemed so long ago….

She hurried through the gate, through the pretty land-scaped bushes nearest the fence and toward the running track. Too bad she was wearing her usual boots, or she could jog around while looking for whoever left the message. Right now she seemed to be alone—

Until someone grabbed her around the throat. Tightened the grip as Cara choked and gagged.

And no matter how much she struggled, the grip grew even tighter.

Chapter Nine

Calm, calm, calm, shouted a voice in Cara's head. A familiar voice. Oh, yeah. *That* voice. Her long-time self-defense instructor.

That recollection was all it took. Not that she could ignore the pressure on her neck that was hurting her. Making her grow woozy. But her training kicked in.

No kicks for this situation. Instead, she drew one arm forward, made a fist that she grabbed with the other hand, then propelled it backward and up. Hard. It connected with something soft. A stomach, maybe.

The person holding her grunted in pain. The grip eased a bit—enough for her to pivot and use her knee, right to the groin.

Her attacker was most definitely a man, for he doubled over in obvious distress. Cara couldn't have told what sex he was otherwise, draped as he was in a baggy black sweatsuit, collar turned up to hide the bottom of his face. The top was swathed in a low-brimmed hat and huge reflective sunglasses.

"Who are you?" Cara demanded, reaching for the glasses. Her hand didn't get far; the guy drew a gun from his pocket and aimed it at her.

Cara swallowed. The element of surprise was gone. He

now knew her skill at self-defense techniques. Could she kick the gun out of his hand? Not before he got off a shot.

"Get down, Cara!" The shout sounded from the distance. Mitch! Cara didn't hesitate. She threw herself onto the ground, landing uncomfortably on her large purse.

"Sheriff's Department," he yelled. How had he gotten here? "Drop your weapon."

As a blast sounded, she winced but realized she wasn't her attacker's target. Mitch was. She reached beneath her into her bag. Groping, she immediately found the thing she sought. But where the heck was her mace?

Too late. The guy ran down the track. Mitch broke through the trees, his eyes narrowed in concentration, his pace sleek and fast and sexy as hell as he followed. Despite his confining uniform and heavy utility belt, his pace was faster than most stripped-down runners probably achieved on the high school course. He looked wild and determined and utterly gorgeous—and he held a gun pointed toward the fleeing attacker.

Cara rose, admiring Mitch even as she kept clicking the digital camera she had pulled from her purse. She'd gotten at least one close shot of her assailant, though with him dressed like that it wasn't likely to help identify him.

But then Mitch lost his rhythm, yards down the track. Cara blinked before she realized why he'd hesitated.

Kids. Two students in T-shirts and shorts jogged along the path in front of him, between Cara's attacker and Mitch. He dodged, but his pace slowed as he put himself between the kids and the guy with the gun. When the joggers passed, Mitch stopped and aimed at a car exiting the student parking lot as another car pulled in.

Cara couldn't hear Mitch's swearing but sensed it by his body language—stiff, shaking, enraged. He shook his head as he put the safety back on his gun and returned it to the holster at his hip. He reached into his pocket and jotted something into a notebook—undoubtedly the description of the car, a license number, whatever he needed to identify the guy. Then he spoke into a radio slipped from his duty belt.

To no avail, Cara was sure. The guy had a head start. Since he'd set her up, the car must have been part of his plan, and untraceable to him.

Mitch turned and walked back toward Cara, his posture slack and defeated.

"YOU'RE ALL RIGHT?" Ignoring the couple of huge-eyed young runners who'd joined them, Mitch looked Cara up and down. Her skirt was wrinkled, her vest askew, her hair a mass of untamed red curls.

But she was alive. And beautiful.

"I'm fine," she said, though the raspiness of her voice drew his gaze to her throat. It was red.

"He choked you?"

"Before I elbowed him, then kicked him where it hurt." Her grin was so delighted that it almost lured him to smile back—though he wanted to kick *her* butt. Kick some sense into her.

Kiss that adorable, grinning mouth...

"But you're all right?" he repeated gruffly.

"Of course." She swallowed, and it was obviously painful. Her smile faded. "Thanks for coming to my rescue, Mitch." This time her voice quavered. Her eyes widened, and he could tell that the shock of what had almost happened was finally sinking in. Her breathing sped up, her breasts rose and fell faster and she looked up at him fearfully. "He tried to hurt me." Her voice was barely a whisper.

The urge to comfort her warred with his need to do his job. He nearly took her into his arms before he got control. "What the hell you were doing here?" The words burst from him so angrily that the kids muttered something and stepped back. Mitch was as angry with himself as with her, but she didn't need to know that.

"Taking pictures." Her attempt to sound proud as she held out a small camera seemed a huge effort. "I'll even let you download copies for your report."

"Hey, cool," said one of the kids, reaching for it. "You got pictures of that dude with the gun?"

"Sure did," Cara said, her tone more confident. "Watch tomorrow's *Gazette*. First, I'll want to interview both of you and—"

Good thing a patrol car pulled into the parking lot. Mitch might have done something he'd regret later, like dragging Cara off somewhere to slap her with a sense of reality. Give her a blow-by-blow description of what the suspect who'd grabbed her might have done with her— and that *before* he blew her brains out. He closed his eyes to absorb the agony the image caused him.

"What happened here, Deputy Steele?" It was Deputy Stephanie Greglets. She stood tall in her immaculate khaki uniform, her hair pulled into a bun at her nape.

Mitch recounted what had gone on. "Anything on the radio about apprehending the suspect in his car?"

Stephanie shook her head. "No one's spotted him."

"Damn." Mitch resisted the urge to slam a fist into something. There was nothing suitable around anyway— a couple of trees, a chain-link fence, some cars. And people.

Including Cara, who watched silently, as if studying him for her next damned article.

"I'll write up my report later, Deputy Greglets," Mitch said to Stephanie. "Right now, I'd like you to get statements from these witnesses." He nodded to the joggers.

"Sure."

As Stephanie took the two youths aside, Mitch approached Cara. Her sidelong glance evinced her apprehension. He glanced at his watch. His shift was nearly over. "We're going to have dinner together, Ms. Hamilton."

He could have laughed at the surprise that caused her full lips to part. Could have, but didn't.

Instead he surprised her all the more. "You're going to interview me for that article you're writing for your paper tomorrow. Okay?" Not that he'd allowed her to decline. But the curiosity that seemed as much a part of her as her rich red curls obviously kicked in.

"Sure," she said.

CARA WASN'T SURE what she'd expected of Mitch's dinner invitation, but it wasn't this.

They'd brought a large order of Tex-Mex food in from Mustang Valley's most popular barbecue restaurant.

Now they sat at her kitchen table. She wondered whether her drooling was obvious to him. If so, she'd explain it as a reaction to the wonderful, spicy aroma wafting around a room compact enough that her tile counter and pine cabinets were efficient, yet large enough to fit a small oak table with matching chairs. But what she really drooled over was Mitch.

He had changed clothes. She didn't remember seeing him out of uniform before. Certainly not in anything as tantalizing as a muscle-hugging black T-shirt and matching black jeans.

He'd made himself at home, helping her put out her bright-red placemats and set the table for two. Now he sat across from her, stripping meat with his teeth from a beef rib bone.

She'd never considered such a thing sexy before. But then, she'd never before sat across a table from a handsome, dark-haired lawman who had saved her life.

That was the sexiest part. That and Mitch's broad shoulders, seductive golden eyes, large, muscular build...

Everything about the man was sexy! Especially because they were alone here, in her apartment.

That had to be why he'd invited her to dinner; this was part of a planned seduction.

Would she participate? Maybe.

Jerry Jennings had tried to seduce her before he'd stolen her research, but she had been young, naive and unwary then.

"Okay." Mitch put the bone he'd been holding down on his plate and wiped his hands on a textured paper napkin.

She regarded him skeptically. Was he getting up the nerve for his seduction?

No, Deputy Mitch Steele had nerves of...well, steel. He'd proven that today when he had faced down an armed thug for her. A thug who'd tried to hurt, maybe kill her.

But as enticing as being seduced by him sounded, she might not be ready for it. And that had little to do with Jerry's attempt at manipulation.

She didn't have the chance to decide about Mitch. "Okay," he said again. "I wanted us to be alone when we talk, and dinner's as good a way to be by ourselves as anything."

"Talk about what?" Cara asked. But she knew from the seriousness of his expression what the topic would be—what she wanted to avoid talking about. What she wanted to forget but couldn't.

"First, I want an explanation of how you happened to be on the high school track with that suspect."

Suspect? Heck. She knew that was police lingo, but the guy had been more than a *suspect*. He'd tried to kill her.

"You tell me first," she insisted. "How did you just happen to be there to save me?"

"Because I had a feeling, when you left me this afternoon, that you would do something stupid out of spite."

"So you followed me?" Outrage swamped her. "Because you think I'm stupid?"

"Foolish," he said. "Not stupid."

If her glare had been as razor sharp as she intended, it would have inflicted mortal wounds.

Only, she didn't want to hurt him. No matter what his rationale for tailing her, he had saved her life.

"Your turn," he said, his tone mild. Her enraged stare obviously didn't bother him. "Why did you go there?"

She took a deep breath, got control of her injured pride, then said, "I received a phone call." She proceeded to explain what she'd done and why. "The thing is, the guy mentioned Ranger Corporation, said he had information for me. Since I'm all but sure Ranger has something to do with Nancy's death, and the other killings, too, I had to go find out."

"Without calling me first." His voice was too low, his golden eyes too blank. He was angry.

And she probably deserved it.

"We'd just argued. Again. And I thought—"

"You thought it would be better to put yourself in danger than to call for backup."

"If you put it that way—"

"Of course I do!" He stood as he exploded, glaring down as furiously as if he wanted to throttle her. Judging by the way his large hands formed fists on the back of his chair, he *did* want to throttle her. He looked damned sexy that way. And intimidating.

But Cara wouldn't let herself be intimidated. Someone else had tried it that day and gotten a jab and a kick where it hurt for his trouble.

"We'd better end our collaboration," she said coolly. "It isn't working."

"No, it isn't. But if we end it, we'll both be sorry."

She felt her eyes widen as she stared. Was he insinuating he was attracted to her, too? There was something molten in his eyes. Desire so wanton that it stoked her own. And yet—

"If we end our collaboration," he continued in a voice as icy as hers had been, notwithstanding the heat in his gaze, "I won't help you find information, and you'll always be in danger of my arresting you for obstruction of justice if anything—" he paused and stepped around the table toward her "—if *anything* you publish in an article hinders my investigation or apprehension of a suspect in Nancy Wilks's murder. Do I make myself clear?"

"Sure, but I've heard it before."

"Before, it was a threat. Now it's a promise."

She swallowed, studying his face for any chink in his sexy but steadfast armor. She looked down the length of his body, let her gaze linger along the portion of his dark jeans that swelled, then drew her eyes back up again. He was turned on, too. That was obvious. "Look, Mitch," she said softly, "I'm not trying to get in your way. I just want—"

"Your story at any cost." His words were blunt, and whatever hint of need she thought she'd seen in his eyes was concealed behind his hard, determined stare. "*Any* cost. Like getting yourself killed. I'm not going to let that happen, Cara, even if I have to incarcerate you to prevent it."

"Then you do like me!" she said triumphantly, though she could have kicked herself. This wasn't the time to tease him.

To her amazement, though, his gaze did soften. "Yeah," he said. "The hell of it is, I do like you. So here's what we're going to do."

MUCH LATER, after she'd heard him out and given her agreement—as if she'd had any choice—she saw him to the door.

"So, we're all set?" he asked.

"Sure," she began, "but you have to understand—"

Apparently he didn't want to understand, for Cara suddenly found herself in his arms. She looked up, trying to stick both defiance and a promise of limited cooperation in her gaze. All her intentions melted away under the heat of his molten golden eyes. And then his mouth met hers.

Their lips merely touched. Skin on skin, brushing gently, and she trembled as he grew totally still. And then, as if the gentle flame of their kiss had ignited the dry brush of desire within her, she felt herself blaze deep inside.

He, too, must have felt the conflagration. Instead of pulling away, he deepened the kiss, stoking it with the strokes of his searching tongue. He murmured something against her that could have been endearment or epithet, she didn't care.

She pressed against him, reveling in the hardness of his chest and the bulge against her belly, wanting more. Wanting— He pulled back. His breathing was uneven, but his gaze was so blank she wondered if only she had been shaken by that kiss.

"We'll talk tomorrow, Cara," he said much too evenly. "After the morning's *Gazette* comes out."

MITCH DIDN'T GET the newspaper delivered to his home. It was a small house located only a few blocks off Main Street. Not the best area of town—too close to the honky-tonk strip where places like the Hit 'Em Again Saloon, the bar owned by Wade Lansing, was located. Wade, who, with his new bride Kelly McGovern, the first victim's sister, had helped to expose that Mayor Frank Daniels had committed murder a couple of months ago. But the Sheriff's Department was not far away and the neighbors here were friendly, if not well off, and seemed to appreciate having a lawman nearby.

This morning he got up early and threw on jeans. He'd have to change before going to work but wasn't on duty for a while. He walked to Main Street and bought a copy of the *Mustang Gazette* from a convenience store. What he was looking for was right on the front page.

Hot damn! Cara had kept her word.

He bought a cup of coffee and stood outside on the sidewalk as he read the article.

The byline was Beau Jennings, but Mitch figured Cara had done all the work. She must have stayed up damn late to write it, while he had lain in bed thinking of her....

The story described what had happened to her yesterday. The account, in journalistic, nonemotional style, still made his teeth ache as he gritted them hard.

Included was an interview with the kids who'd witnessed his futile chase of the suspect. Damn, but that had frustrated him! He'd have at least shot out the punk's tires if that other vehicle hadn't gotten in the way.

Next time, the creep wouldn't be so lucky.

Not that he'd allow a next time with Cara involved.

The article went on to say what Cara and he had discussed: a representative of the Sheriff's Department had given a statement accusing Ms. Hamilton of interference in an ongoing investigation. Stated that the *Gazette* was on notice to cease intrusive practices that got in the way without yielding useful information, as evidenced by its shallow reporting so far.

Of course, in the interest of unbiased journalism, it also contained quotes from her, as if she'd been interviewed by her boss, Beauford Jennings. She expounded upon freedom of the press and the unwarranted arrogance of the Sheriff's Department, one deputy in particular. It named no names, but he knew who he was.

She'd discussed that with Mitch, too, the night before. The idea was to show the suspect and the world that she'd been chastised, and though she'd had a bone to pick with the deputy in charge, she had agreed to back off. Would it work? Who knew?

He sure didn't.

And was Cara actually going to back off? Hell, no. He knew better.

She had included a few paragraphs about the other murders—excluding his father's—reiterating who the victims and their killers were, describing without pointing fingers the links to Lambert & Church and its client Ranger Corporation. The story also hinted that more details were pending.

This went further than they had discussed, but at least they had resumed their uneasy alliance. And after yesterday's attack on her, maybe she would take it more seriously.

Mitch whistled as he strode back home to dress for work.

Until he let himself consider what else had gone on at Cara's home that night.

He'd seen the look in her eyes when she'd thought he'd invited himself home with her for sex instead of scolding. More than he wanted to eat, drink, sleep—heck, anything necessary for living—he'd wanted to forget his purpose and oblige.

Instead he'd kept his pants on. At least he hadn't been in his uniform pants then, which he had no business even thinking of removing while he was on duty. Or at any other time with a witness who happened to also be a reporter.

He'd also intended to give her just a small, cool kiss

when he'd left her place. One that simply cemented their agreement. Except… It had erupted into a *kiss.* A real one that had rocked him. Fortunately, he was used to asserting restraint over every conceivable emotion. He had backed off before losing control altogether…this time.

"Next time, Cara, if you tease me, be prepared to follow through." He spoke aloud as he entered his small, shabby but clean living room. "That's another threat. Another promise. Count on it."

He would.

CARA FOLDED the morning's *Gazette,* sat back in her desk chair and laughed. The sound was still hoarse after yesterday's ordeal, but she was trying to put that behind her. Most of it.

Except the recollection of Mitch Steele coming to her rescue against an armed assailant.

Coming to her home for dinner.

Negotiating the contents of this very article with her.

And that wonderful, too-brief kiss.

"Are you watching, Sally?" Cara demanded aloud.

She was alone in her cluttered office so she could talk to her idol Sally without anyone knowing. Sally would have appreciated the article she'd ghostwritten for Beau. It was just as Mitch and she had discussed. As *he'd* suggested.

Had he recalled, in the recesses of his mind, that Shotgun Sally had had such a public feud with her lawman lover in the story they'd discussed?

Of course, it had been contrived. They were close by then, and the idea had been to convince folks they hated each other's guts. That way Zachary could disavow knowledge or approval of Sally's roughshod ways as she ignored laws and conducted her investigation into who killed her sister. Who had wanted, instead, to kill *her.*

Not that it had any bearing on the present situation, which in some ways was too bad. Though the story had a couple of conflicting endings, one thing was certain— as certain as any of the Sally stories were. Sally and her lawman had had one heck of a passionate affair.

And Cara? Mitch Steele was hardly *her* lawman. But the idea of a passionate fling with him was more than a little appealing.

Especially now, when they were working together again. Sharing information.

Not that she would fully trust him to do as he'd promised. Not any more than she figured he trusted her.

But, oh, how she'd enjoyed being alone with him in her apartment last night. She'd been incredibly turned on by him. She'd seen in his eyes that he wanted her, too.

And to top it all off, there'd been that kiss, full of promise, passion...and, ultimately, kiss-off.

He wasn't seducing her to steal a story or even information. He wasn't seducing her at all, damn him!

"Enough," she said aloud. She wouldn't keep thinking about Mitch. Instead, she'd focus on the similar Sally story. Though she knew how it ended, she forgot some of the details. Her curiosity was piqued. It would prod at her till she got the answer.

Rather than be ruled by discomfort, she took a sip of tepid coffee from a white mug on her desk, then lifted the phone. But Della Santoro wasn't in her office.

"Hi, Della, it's Cara," she said into the machine. "I've got some Shotgun Sally questions for you. Call when you get a chance." She left her work and home numbers, though Della already had them both.

And then Cara sat still at her desk, frustrated. What was she going to do now?

Research her primary story, of course. And if she used

methods that rubbed Mitch the wrong way? Well, they'd already prepared for that. That's what the article was for.

Except…she'd learned her lesson. If she was going to do anything that even hinted at danger, she would call Mitch and let him know first.

Her next step, then? She reached for the phone, just as it began to ring. "Cara Hamilton," she answered as she always did, also checking the caller ID as was her habit. It displayed Unidentified Number.

"You got away yesterday, Cara," said a distorted voice on the other end. "Again."

"Who is this?" Cara demanded, though of course she knew. Her hand lifted to massage her still-aching throat. It was the person who'd attacked her yesterday. Except he sounded different. "What do you want? Did you drive that truck, too?"

"I want to make sure the *Gazette* corrects an inaccuracy in the article about the attack on you yesterday," the voice said.

"What do you mean?"

"It implies that the *Gazette,* and one particular investigative reporter, is continuing to look into the Nancy Wilks murder and ties between it and other crimes in the area."

"So?" Cara said coldly, forcing herself to hide any sign of fear. "There's nothing inaccurate about that."

"Oh, yes, there is," said the voice. "That is, it's inaccurate if you want to stay alive." There was a click as the caller hung up.

Chapter Ten

This was one of those times Mitch wanted to shove Hurley Zeller right in his ugly face. But it was also a time he had to take it and act as if nothing was wrong. Be stoic, or pretend to be, as his mother's people had to do when defeated by the intruders in their world.

Not all had succeeded. Mitch would. Outward serenity was a ploy he had learned long ago.

Inside was a different matter.

They sat in Sheriff Ben Wilson's large office. Ben acted as officious as always, backed by the revered flags of Texas and the United States on the wall behind his desk.

The sheriff was not happy. Resembling a straw-deprived scarecrow in his loose khaki uniform, he clutched a copy of that morning's *Gazette* in one hand. His other was clenched white-knuckled on his desk.

Mitch could have gagged from the strong fumes of old cigars that hung in the rank air of the office. He took shallow breaths.

"So now the department is the butt of jokes all over town," Hurley Zeller was saying. He'd brought Ben the paper. Sitting on a low-backed chair beside Mitch, he had pasted a hurt and self-righteous frown on his fat face. He knew exactly what buttons to push to rile Ben further.

"Not bad enough that you haven't found the Wilks

murderer yet," Ben growled, his thin face a mass of angry wrinkles. "But you were right there and still didn't nab a suspect who was in front of you, attacking that big-mouthed-bitch reporter, of all people. Of course she'd write an article that makes us appear like fools, even if it's got Beau Jennings's name on it. To top it off, it makes us look even worse that you blamed her for your own foul-up. She's retaliated in print, made it clear where the fault lies."

Just as Mitch had told her to do. Any indication they were working together could create even more problems for him.

"You blew it bad, Steele," Wilson continued. "Real bad."

"Reminds me of someone else he knows," Zeller said, a barely suppressed guffaw in his tone. "*Used* to know. You gonna take the easy way out like your old man did, Steele?"

Before he realized what he was doing, Mitch leaped to his feet. "You—" He stopped himself. The ass was trying to get him mad. He wouldn't give him the satisfaction.

Instead he turned back toward the man he figured had murdered his father, if only he could prove it. "You're right," he said to Wilson. "I blew it. Of course, we'd have gotten worse publicity if I'd blown away a couple of high school kids to make sure I took down the suspect. But that's what I should have done." He hung his head as if in remorse, forcing his fingers to remain loose when what they wanted to do was turn into tight, lethal fists.

"Don't get sarcastic with me, boy," Wilson hissed.

"No, sir. And I won't even mention how bad the department looked when the media reported that one of its own dated a murder victim just before her death." Mitch didn't look at Hurley, but if that jerk thought this new problem would overshadow what he'd done, he now knew otherwise.

"Here's what you're gonna do to fix this, Steele," Wilson said without responding to Mitch's digs. "First, you'll stay out of that reporter's sights. If she wants an interview, you send her to me, and I'll set her straight. If she's being attacked right before your damned eyes, you call for backup and let someone else deal with it. If she—"

Mitch's cell phone rang. Damn. What a miserable time. "Excuse me, Ben. I'll make it quick." He flipped his phone open. "Deputy Steele here."

"Mitch? It's Cara." There was an uncharacteristic edge to her voice. Excitement? No, it sounded more like fear. "I need to talk to you."

Despite how badly he wanted to walk out of there right now, it would do no one any good if he got fired for insubordination. Not if Cara wanted any cooperation at all from the Sheriff's Department. And not if the Sheriff's Department had a hope of getting relevant info from the indomitable, exasperating, beautiful investigative reporter who'd burrowed so deeply under his skin that he jumped when she hiccuped.

But he couldn't jump right now, no matter what her stimulus.

"My laundry's ready?" he said, picturing the shock and outrage on Cara's pert face. "Good. I'll call later to arrange to pick it up." And then he hung up on her.

CARA GLARED at the phone. She gathered that Mitch couldn't talk right now. But right now was exactly when she *needed* to talk to him.

That damned phone call had really unnerved her.

She leaned over her cluttered desk, breathing too fast. Tears burned her eyes, though she refused to let them fall.

Mitch and she were supposed to be partners of sorts. But he had let her down—whether or not he'd intended to.

She needed to talk to someone. Right now. Someone on her side, who'd be there for her no matter what else was going on.

Not Beau. He would compare her with his back-biting nephew, Jerry, or at least his illusions about him. *Jerry* never got scared off by anonymous phone calls. *Jerry* never let anything stand in the way of a story. Not even integrity.

The fact that Jerry got his start by stealing from her had never mattered to Beau, who'd put his pet relation on a pedestal.

Cara sighed. What was she going to do? Sitting there thinking about being scared wasn't an option.

She'd done what she'd promised: called Mitch. And look where that had gotten her. He'd just hung up on her.

She knew exactly who she wanted to call, her dearest friend, Kelly McGovern Lansing. But Kelly and Wade were still in Hawaii on their delayed honeymoon. Cara wasn't sure where they were staying even if she wanted to interrupt them. And she needed to do more than send an e-mail.

Instead she called a number she'd used just the other day. She nearly hung up after two rings, though. Heck, she'd already interrupted Lindsey Wellington once at a time she wanted least to be bothered. That was almost as bad as busting into a honeymoon.

"Hello?" A man's voice answered. It had to be Bart Rawlins, Lindsey's guy.

"Bart, it's Cara Hamilton. How are you?"

"Probably better than you sound, Cara. What's wrong?"

Damn. Was her distress so obvious? She knew Bart, of

course, but not that well. "Nothing," she lied. "I just had some questions to run by Lindsey. Is she available?"

"Sure. Just a minute."

Though it was less than a minute before Lindsey picked up the phone, it was long enough for Cara to wonder what it would be like to have found one's soul mate, as Lindsey had. Sure, Bart had gone through hell and Lindsey had nearly followed before they realized what they had together. After all, Bart had been in jail, awaiting trial for the murder of his uncle, when Lindsey, a new lawyer, had been assigned to defend him.

And Kelly, too, had found the right man for her—Wade Lansing, a guy they'd both known forever. Cara had never even considered looking beyond his bad-boy image, but Kelly had...

"Cara? What's wrong?"

Suddenly Cara didn't want to go through with what she'd called to do—cry on her friend's shoulder.

She wasn't a wimp. She was like Shotgun Sally, a damned fine investigative reporter.

So act like it, she ordered herself.

"I'm still struggling with trying to figure out what poor Nancy wanted to show me," she said. Not that it had been at the forefront of her mind right then. "We've talked before about what's ethical, but is there any way for me to look at the Lambert & Church files?" After Andrew McGovern's murder, Lindsey had turned over to his sister, Kelly, what she'd thought were his personal effects. Some of his working files were in those boxes, and Lindsey had been uncomfortable about having unwittingly put them into the hands of someone outside her firm.

"You know it wouldn't be ethical of me to hand them to you or discuss them, but I've no problem telling you where they probably are right now."

"Really? Where?"

"Since the firm is disbanding, most have been sent back to the clients whose files they were."

"Oh." Cara's sudden bubble of excitement burst and oozed into dejection once more.

"If the clients want to reveal the contents, they're the ones who hold the privilege, so…"

"So all I have to do is to convince someone like Roger Rosales to hand over the Ranger Corporation files."

"Right," said Lindsey.

"Sure," said Cara.

After saying goodbye to Lindsey, Cara took a deep breath and thought of Shotgun Sally. Nothing ever stood in the way of her getting a story. She lifted the phone and made another call.

"Roger? This is Cara Hamilton. I'd like to make a deal with you."

"So you're the deputy I wrote that article about." Beau Jennings peered over the top of his silver-rimmed glasses at Mitch. "You want to tell me what really happened at the high school yesterday? Cara wrote part of the article and really cut you to shreds. I respect our law enforcement officers, so I figure it wasn't really as bad as she said."

As soon as Mitch broke free from his chewing out by Ben Wilson, he'd come to the offices of the *Mustang Gazette*. He hadn't gotten farther than the tiny reception area, its walls plastered with dozens of framed certificates of merit for the small-town paper and pictures of reporters receiving awards.

Some were of Cara, he'd noticed immediately, suppressing his smile. He wasn't surprised.

When he'd asked the skinny young man behind the front desk for Cara and identified himself, Beau Jennings had come out. Now, the plump, suspendered editor of the town paper was acting too smug. Once again, to get what he wanted, Mitch knew he had to take it.

"I happened to be patrolling the area around the school and thought I saw a citizen in trouble. It was Cara, and she'd pretty much fought off her attacker before I got there. The guy pulled a gun, so I drew mine but couldn't use it for fear of endangering other citizens."

"Yeah? Then what? Why did Cara insist on giving you a hard time in the article?"

"Because I made it clear she wasn't to take the law into her own hands. She's got the idea that she's a superwoman and that she'll solve the Wilks murder all by herself. I told her that getting herself killed might be one way to do it, as long as she fingers the perpetrator first, but that the town would much rather have her around writing her vicious stories."

To Mitch's surprise Beau Jennings laughed. "You're okay, Deputy, no matter what Cara says."

The idea that Cara had probably gone further than her article and criticized him to her boss didn't please Mitch. Did it further their alliance for her to put him down? Could be. If their cooperation wasn't obvious, maybe they could each extract more from people they were investigating. Someone who craved publicity but hated the law might talk to her, while a different person might cooperate with the Sheriff's Department anonymously, out of media scrutiny.

Right now, though, it wasn't philosophy motivating Mitch but concern for Cara. "Do you know where Cara is right now, Beau? She called a while ago and said she had some information to share with me." An exaggeration, of course.

Beau's eyes narrowed shrewdly. "That's what she said? Well, even so, I suspect she's changed her mind since she left before you got here."

"Any idea which way she went?"

"Northeast, I think. Or is it Midwest?"

Mitch's puzzlement must have shown, for Beau Jennings's large teeth emerged as he smiled hugely. "Ranger Corporation," he said. "I don't know where their headquarters are, but Cara was heading for their local offices."

CARA WAS BACK in the small yet prestigious Ranger Corporation local headquarters. Once again she faced Roger Rosales in his own well-appointed office, asking questions.

He still looked like a boy who'd rather pull pranks than run a national company's local offices, his youthful look emphasized by his attire, more casual than the last time Cara had seen him. Today, he wore a blue buttoned shirt without a tie, and his suit jacket was over the back of his tall leather desk chair.

"What kind of deal do you have in mind, Ms. Hamilton?" Roger sat forward, folding his hands on his pile-laden desk. Interested, but not too interested, his body language said to Cara.

"Have your records been returned to you from Lambert & Church?"

"Our legal files? Could be, but what business is it of yours?" His smile didn't falter. But was that a tinge of uneasiness Cara detected in his otherwise cheerful brown eyes?

Cara bent forward till she, too, leaned over his desk. She hoped her body language suggested sincerity. "I'm not asking for information that's strictly between your company's lawyers and you."

Not exactly true. She'd love to see it all. Would she be able to tell what documents had passed over Nancy Wilks's desk? Would she finally learn what Nancy had wanted to show her? Or would she simply be able to rule out that Nancy's find involved Ranger Corporation?

"I also know that if I dig deeply enough into public records I'll find what I need, but that could take time." Mitch was trying to get it for her, too, but she had no guarantees as to if and when he'd succeed. "Here's what I suggest. I don't know for sure why Ranger Corporation has a presence in Mustang Valley, though I'll know eventually, since for any development to be built it'll need government approvals. That process can be smoothed by good publicity and made bumpy by bad."

"So if I give you what you need, you can promise your paper will get behind whatever our project is?"

How she despised his smile! It didn't reveal a thing about what was really on his mind. She had to look away before she gagged. "I didn't say that." She again met his stare. "I can't promise anything, since the *Gazette* isn't my paper. I don't determine editorial policy. But I can make strong suggestions. And if your project will benefit the citizens of Mustang County, bring jobs, that sort of thing, then I'll urge that the paper run favorable editorials. Maybe charge lower advertising rates."

"And all that just for letting you in on what's already public record?"

"Right. Like whether Ranger Corporation is affiliated with Eastern Mustang Property Acquisition or Texas Mustang Valley Sites, the companies that own land in the vicinity of the Rawlins ranchlands that Ranger was trying to buy a month or so ago."

"And that's all you want? You're not here to twist something out of me like you tried last time, when you insinuated Ranger was involved with unsavory things like Mayor Daniels's or Paul Lambert's sins?" The gleam in his eye was a penetrating dagger of contained fury.

That didn't deter Cara. "You mean murder? Including Nancy Wilks's?"

"Exactly."

"You brought them up this time, Mr. Rosales, not me. I asked before if Ranger was connected and you neither confirmed nor denied it. I didn't expect anything different now, unless…" She let her words taper off.

"Of course I'm not going to confirm or deny. That's too much like asking if I've stopped beating my wife. Damned if you say yes, damned if you don't." He paused. That despicable grin reappeared, this time with something more behind it. He scanned Cara with glittering eyes that overtly undressed her before rising again to meet her gaze. "I'm not married, by the way."

"Glad to hear it." Cara smiled. She knew the value of flirting, but it wasn't easy with this slick and slimy corporate executive from whom she needed information. His damning question was more like: Did you steal what Nancy Wilks had to show me before or after you killed her?

"So if you confirm a connection," she said, "you admit the company's somehow involved with murders, which of course you won't do. But if you deny it, why does that harm you?"

"It's gracing a totally inappropriate question with a response." His words came out one by one, and she had a sudden uncomfortable feeling he'd switched from flirtation to threatening her in a covert manner she didn't quite get.

"I don't agree," she said. "But in any event, do we have a deal?"

"I'll think about it, Cara. Talk to my superiors. They'll check with our corporate lawyers."

In other words, they'd have a deal when hell froze over.

Or when Cara got this too-slick company executive to dance a jig on Nancy Wilks's grave.

Still, as Cara left the office, wishing she had time to jump into the shower to wash the slime off, she grinned.

Deal or not, she'd gotten more leads from her visit to the Ranger offices.

MITCH CAUGHT UP to Cara at the Main Street curb as she opened her car door.

"Mitch. What are you doing here?" She smiled as if pleased to see him. Damn, but that made him feel good.

But he knew her welcome wouldn't last. "Why did you call me before? And why didn't you wait till I got back to you?"

Sure enough, the glow in her joyful hazel eyes flickered into defensiveness. "I had some information to share, per our deal, but you obviously weren't interested."

"I obviously couldn't talk then. You're smart enough to have realized that."

"Yeah, I did. Anyhow, it doesn't matter now." But her face paled suddenly as she was reminded about whatever it was. And that told Mitch it definitely did matter.

"Tell me anyway," he said.

"No need. We'll touch base later." Cara slid into her car.

Good thing it was one where all the doors opened with a flick of a switch on her key ring, since before she could start the engine Mitch had moved around it, taken off his hat and slipped into the passenger seat.

Cara glared. Her blouse beneath her beige vest that day was rust colored, a few shades darker than her hair. He liked the contrast, even as a clashing pinkness rose up her cheeks. Good. He was glad her color returned, and then some. "What are you doing?"

He countered with a question of his own. "Where are we going?"

"We?"

"Yeah, partner. And by the way, we're not going anywhere till you tell me what you called about earlier. Your voice then and your reaction now have told me it's something I want to hear."

Her shoulders wilted, and the defeat in her eyes made him want to draw her close. Wring it out of her.

Hug it out of her...

"You don't want to hear." Her voice cracked. "I sure didn't."

"Tell me anyway."

"It was another phone call. I don't think it was the same person as last time. But whoever it was knew details about the attack on me yesterday that weren't in the article. Maybe it was even the attacker. And he—or she—threatened me if I continue to work on the exposé about Nancy's death."

"Damn it, Cara, you should have told me right away. Do you have caller ID on your phone?"

She nodded. "It's a fixture at the *Gazette,* but it was blocked."

Mitch knew that even as a peace officer he couldn't fix everything. Be everywhere at once. Save everyone. He'd told himself so often.

Especially after his dad died.

He didn't believe it then. He didn't believe it now.

And he'd failed to be there for Cara when it really mattered at least twice in only the past two days—once in the park and again with this damned phone call.

That was two times too many.

His objectivity in this case was stretching thin. He never let feelings for victims develop, let alone get in his way. But Cara wasn't an ordinary victim. She refused to be a victim at all. And admiration was leading to other unwelcome feelings.

His training kicked in automatically. He questioned her about the call. But she hadn't recognized the voice, nor had there been any distinguishing sounds in the background.

"I thought of all that," she said grumpily. Good. He preferred her spunk to show through instead of fear—even when it was turned on him.

"I'm sure you did. Look, you feel like some coffee at the Lone Star Lodge? We need to talk."

"Later. I have someplace to go right now."

"Like?"

"Well, I just visited Roger Rosales in the Ranger Corporation office."

"Yeah, I kinda figured, since you happened to be right outside his office. But did you clear it with me? Cara, I told you—"

Both her words and her cat-and-canary smile stopped him. "I told him I wanted to make a deal with him. As if I thought I could trust him. What I really went there for was information."

"And he handed it to you?" Mitch didn't believe it.

"Not exactly. But journalists learn all sorts of unusual skills."

"Like?"

"Like reading upside down."

CARA DROVE IN SILENCE, sneaking looks toward Mitch.

Most of the time he was looking right back.

Darn him. She'd always considered her compact car roomy enough, but Mitch seemed to occupy the entire passenger seat and then some. He'd pushed the seat back as far as it would go, and still his uniform-clad legs seemed cramped.

Not to mention that his presence heated the entire car. Or maybe it was just that she always seemed to warm up when he was around. And not just with body heat. Desire for this man did strange things to her, at all the wrong times.

As if there would ever be a right time. He was her ally in an investigation. That was all. And as with all allies, she could not let her guard down and trust him.

He'd brought back to her mind much too forcefully that damnable threatening telephone call. And her frightened response. She wasn't a fool, but neither would she let someone scare her off by threats that made it even clearer to her that she was on the right track. If someone wanted to scare *her,* that meant she was scaring them!

She pressed the button to roll down her window partway, but that didn't help. The outside air was hotter still. She put the window back up and turned on the air conditioner.

She didn't want the stubborn, interfering deputy with her right now, and not just because his sexy presence was a distraction. The person she was going to see would undoubtedly have nothing to say with the law there.

Not that he was likely to say much to the media, anyway.

Especially her.

And she had to admit—but only to herself—that she felt safer with Mitch along.

"Exactly what did you see as you read the papers on Roger Rosales's desk upside down?" Mitch asked. She'd explained what she meant. While Roger and she played their cat-and-mouse games in which she'd seemed to have gained nothing, she'd taken the opportunity, in a seemingly sincere moment leaning toward him, to scan the pages on top of the stacks on his desk. Most were letters. She'd memorized the addressees.

"I gathered he was interviewing contractors for his mysterious development," she said. "I saw five names, and most weren't local."

"But some were."

She nodded. "That's where I was going when you caught up with me, to see one."

"You made an appointment?"

"No, but he won't be surprised to see me." She laughed at Mitch's puzzled expression. "He owes me a phone call," she explained. "I tried calling him the other day and left my name, but he never got back to me."

"And just why did you call him before?"

"Because he's on that handy-dandy list you told me to make. You know, the people likely to have grudges against me since I exposed their shoddy practices in one of my articles. One of them just happened to be a contractor—Shem O'Hallihan."

Chapter Eleven

The offices of O'Hallihan Construction, on the outskirts of town, were in a building that resembled a huge garage. Not surprising, Cara thought. It probably housed a lot of machinery. O'Hallihan was the busiest contractor in Mustang County.

If she hadn't known better, she'd have hoped, for its customers' sakes, that the company did better with other people's projects than with maintaining its own premises. The wood frame structure hadn't been painted in years. Of course, she knew how O'Hallihan treated its customers—and it wasn't good.

She parked in a visitors' spot between a red pickup truck on wheels practically as tall as she was and a shiny green SUV.

"You don't happen to see an old blue truck here, do you?" she said, turning her head as she got out of her car.

"Reading my mind?" Mitch, too, scanned their surroundings. "I don't see anything matching your description."

She headed for a door toward the building's left side marked with a big red sign saying Office. Mitch was beside her. This close, she was very much aware of how much taller he was than her. And how much safer she felt in his presence.

If she weren't careful, she'd be stupid enough to start liking that feeling. Liking him.

Oh, hell. She already did like him. Too much.

"Let's discuss strategy," he said.

She looked sidelong at him, only to find his gaze on her. She appreciated that he actually waited for her input. There was a heat in his eyes—a reminder of last night's kiss—that suggested he wanted to tear her clothes off. Yet at the same time he respected her for her mind.

Was she reading too much into this look—like her own libidinous reaction to him?

Later, she thought. Now wasn't the time to think of anything beyond their current mission.

"Not much to strategize about." She drew her concentration back to the door in front of them. "You'll listen, I'll talk and Shem O'Hallihan will scream."

Mitch's brief laugh was rich and hearty and curled around her like an appreciative hug. "And you know this because...?"

"I've interviewed the man before. I've even been one of his employees, or so he thought. I put on a hard hat, a work shirt and jeans and applied for a job as a drywall installer."

"He took you on?"

"After I proved I could install drywall. That's one of the ways I learned how he skimped on materials. The drywall he used stank. Literally."

"No kidding? And of course you know how to install the stuff." Was he was patronizing her? Instead his expression still seemed amused. "Let's see if we can find out why Ranger Corporation is thinking of hiring him," he finished.

Cara recalled these offices—small rooms connected by a narrow hall with gray, stained walls.

"Which is O'Hallihan's?" Mitch asked. None of the three doors was marked.

"The last one." Cara also remembered—too well—being in O'Hallihan's office, especially the last time. It was uncomfortably small, as they all were. But what made the others cramped was that they were always filled with files and tools and people. The dozens of company laborers hung out here between jobs, sometimes in the warehouse, but often in these close rooms that contained uncomfortable benches and coffeepots kept bottomless by constant brewing.

Cara hadn't gotten to know her temporary co-workers well, despite working with them for several weeks. Employees seemed to change nearly as often as pages on a daily calendar. She'd gathered physical proof of the allegations she later made in her story, but no one had enough knowledge to provide an in-depth interview.

Except, of course, Shem O'Hallihan himself. He hadn't realized that his flirtation with Cheryl Hazleton, as Cara had called herself, was a dialogue and that most unsavory points would appear in an article that exposed his corrupt business practices.

His obvious lust for her was why his office had seemed the tiniest of all, for she'd wanted to put as much room between them as possible.

And now? Her skin crawled at the thought of seeing him again, but she wanted to get it over with. Besides, she wasn't alone.

She was surprised there weren't as many people around now. Maybe they were all out in the field, at work. Or at lunch. It was just after noon.

Was Shem in? Probably. He usually didn't grab lunch

till late afternoon, when he also visited job sites to check on the progress.

Cara edged around Mitch in the narrow hall. His body heat mingled with hers as she brushed by. Ignoring her too-powerful awareness of the uniformed deputy, she knocked on the door.

"Yeah?" Cara recognized the familiar, gruff voice. Taking a deep breath, she pushed the door open.

Shem O'Hallihan sat behind his desk, dwarfing his office by his presence, though not by his size. He'd always seemed surprisingly flimsy to Cara for a guy who purported to work with his hands and heavy materials all day.

As in the other times she'd seen him, he wore dark glasses. The puffy style of his light hair seemed to flaunt that his hairline hadn't begun to recede, despite his being middle-aged. But his body was skinny and his usual white T-shirt didn't hide that he lacked muscle tone.

He might be great at hiring people to do his company's work, but Cara hadn't seen him do an hour's worth of labor himself.

Shem stood up. The expression on his face suggested he wanted to tear her apart. "What the hell are you doing here?"

She refused to let herself be quailed, but before she responded, Mitch moved around her. "She's assisting on an official investigation, Mr. O'Hallihan." His uniform said it all.

"Yeah, officially printed lies," he spat.

Cara conjured a friendly smile. "Good to see you, too, Shem. And you're right that I'm here as a reporter, though I'm cooperating with Deputy Steele as he looks into the Nancy Wilks murder. Did you know Nancy?"

She thought Shem's small eyes would leap from his head the way he glared from behind his glasses. "First you accuse me in print of cheating customers. Now you're accusing me of murder?'' Leaning on his fists on his desk, he turned to Mitch. ''Isn't it a crime to tell lies about a citizen, Deputy? If so, I demand that you arrest her.''

Cara sat on a small wooden chair near the edge of Shem's filthy desk, which looked as though a hurricane had gone through the office. ''I didn't lie in my article. I laid out facts as I'd discovered them. And, gee, what a surprise. They formed one, big, interesting pattern that suggested your customers were not getting what they paid for. And right now I merely asked if you happened to know a murder victim.''

''Of course I didn't—'' He stopped, glaring from Cara to Mitch, then obviously thought better of lying. ''Yeah, I knew her. But Mustang Valley's not a big town. People know people here.'' He slipped back onto his chair. ''And Lambert & Church was my law firm—at least till a few weeks back, when they filed for bankruptcy. I knew Nancy from when I visited their offices, but not well. And I sure as hell didn't kill her.''

From the corner of her eye, Cara noticed Mitch's mouth open. ''No one suggested you did,'' she said smoothly, cutting off whatever Mitch was about to say. Arms crossed, he leaned against the wall beneath a picture of Shem shaking hands with the now-deceased mayor, Frank Daniels.

Was the former mayor the Ranger Corporation connection? If so, what did it mean?

''Actually, Shem,'' she continued, ''we're here following a lead on another matter that probably has nothing to do with Nancy's murder.'' She hoped he'd be so relieved not to be under suspicion that he would cooperate.

''What matter?'' He crossed his skinny arms belligerently.

''Unfortunately, we can't reveal it yet. But it has something to do with a contractor that's not local.''

Indirectly, Cara thought. Maybe. She glanced at Mitch, prepared to send him a look begging him to let her run with what she made up as she went along. His face was impassive—except for a slightly raised dark eyebrow that gave him both a quizzical and a deliciously rakish look.

"Although I can't identify that contractor," she continued, "we've just come from the Ranger Corporation offices and believe your competitor may be engaged in unfair business practices. Perhaps is even ready to use extortion to gain Ranger as its account. We just wonder what criteria you've used for submitting your bid for Ranger's project."

"You mean some out-of-town slimeball's trying to muscle in here based on lies and blackmail?" Shem, tense once again, stood and paced behind his chair. "Hell, Roger Rosales at Ranger hasn't done much with me so far beyond tossing me a crumb or two and checking on my availability for a project so big he won't even tell me what it is. But I've assured him we'll make the time. He said there'll be a lot of excavation, so I quoted him a per-unit price based on cubic yards of dirt we'd move and dispose of. And gave him references that show we do a damned fine job of conforming to an architect's plans for constructing commercial stuff, like office buildings, shopping centers, schools, playgrounds, whatever."

Interesting, Cara thought. Though it still didn't tell her what she wanted to know. "No residential?" she asked. In her mind, she'd assumed Ranger Corporation was buying land in Mustang County to build a huge, amenity-filled bedroom community for the Dallas/Ft. Worth area an hour away.

"Sure. That, too, though Rosales seemed more interested in commercial."

Cagey Roger might be hiding his real interests by pretending Ranger's focus was on something else.... Cara wouldn't put that past him.

"I see." Mitch took a few steps away from the wall. Cara shot him a warning glance. She was in charge of this interview. But he wasn't looking at her. "Then you don't know any vulnerabilities Ranger has that would leave them open to being strong-armed into hiring the wrong outfit?"

Hey! Cara liked that question. The right answers could steer them toward any number of useful leads: rumors in the construction industry about Ranger. Things Shem liked and didn't like about the secretive development company—hopefully supported by facts or innuendos he'd reveal. Score one for Mitch.

"Vulnerabilities?" Shem repeated. He shrugged and again took his seat. "Well, any outfit as big as Ranger sometimes gets involved with projects that don't pan out. Too much government regulation, that kind of thing."

"Do you know of specific ones that failed lately?" Cara asked.

Shem looked up, as if trying to find the answer written on one of the stained acoustical ceiling tiles. "Yeah," he said slowly. "There was a big housing development back east somewhere last year that tanked. Boston? Baltimore? I don't remember. But it was too close to the city, and activists got involved, everything from tree huggers to guys who insisted that half the homes be designated low income. That kind of thing. It could have made Ranger go a little nuts if they came up with another pet project and some contractor threatened to make enough noise to crater that one if they didn't get the work, right?"

"Maybe," Cara said. Her mind whirled. She'd done some research into Ranger but had missed this, despite how big it had been. "You said this was a Ranger project. Was it in the name of some subsidiary?"

"Yeah, I think so. Something with the name of the city in it, maybe."

Something similar to Eastern Mustang Property Acquisition or Texas Mustang Valley Sites, but local to that project? Cara would have to see.

"I don't suppose Ranger has hired you yet for a portion of the project, like getting a surveyor onto the site?" Mitch asked.

"Actually, it has," Shem said. "A small thing like that, to see how well we work together. We're checking out water rights."

"Are any other contractors being tested like that?" Cara kept her excitement inside.

"We weren't told, but I've heard rumors that a couple guys out of Dallas are getting Phase I environmental reports started. You know, the historic background of properties in that area for uses that could have caused contamination, like oil production, that kind of thing."

"You've been a big help," Mitch finally said, pushing off from his backrest along the wall. "If you think of anything else to help us help Ranger Corporation, please give me a call." He handed Shem a card.

Cara considered doing the same, but figured that the chances of Shem calling her for anything except to swear at her again were slim. She was surprised that he'd been as cooperative as he had. Or maybe he'd been relieved that he wasn't the subject of their investigation.

Not that Cara could absolve him from all suspicion.

They now had a good reason for O'Hallihan Construction's name to have been on a letter on Roger Rosales's desk. But the existence of these tenuous connections didn't mean there weren't stronger ones.

Shem O'Hallihan had known Nancy Wilks. But he was right. Lots of people in a small town like Mustang Valley had known her.

At the door, Mitch behind her, she turned. "Bye, Shem. Thanks for the help." She reached for the knob, then again turned back. "By the way, in case you did kill Nancy Wilks, or know who did, keep in mind how fast I was at digging up the facts about your drywall before."

Before either Shem or Mitch could react, she was out the door.

BACK IN CARA'S CAR, Mitch was proud of himself for not blowing up at her. Even so, when he not so gently pointed out her imprudence, the beautiful but brutally forthright reporter was having none of it.

"Of course I doubt O'Hallihan killed Nancy," she admitted to his frustrated question, glancing over at him at a stop sign. Her tone was as exasperated as his.

"Then why did you accuse him that way? You're not keeping something back from me, are you?"

"I don't do things like that," Cara snapped back as if accusing him, then cooled her tone a bit. "I thought my rationale was obvious."

"So pretend I'm a dense son of a bitch and enlighten me."

She shot him a grin. In the close quarters of her car, he breathed in her soft scent that reminded him of the fresh-washed sky after a rain or a flower-laden mountain. How could someone who smelled so lush yet innocent be so irritatingly reckless in what she said?

"I want to make sure everyone stays on his toes," she said. "As an officer of the law, you can't use poetic license or imagination to stir up suspects till one rises to the surface as the killer, but as a reporter, champion of First Amendment rights, I can." She frowned. "Speaking of poetic license, I can't even count how many metaphors I just mixed."

Mitch didn't want to laugh, but he did. In fact, he

wanted to reach across the seat and play with a couple of red curls that bobbed each time Cara swung her head from watching the road then back to him. The strands just seemed to beg for him to try to tame them.

Sure. Like he was going to tame Cara. Get her to keep her lovely lips closed instead of goading everyone in town to want to do her harm. That might nab them a murder suspect, and it might just push someone otherwise innocent to kill Cara.

Mitch felt grimness settle over him like a filthy old blanket. He wouldn't let that happen. He would make sure Cara stayed safe.

And he wouldn't give up trying to get her to tone down her provocation of everyone she met.

"Should I just drop you off at the Sheriff's Department?" Cara asked.

Not hardly. At least not right now. It was barely lunchtime, and she'd already received a threatening phone call that day and goaded a man who had previously loathed her to breathe fire at her. Shem O'Hallihan had sworn like a demon at Cara's last words to him, even though, outside the office, she probably hadn't heard. Mitch wasn't about to let her out of his sight.

"I'm hungry," he said, noticing they had reached downtown Mustang Valley. "Let's grab lunch." He pointed at Dot's Sandwich Shop, practically beside them.

"Okay," Cara agreed, and parked her car. Joining him on the sidewalk, she said, "You know, according to my article we're supposed to be sworn enemies. Our being seen together in town so much may not be a good idea."

An understatement, Mitch thought ruefully. And not just because of their manufactured feud. Ben Wilson had made it clear he didn't want Mitch hanging out with Cara. Hadn't Ben said something like, if Cara insisted on interviewing a member of the Sheriff's Department, she was to be sent up the ladder to him?

And Mitch was in uniform, as he too often was when he met with Cara. Everyone would assume he was on official business, on duty.

But like he'd told himself, he wasn't going to leave her alone when everyone she knew and probably some she didn't were pissed off with her. And one was a killer.

"We'll deal with it," he said. "We can always stage an argument for effect."

A minute later, after alerting the dispatcher he was on break, he pushed open the restaurant door with one arm extended so Cara could slip by him and enter. Except, she brushed his chest with her arm, bare beneath her short-sleeved blouse, as she walked through the open door, and the soft, quick touch nearly drove him nuts. He wondered, as he had so often before, what it would be like to touch more of her bare skin, other even more sensual places, when he was so awake after innocent contacts like this one.

Stay focused, he commanded himself. Entering after her, Mitch did his usual scan of his surroundings. Dot's, a popular local hangout, was busy, despite it being later than the traditional lunchtime. A Lee Ann Womack country song filled in the few spaces between the sounds of the conversing patrons. At least there was one high-backed booth available along the wall. He gently took Cara's elbow and steered her toward it.

Only after they sat down did he notice that his inspection of the place had been faulty. A couple of other deputies were seated at a booth way over in a corner. One was Hurley Zeller. And his stare at Mitch was one unpleasantly pleased sneer.

CARA HAD TO ADMIT to herself that lunch with Mitch was delightful.

Whether or not it was advisable for them to be seen together, there they were in public, so they agreed not to discuss the murder investigation. Despite how busy the place was, someone might overhear, and she didn't really want to stage a fight. Though Cara knew maybe half the patrons and didn't see a known suspect among them, people around here had big lists of friends, and even bigger mouths.

They kept their conversation light. Somehow it wended its way to a discussion of Shotgun Sally legends.

"Do you really think she was involved in half the escapades the stories told about her?" Mitch asked, then took a bite of his barbecue sandwich.

"Sure," Cara said after chewing a bite of her turkey croissant. "And most, even the ones that contradict each other, can be explained by her being a crusading reporter, out to expose all sorts of corruption in the Mustang County of her time."

There was a wistfulness in Mitch's grin that made Cara want to stroke his dark hair. Maybe give his large and altogether too sexy body a hug. "My mother told me a lot of stories when I was a kid," he said, his voice so low she had to strain to hear him in the noisy restaurant. "Most were outrageous, fables about coyotes outwitting foxes, and our Earth Mother teaching them both lessons. I don't know whether she took them from stories of her people or whether she made them up, but they always contained the lessons she wanted to teach me."

"Your mother's Native American, isn't she?"

"Yes." His face was suddenly expressionless. Wasn't he proud of his heritage? Cara knew that, even these days, there were too many prejudiced jerks who scorned people of American Indian ancestry. She'd even heard some of the bigoted gibes against his father for having a Native American wife years earlier. How had that affected Mitch? She was suddenly eager to know.

"Tell me about her," Cara urged.

Mitch blinked as if just recalling who he was with. When he smiled, it was rueful. "She always kept me guessing. She'd use her heritage to tell me those wonderful stories that made me proud of where she came from, but then, almost in the next breath, she'd say something scornful about people who were defeated and refused to live in the real world of their conquerors."

Compassion flooded through Cara at the thought of the confused little boy he must have been. "I'll bet that was hard for you," she said.

"Sometimes. But she said she'd always intended to live in a town, with different kinds of people around. And she and my dad were close, and he was always there for her, until…" His voice tapered off, and Cara knew he was thinking of his father's suicide. Before she could say something sympathetic, Mitch continued, "She came from hardy but mixed stock herself. Though she was all Native American, her background was a combination of Chickasaw and Chocktaw and maybe more. That gave her a lot of understanding of what it was like for me to be of mixed heritage, and she talked about it a lot, helped me to be proud of having the best characteristics of all my ancestors. Except…"

"Except?"

He shrugged again. His eyes rested over her shoulder for a moment. She turned and glanced in that direction. Some deputies were rising from a booth. One was that lout Hurley Zeller, who'd burst in on her interrogation after Nancy Wilks's murder. She knew that Zeller was no friend of Mitch's.

Mitch nodded coldly toward Zeller as he passed. He

must have made a gesture Mitch didn't like, for Mitch's eyes narrowed angrily, but he said friendly things to the others as they left.

Cara figured, with the stiff set to Mitch's shoulders, that their conversation was over. That he might just want to leave, possibly without saying anything else to her.

Instead, he said, "You're a good reporter, you know?" He didn't sound especially pleased about it, and the gold in his eyes glinted irritably. "You hardly have to say a word to get people to spill their guts to you."

"Thanks," she said.

"But this was just a discussion," he said coolly. "Off the record. You're not going to do any story on me, only on the investigation. And then only things that I agree you can print."

She blinked, reeling under his sudden attack on her and her integrity. And the unjustness of his insistence that she write only what he permitted.

She'd ignore it, of course. As much as she could get away with.

"I'll comply with the terms we agreed on before," she said, keeping her tone much more level than her angry glare at him.

She finished her sandwich in silence. Damn him! And now she missed their earlier camaraderie. She at least wanted him to finish his earlier sentence: "Except..." She realized how much she didn't know about Mitch Steele and where he'd come from, who he was now. It seemed very important for her to know.

Because, despite his commands, she would need information when she wrote the story in which she'd describe the Nancy Wilks murder investigation, and how it was solved, and how Deputy Mitchell Steele—with her help, of course—tied it to the other murders.

More realistically, she knew she was totally, foolishly

captivated by Mitch. She wanted to know what he was thinking. What made him tick.

As she reached for her purse, intending to pay the check, her cell phone rang. She dug only a few seconds before she found it. Oddly, the caller ID indicated the source of the call was the line in her own office at the *Gazette*.

"Hi, Cara," said the voice at the other end. "It's Della Santoro. I'm in your office. I've collected some stuff about Shotgun Sally to show you."

"Great. I'm on my way."

"Good." Cara was about to hang up when she heard Della's voice again. "I skipped lunch today, so is it okay if I have a piece of the candy that's on your desk?"

"Of course." Good thing she'd loaded up earlier on the malted milk balls in her glass jar.

Cara again tried to drop Mitch off at the Sheriff's Department, but apparently he'd decided to become Velcro to her—the prickly side that nettled her. She wished she understood him. One moment he was issuing her orders, impugning her honor as a journalist. The next he was sticking to her side as if he gave a damn about her.

More likely he was making sure she didn't unearth a clue in the investigation without sharing it with him. Never mind that he was the one guilty of that little sin.

But she was glad after all for his presence when she pulled into the *Gazette* parking lot—after edging around the ambulance waiting there.

"What's going on?" she demanded of one of the interns who stood outside the door, tears rolling down her pink cheeks.

"Someone collapsed," she cried. "In your office."

"Oh, my Lord! Della!" Cara pushed past the intern, feeling Mitch close behind her.

As she reached her office, she had to buck her way through the crowd at the doorway.

"What's wrong with Della?" she asked Beau, who stood right inside the door, his drooping shoulders making his suspenders slack.

"We don't know yet," he said.

That wasn't good enough. Cara drew closer, close enough to see that the EMTs had Della down on the floor.

"Stay back," one yelled at her.

"What the hell?" Mitch said. He flashed his badge— unnecessary since he was in uniform, Cara thought. He approached her desk.

As she watched, he used a manila file folder to move something right in the middle, a red box.

"Check her for poison!" he ordered the paramedics.

"What are you talking about?" Cara demanded.

He nodded toward the box. A candy box.

On its top was glued an open card that said, "To Cara, from Mitch."

"I didn't send this," Mitch said, his mouth in a grim line.

But Cara's knees went weak as she realized who probably had sent it. A killer.

For if the candy was poisoned, it had been meant for *her*.

Chapter Twelve

While the EMTs did their job, Mitch did his. First he called the matter in, requesting back up and a Forensics Division team. Then he commenced his investigation of this latest incident, all while keeping watch over Cara.

Her hazel eyes were wide and frightened as she leaned against her office wall, the taut fold of her slender arms suggesting how hard she worked to keep her emotions in check. He gauged her trembling by the shimmy of her long blue skirt, but she refused to leave the room while Della was being treated.

He wanted to take her into his arms, comfort her. But, as often happened lately, his wants conflicted with the actions he let himself take. For one thing, he didn't want to embarrass her in front of friends and co-workers. For another, he had work to do. Besides, the best comfort he could give would be to find the truth.

Who had wanted to harm Cara? Those candies had been meant for her. And the card had said they were from *him*, damn it. Whoever had done it, Mitch wanted to shove those cursed chocolates down the SOB's throat.

Outside the door, Mitch asked Beau Jennings if he knew where the candy came from. His answer was negative. No surprise.

No one else at the *Gazette* remembered any unusual

deliveries, either. There were always plenty of things being brought to the newspaper office: mail, advertising art,
paper, printing supplies. Everyone was supposed to check
in at the desk by the front door, but a messenger with a
potentially deadly package could easily have slipped by.

Mitch was in the brightly lighted hall outside Cara's
office talking to a proofreader when a paramedic hurried
backward through the door, guiding a gurney carrying
Della Santoro and holding a plastic bag hooked up to an
IV tube. Della, though still alive, was nearly as pale as
the bleached sheet covering her, and her eyes were closed.

Mitch had questions for her. He hoped he'd get the
opportunity to ask, but it wouldn't be now.

Cara followed the second paramedic out the door.
"Where are you taking her?" she asked.

The EMT named the nearest full-facility hospital, in a
larger town close to Ft. Worth. Good. That meant Della
was stable enough for the ride that would take half an
hour even at top speed, siren shrieking. Mitch had seen
accident victims who were taken to the town's primary
emergency clinic die before they could be transported
elsewhere. Maybe they'd have died at any facility. But it
didn't speak well of the skills of Doc Swenson, whose
clinic it was—and the doc was also the local coroner.

"Can we follow?" Cara asked.

By then, the forensics techs who'd come to the scene
of Nancy Wilks's murder had arrived. They took charge
of the candy and checked Cara's office for fingerprints
and other evidence. Deputy Stephanie Greglets had come.
So had Deputy Hurley Zeller.

It was getting late. Mitch should be off duty. But if he
left now with Cara, he'd never hear the end of it. Zeller
would report to Ben Wilson that Mitch disobeyed the
sheriff's direct orders by not handing Cara Hamilton off
to him to deal with.

Yet Cara, her chin high but her sweet, slender body shaking, couldn't stay here.

To accomplish his own key goal, Mitch had to hang on to his job as Mustang County Deputy Sheriff. But if he blew it, so be it.

"Yeah," he said to Cara. "Let's go."

"DELLA, THIS IS Deputy Mitch Steele," Cara said to the slight woman with messy dark hair and hazy eyes who was propped up in the mechanical bed. "He has some questions for you."

Her voice was gentle, but at least it was stronger than any other time since she got the call about Della. Mitch was glad. Maybe she was snapping out of her earlier shock. Sure, he found her usual intrusiveness and insistence exasperating. But that was the Cara he'd come to know. And appreciate. And care about.

Where the heck had that come from? He shelved it in his mind to chew over later—and spit out, before it caused him further trouble.

He approached the bed, sliding slightly on the slickness of the polished hospital floor despite the rubber soles of his work shoes. "Hi, Della. I'd like you to help me find out who did this to you by answering some questions."

"I'll try." Her voice was weak, and Mitch leaned over. He smelled the too-clean scents of disinfectant and bleach intermingled with a more sour smell, like vomit. Well, they had pumped the poor woman's stomach, after all.

The brief interrogation turned out what Mitch anticipated: nada. Zilch. The candy was on Cara's desk when Della came in. She'd been sure to ask Cara's permission before taking any.

"I'm so sorry, Della," Cara interjected. "I didn't even know about that candy. I assumed you were talking about my regular supply of malted milk balls."

"You're not to blame, Cara," Della said.

But by Cara's sorrowful expression, Mitch could tell she was riddled with guilt. He'd talk to her about it, but that was something he understood well—a person's assuming he had control over everything in his life, so if something went wrong, it had to be his fault.

Of course, sometimes it *was* his fault. But not this time. Nor Cara's.

He gently insisted that Della go on with her story.

She'd eaten the candy. Then there'd been pain and she'd passed out. "That's all I know, Deputy." She sounded apologetic.

"You've been helpful, Ms. Santoro. And to Cara's friends, I'm just Mitch."

"I didn't think police gave interviews about ongoing cases, Mitch." Della's brown eyes focused on him for the first time. "Cara told me you're the deputy in charge of the investigation of poor Nancy's death. She's looking into it, too. And I gathered from the *Gazette* article that you disagreed about how the press was handling things."

Della was an attractive woman, or she would be when her dark brown hair was combed, her mascara not blotched and her complexion less pale. Her bone structure was fine, though her chin was a little too flat. And no one looked good in those ugly, thin hospital gowns.

Mitch knew she was a professor. Cara had told him that. But he wished the woman would keep her lectures to herself.

Before Mitch responded, Cara broke in. More effervescent now, she paced the short length of Della's hospital room. "I'm not interviewing him about Nancy's murder," she said, though she stumbled over the last words. As professional as she was, she apparently couldn't detach herself emotionally from her friend's death. It suited her. But Mitch, of all people, recognized how much harder it made her job. "We've worked it out for now," Cara continued. "I won't quote him unless he approves, which he won't, I'm sure, till something breaks. Meantime, we're conducting independent investigations and sharing what we learn."

Mitch tuned out most of the rest of the conversation, though he listened for any speculations about who had left the candy for Cara. The chocolates would be sent to the lab in Dallas for testing, then they would see.

"I had more background for you on Shotgun Sally," Della was saying. "You wanted to know where she lived, her family's property? I researched it and came up with something, though it's not substantiated yet. The site was on the east side of town. I laid some printouts on your desk."

"Hopefully, they'll still be there," Cara said. "Don't worry about it now. Just concentrate on feeling better, okay?"

"Sure." Della sank back into her pillows, her eyes closed.

"I'll call tomorrow," Cara said. "For now, get some sleep."

IT WAS MIDNIGHT before Cara returned to her apartment complex. Surprisingly, she slept part of the ride back. When she'd opened her eyes a few minutes ago, she'd seen the familiar streetlights of Mustang Valley.

Mitch had driven the whole way to the hospital and back. Sometime, while she'd stayed with Della, he'd changed into civilian clothes—jeans and a T-shirt.

He parked in an empty space in her complex's lot.

"Thanks." Cara rolled her head along the headrest and found the energy to smile at him. "For everything." She meant it. His presence had made bearable all the miserable things that had happened that day—the menacing call, the ugly interview with Shem O'Hallihan, the attempt on her life that had harmed poor Della instead.

"You're welcome." He opened his door and got out. Nice man. He was probably going to open the door for her, though it wasn't necessary.

In a moment he helped her out of the car. She looked up into his face under the sodium lights near her building. That last kiss they'd shared—it seemed a long time ago— still sang show tunes in her mind. She wanted him to kiss her again. Could he see that in her eyes?

Oh, yes. In a moment his arms were around her and his lips on hers. Lord, the man could kiss. His hard body rocked against her as he tasted her, using his tongue as a thrusting hint of what he really wanted.

What she really wanted, too. This irritating, officious, sexy deputy had really gotten under her skin.

Heat curled like smoke all through her, particularly where need pulsed inside her.

She smiled against his mouth as she gently pulled away, knowing it was one of the hardest things she'd ever done.

Speaking of hard… Maybe her mouth had moved away, but her hips hadn't. She closed her eyes, gathering strength. And then she pulled back. "Good night, Mitch," she whispered.

"We'll say good night in a little while," he said.

Her eyes popped back open, and she narrowed them when she saw mocking humor in a gaze that otherwise mirrored the desire inside her. "What do you mean?" she demanded. "Just because I let you kiss me good night isn't an invitation for anything else."

"Let me? I'd say you were more than a willing participant." He moved closer again and took her into his arms.

Cara didn't resist when he kissed her once more. Why should she? She enjoyed it. *Really* enjoyed it. Ached for more—and not just kisses. But that was an urge she wouldn't give in to.

She wasn't in a hurry to end this kiss. But eventually she murmured once more, against his lips, "Good night, Mitch."

"I'm coming inside, Cara," he said, his words reverberating from the contact with his mouth all the way to her toes.

Temptation? Sure. But she said, "Like hell you are."

"If you think I'm going to leave you alone tonight after all that happened today, you've got a lot to learn."

Her body stiffened, and she tried to step back. "I don't need—"

"Yeah, you do. And if you don't want me to touch you, I won't. Though if you can be convinced—"

"In your dreams, Steele." Cara tried hard to still her heavy breathing as she glared at him.

"Most definitely," he agreed.

THE HELL WITH THIS TORTURE, Cara thought a while later. She lay sleepless in her bed. Her place had only one bedroom, so Mitch was on the couch in her living room. Since he'd been so insistent on staying, she had finally agreed, though she hadn't offered him her bed.

Suffer! she had thought. He was too substantial a man to feel comfortable on her sofa.

But she was the one who was suffering. For that last kiss kept replaying in her mind. And the fire inside her refused to be snuffed out, even after a lukewarm shower. She hadn't resorted to a cold one, but that might be next.

Better yet, she'd handle the fire a different way.

Since it was summer, she slept in a short silky nightgown that left her arms and legs bare. It was light blue—not the most seductive color, but so what? She got out of bed and headed for the door.

She pulled it open and listened for a moment. The only illumination was the apartment complex's light, barely shining between slats of the vertical blinds on her living room window. If Mitch snored, she didn't hear it. She padded in her bare feet, cool against the hardwood floor, toward the sofa.

"Mitch?" she whispered, unsure whether she wanted to wake him if he was asleep.

"What's wrong?" he demanded at once. His deep voice wasn't coarsened by sleepiness.

"What do you think?" She moved to the front of the couch. "I've only been threatened by at least two people in the past few days, and one or more actually tried to kill me."

"I know." There was a grimness in his tone and utter sexiness to his appearance in the shadows of her apartment. He sat on the sheets she'd proffered as her only concession to making him comfortable. He'd stripped off his clothes, except for white boxers. They seemed to glow in the faint light, calling attention to that part of his body—quite an exclamation, considering the appeal of the breadth of his chest, sprinkled with hair as black as the mussed mop on his head. "That's why I'm here," he continued. "I promise, I'll keep you safe. You can relax."

"No, I can't. That's not the only reason I couldn't sleep." She sat down close to him. "Care to guess why?" She let one hand range over the tight muscles of that incredible chest.

Mitch groaned. "Cara, you don't want to do that."

"As a matter of fact, I do."

Maybe she'd come in as the aggressor, but he jumped immediately into her game. Prey became hunter as he wrapped his arms about her, pulling her close. He was warm, with a faint sheen of moisture on his skin. He smelled of the familiar soap she had in her shower, but the scent blended with his own masculine aura of tartness and temptation.

"This isn't right, Cara," he whispered, but before she could contradict him, he lowered his mouth to hers once more.

She'd thought his earlier kisses had been sexy, but they were chaste compared with what he did to her now. His tongue was an erotic taunt, thrusting and parrying and driving her wild with desire.

Or maybe that was because he was touching her now, no holds barred. His fingertips plunged below the neckline of her gown, finding her breasts, teasing one nipple, then the other, till she moaned from the sensation. Moist heat oozed from her, down below. She wanted more.

She wanted Mitch.

She showed him so, the best way she knew how. She moved her hands from the taut planes of his back, down, down over his tight butt and around, over his shorts, till she found what she wanted—what she'd already felt pressing against her. His length was thick and rigid and showed he wasn't kidding when he licked her earlobe and whispered huskily, "I want you. Now."

Now, that turned up the thermostat of her already burning desire. Still, she wouldn't give in that easily to temptation. To allow him to think *he* was in charge.

"Nope," she said aloud, ignoring how fast and hard her breathing was. Although she didn't stop stroking his erection, she otherwise pulled back. Just a little.

"No?" He sounded shocked back to reality. With a groan, he tried to pull away. But she didn't let him. She held on with gentle strength. "Cara, if you don't let me stop now, I won't be able to."

"Really?" she murmured. "You mean, if in three minutes I stop, you'll force me to go on?"

"Don't tease," he warned. And then she gasped as she

felt the roughness of his hand grasp her below, where her ache for him was already intense. He stroked her, teasing her with two fingers where she wanted another part of him to be. Fast.

"No," she said.

"No?" His voice was ragged, and his stroking stopped.

She grabbed his hand and moved it until he continued. "No, I won't tease," she said in explanation. And then she didn't say anything for a very long time, as he heated her to her boiling point and beyond, stopping only once, to grab protection from a pocket of his pants on the floor.

When he entered her, she cried out. And very soon, she reached the fulfillment she'd yearned for, even as she heard Mitch's gasp and felt his satisfaction, too.

MITCH WAS NOTHING if not creative. And his stamina? Incredible. They made love at least three more times that night. Cara lost count. She lost track of time and place, too. When she awakened the next morning she discovered they'd somehow made it into her bed.

Which was a good thing, as she was right beside the phone on her nightstand when it rang. This early in the morning, she knew who it had to be. No one else called at this hour.

"Hi, Mom," she muttered into the receiver, turning slightly to meet Mitch's grin as he awakened, too.

"I've heard some terrible things about yesterday, Cara." Cara could picture her mother standing by the wall phone in her kitchen, clutching it, her face filled with worry.

"Probably all an exaggeration." Cara loved living in Mustang Valley, where she'd grown up. But there were times she wished she lived in Dallas or Ft. Worth or any fair-size town where rumors didn't circulate like dust in a windstorm.

"Can you come over for breakfast? I want to make sure you're all right."

Cara glanced at Mitch. A sheet covered him from the hips down—darn it. But the view of his muscular upper body, his sleepy, smiling eyes, was highly enticing, too. Still, she didn't have much choice. "Sure, Mom." As Mitch's hand began stroking her side, then rose to cup one breast, she forbore from sighing or moaning into the phone. Keeping her voice level, she said, "I've got…something I need to take care of here first, but I'll be there as soon as I can."

MITCH WAS LATE arriving at the department that morning.

He'd showered at Cara's, which had turned into yet another irresistible interlude that kept the water running for half an hour. Maybe longer.

He'd followed her to her folks' place, after extracting a promise that from there she'd go straight to the paper. Call him if anyone looked suspicious on the way. And stay there till they talked again. Better yet, till he came for her.

Then he'd had to stop at home, put on a fresh uniform, grab a cup of coffee and try to get his head on straight.

What had he done?

He'd let himself be seduced by that sexy little fireball Cara Hamilton. *Let* himself? Hell, he'd welcomed it. Jumped in with both feet and enjoyed every hot and hungry second of it.

They'd known each other days, not weeks. She was a victim and a witness in matters he was investigating. She was a reporter bucking against his need for confidentiality. What he had done with her was highly unprofessional.

And he'd do it all over again, given the chance. In fact, Cara and he had already discussed getting together that night and—

"Hey, Steele. You telling time by the sun these days?" Of course it would be Hurley Zeller who'd spot him coming in behind schedule. "There's such a thing in our world as the clock, but that's only in civilization. Something you know nothing about."

"Cram it, Zeller," Mitch growled. He knew better than to react, but he was reaching the end of his patience with Zeller and the sheriff's tolerance of him.

Hell, he had little tolerance for Sheriff Ben Wilson, too. Suspicions notwithstanding, was he deluding himself into thinking he'd eventually find evidence to clear his father? Even his friend Assistant Attorney General Tim Bender seemed merely to be humoring him now.

Maybe he would just quit, once and for all. Get a job someplace where fellow officers really *were* civilized, instead of ignorant apes like Hurley Zeller.

Ignoring Zeller's ugly grin, he edged past the others in the deputy admin room and slipped into the chair behind his desk.

Who was he kidding? There was no way he was leaving Mustang County till the Nancy Wilks matter—this case—was solved. And certainly not while Cara remained in danger.

And who knew? Maybe by the time he got that all wrapped up, he really would find the smoking gun to unearth the truth about his father once and for all.

Yeah, right. After two long years, some piece of evidence would drop from the heavens into his lap. Maybe Zeller was right about him and his Native American background. Of course these days, he figured that damned few Indians accepted that their Mother Earth or any other deity would drape miracles about them just for the asking.

Though maybe his mother did. He would have to track her down and visit her one day. Maybe then he would find peace with his ancestry. With her.

There was a large, sealed envelope on his desk, labeled as originating from the lab. He opened it. It was the report on the crime-scene analysis at Nancy Wilks's place. Nothing noteworthy other than that the poor vic's body had been found. No murder weapon. No fingerprints of potential suspects. All those identified had been accounted for as Nancy's, Cara's, friends with no motive or opportunity to murder and a maintenance guy hired by her landlord, the ill-tempered John Ayres.

There'd been no indication of a break-in. Nothing missing that anyone could tell. Nothing broken or trashed to indicate a crime of passion. Nothing identified as important enough that Nancy had called Cara to come over to see it in the middle of the night.

Nothing.

Not good enough.

Who were his main suspects? Well, only one person left at Lambert & Church could have done it: Donald Church. But what motive would he have had?

It all hinged on what Nancy wanted to show Cara. Something to do with a client? Linked to the two prior murders, Ranger Corporation was obvious. Too obvious? Still, he wouldn't rule out Roger Rosales. But he wouldn't ignore the possibility it was Shem O'Hallihan, either. The contractor was a nasty SOB who'd threatened Cara. And he had ties to Ranger Corporation.

It was long past time to pull this all together.

Mitch signed out on official department business and made sure the dispatcher knew he had his cell phone on in case anyone needed to contact him. Then he stalked out of the station.

Something at Nancy Wilks's place would give a clue about who killed her and why. And Mitch was going to find it.

IT WAS CLEAR whose genes ruled Cara's family. She had known that from when she was a kid, particularly when her brother, and then her sister, were born with fuzzy red hair. Hair that grew curly like hers as they got older. Like hers and their dad's, Charley Hamilton.

Great hair. Unique hair. Cara loved it.

Their mom, Ada, had ordinary hair that was light brown way back when, but got progressively more blond as she grew older and more experimental. Now, it was a soft-platinum cap framing a face that was quite youthful for a woman nearly fifty.

Except when she frowned, as she did now, over the breakfast table at Cara. They sat in the roomy kitchen in the Mustang Valley house where Cara grew up, a sprawling ranch-style with bedrooms for each of them. Now just Cara's folks lived there, and she was the only one of her siblings who remained in town. Her brother, Allen, was an accountant in Austin, and her sister Leona was studying for her master's degree in Dallas.

"Is it true that poor Della Santoro got sick right in your office?" her mother asked.

"Unfortunately, yes." Cara prayed the rumor mill hadn't gotten wind of the suspected truth. But that prayer was short-lived.

"And it was from eating candy that someone sent to you? *Poisoned* candy?"

"People exaggerate, Mom. The stuff's been sent to a lab, but there's no reason to think—"

"Of course there's reason to think it, or no one would suggest it."

Cara met her dad's eyes, pleading silently with him. But though he was usually able to get Cara's mother to see reason, he looked as troubled as she did. "That truck nearly ran you over a few days ago, too," he pointed out grimly. At least they didn't know about the attack in the park. "Cara, whatever story you're working on, it's not worth it. Back off, will you?"

"I'll be careful, I promise." That sidestepped the issue, and her dad recognized it. He didn't look happy. "How's business?" Cara asked, hoping to change the subject. Her father was the successful owner of his own small furnace-and-air-conditioning company. Cara had helped with publicity from time to time, getting someone from the *Gazette* to interview her dad when something warranted an article.

"Fine, honey." Her dad launched into a tale of how he'd fixed the air-conditioning at a local retirement home before the senior inhabitants fried in this heat, and hadn't charged a cent. Cara made a mental note to make sure his altruism made the paper.

The rumor mill had apparently not gotten wind of her relationship with Deputy Mitch "Sexy" Steele. Thank heavens. She wasn't sure how she'd deal with that. It was a business relationship, founded on a common need to solve poor Nancy's murder. But as of last night it was a lot more. Though, where something as passionate as what they'd shared would go… Who knew? She had no idea where she wanted it to go, except to the nearest bed. Again. But once the murder was solved, then what? Mitch had made no promises. And neither had she.

Cara didn't want to think about that. She'd take things day by day. No, night by extraordinarily passionate night…

"Earth to Cara," her mother said. "More pancakes, honey?"

"No, thanks. They're great, though." Their luscious blueberry scent still filled the kitchen. "I have to run."

She gave them both a kiss, promised again to be careful and to call soon. And then walked outside.

She loved the comfortable, aging residential area where her folks resided. She still knew most of the neighbors.

But right now she was glad she didn't see any in their sun-scorched, browning yards. For, in the interests of finally solving the Nancy Wilks murder and hopefully finding its tie to the other local killings, Cara had come up with an idea worthy of Shotgun Sally. She was going undercover, and for that she needed a disguise.

She headed for the garage, where her father kept a lot of stuff related to his business, including uniforms.

Soon Cara would transform herself into a repair person for Mustang Valley Heating and Cooling.

Chapter Thirteen

Mitch parked his official vehicle at the curb on Caddo Street and approached the converted Victorian house where Nancy Wilks had lived.

He returned the cheerfully inquisitive greeting of Nancy's upstairs neighbor Bea Carrow, but was glad the building's bad-tempered owner John Ayres wasn't around. He unlocked the door with a key from the file at the department and ducked beneath the yellow crime scene tape.

The place smelled musty. He'd get the forensics technicians to make one more sweep after he'd gone over the scene himself, then release it to Ayres.

He strode straight through the pastel-colored entry and down the short hall toward the bedroom where Nancy had been found. There'd been no sign of forced entry, so she'd either shown her assailant into the room or run there from somewhere else in the house. That meant whatever she'd wanted to show Cara could have been anywhere... assuming it hadn't been taken by her murderer—a big assumption. But Mitch intended to search the place minutely, just in case.

Mitch was a professional. He knew how to don detachment the way he did his uniform and Stetson, and the vinyl gloves he pulled on to avoid adding fingerprints in case a further sweep was needed.

But being in the bedroom that had once belonged to a living, breathing woman, a friend of Cara's—it unexpectedly bothered him. Perhaps his background spoke to him here. Both backgrounds. His mother's people believed in spirits, both human and animal. Was Nancy's spirit still here, guiding him?

Or was it his father's spirit—or his training as a peace officer—that led Mitch in his search?

He saw nothing out of the ordinary in Nancy's bedroom. It looked like the refuge of a lonely woman, with books of all types on wooden shelves—biographies, romances, historical epics. The television was large and sat on a stand facing the bed. All were indications of a woman who slept alone.

In the bathroom Mitch scanned the sparsely filled medicine cabinet, the area beneath the sink with its cleaning supplies and female products. Nothing caught his attention. Still, he lifted each item, examining it, examining behind it. And then he headed for the living room.

It contained the usual furniture, plus more bookshelves. Mitch looked just as carefully through them all, again pulling them out to make sure nothing was behind them.

One book caught his attention. It appeared old, with a cracked brown leather binding. On the front was printed, *The Legend of Shotgun Sally.*

Hey, Mitch thought, *Cara would be interested in seeing this.*

Cara would be interested....

Hell, was this what Nancy had for her? Carefully, he pulled it out and thumbed through it.

That was when he noticed the anachronistic twist: some pages were tabbed with yellow sticky notes. Annotated sticky notes. *Whose* notations?

Whoever had made them, Mitch was all but certain this was what Nancy had called Cara about.

Thanks to spirit guides or detective skills or a combination, he'd found it.

And somehow it would lead to Nancy's killer.

SHE SHOULD HAVE BORROWED one of her dad's trucks, Cara thought as she strode down an alley off Main Street, a beat-up old toolbox in one hand. Of course, then he'd know she had the uniform. And he'd suspect what she was up to.

Her mother would have heart failure if she knew.

No, better this way.

She'd driven in a complex pattern, doubling back on herself to make sure no one tailed her. She also kept her eyes peeled for a blue pickup. When convinced no one was following, she dressed hurriedly at an empty rest room in a park outside town. That way, no one would notice that a woman with curly red hair wearing a long skirt went in, and a guy in a heating company uniform and cap came out—both holding the same filled gym bag. She was equally cautious driving back to town and parking in a church's auxiliary lot that was deserted on a weekday.

She'd promised Mitch she'd go straight to work at her office after breakfast at her parents'. She *had* gone straight to work—just not at her office.

He'd be steaming. But as much as the earth moved beneath her each time they'd made love, it hadn't moved so much that she'd suddenly become an obedient little mouse. She had a job to do, as he did. And even he would appreciate it if she found something useful for his case.

I have my own lawman lover, Sally, she thought delightedly. And just as Sally and her man Zachary Gale had done, Cara and Mitch were working together to solve a murder.

A newspaper woman and a deputy, sharing information and more while the world was led to believe they hated each other's guts.

I think I'm in love, Sally, Cara thought. What would Shotgun Sally say to that?

Cara could almost hear her say, "Nothin's sweeter, gal, than havin' a man who can do more than shoot good waitin' for you at home."

Wiping the grin off her face, Cara headed for the lovely old building that housed Ranger Corporation and other prestigious businesses. It wasn't the busiest block in town, and at midmorning she was the only person on this side of the street.

At the aging granite building's outer door, she walked in, head down as she checked her watch for the time.

She'd already called and asked for Roger Rosales. The receptionist, Erma, had said he was out at a meeting, and Cara had extracted from her that he wasn't due back until eleven o'clock—could he return her call then?

She'd thanked Erma and said she'd call back herself. Instead this workman was appearing in Roger's absence.

At the reception desk, Cara prayed that Erma, whom she'd met when she'd visited before in her own clothing, didn't recognize her. Her voice low and gruff, she said, "I'm with Hamilton Heat and Air. The building manager wants the air-conditioning checked in Mr. Rosales's office. He must have complained."

Fortunately Erma, a spreadsheet extended in front of her, barely looked up. "He didn't tell me," she grumbled. She nodded toward the nearest closed door. "Go ahead."

Cara obediently went into Roger's office, glad her hands were too full to pat herself on the back. That would be premature, anyway.

This time she wouldn't have to read the files upside down.

Had Shem O'Hallihan been angry enough about her questioning him that he'd had someone attack her, then try to poison her? Had it been Roger Rosales himself? Cara was determined not to be scared off, especially for Della's sake. She was going to find out who wanted to stop her from researching her article. That way she'd also learn who'd harmed her friend.

She couldn't count on having the full hour till eleven o'clock, so she hurried, every once in a while clumping and thumping in a way that she hoped sounded as if a workman was testing the cooling system.

There was nothing useful she hadn't already seen on top of Roger's rich mahogany desk. There were no file cabinets in this executive office, either. She tested the desk drawers. Fortunately, they weren't locked.

The deep one on the right side contained files. She rifled through them until she found one that looked promising. Yes! It contained a chart of Ranger Corporation and its subsidiaries. Among them were the ones she'd hoped to confirm as being connected to Ranger: Eastern Mustang Property Acquisition and Texas Mustang Valley Sites, the companies that had gobbled up some of the property around Bart Rawlins's ranch outside town.

Then, Ranger *was* making inroads into acquiring land. Why? What was its development going to be?

Was it important enough to trigger three murders?

No business deal could be that important.

Cara glanced around. Unfortunately, there was no photocopier. She'd have to steal the paperwork.

As she folded the page to stick into her toolbox, another subsidiary's name caught her attention: Juniper Holdings. Where had she heard that before?

She quickly closed her toolbox and went out the door.

At the reception area, she mumbled to Erma something about everything looking fine, then headed outside.

As she hurried toward her car, she glanced at her watch. She'd been quick. Fifteen minutes to spare.

How long, though, would it take Roger to notice that the Ranger Corporation family tree was missing?

She got into her car and started the engine. What she'd done wasn't exactly legal. Should she tell Mitch, anyway? Probably, since it could be evidence to show the extent of Ranger Corporation's dealings in Mustang County. And Ranger's name kept cropping up in relation to the first two murders.

Besides, it would give her a good excuse to see Mitch. She couldn't wait to be with him again after last night, and—

Mitch! Oh, heavens. Cara suddenly recalled where she had heard the name Juniper Holdings before. It was the company from which Sheriff Martin Steele had been accused of accepting bribes two years earlier. Supposedly, Juniper had been engaged in a lucrative illegal scheme involving theft of water rights, and to get the sheriff to look the other way, it had paid him a lot of money.

Martin Steele had denied it. Juniper had reportedly cut a deal with the state's attorney general to give evidence against the sheriff. And Martin had killed himself.

And now Cara had evidence that Ranger Corporation had been involved with that, too. Could Mitch take this information and learn the truth—a truth that would exonerate his father?

Cara sped out of town toward where she'd changed clothes before. She was going to resume her identity as Cara Hamilton, ace reporter. And then she'd go see Mitch.

IN THE CLUTTERED FILE ROOM next to the deputy admin room at the Sheriff's Department, Mitch carefully photocopied every page of the book on Shotgun Sally—including the handwritten notes. He needed to send the book to the lab for further handling, but not before he had a copy.

It was tedious work, since the book was old and brittle. He handled it gingerly, touching only outer edges to preserve fingerprints. He carefully removed the notes to make some copies.

He'd started this task nearly as soon as he'd returned to the department, ignoring the stack of messages on his desk. Ignoring Hurley Zeller's particularly viperous grin as he'd told Mitch the sheriff was looking for him.

Deputy Stephanie Greglets came in. "Hi, Mitch. What are you doing?" She eyed the copy machine and the book in his hand.

"Just copying some possible evidence."

She drew closer. "I can help you with that." She glanced down at the book.

"No, thanks." Mitch pulled the copier's cover down low enough that Stephanie wouldn't be able to see the book's cover. He wasn't certain why. Stephanie had offered her assistance more than once on this case.

Maybe that, in itself, made him mistrustful, though he couldn't say what he was suspicious of.

"Steele, what the hell are you doing in this room?"

Damn. Mitch turned at the sound of Ben Wilson's voice. The sheriff stood in the doorway, his narrowed eyes and compressed lips making it clear he had something on his mind.

Stephanie stepped back, leaving them both at the machine.

"I found something at the Wilks murder scene," Mitch replied to Ben's question. "I'm making copies before sending it to the lab for analysis."

"What is it?" As Ben reached out for the old book, Mitch stopped him with a gloved hand.

"We need to check for prints," he reminded his boss.

"Yeah. So what's its significance?"

Aware that Stephanie was listening, too, Mitch explained his theory that the book was what Nancy Wilks had called Cara about. "I don't understand the notes, though," he admitted. "We need to find out if they were Nancy's or someone else's. They seem to tie the old legends in the book to Ranger Corporation, but I don't follow the significance. Like this one—'Consider this for Ranger's best yet.'"

"Best what?" Stephanie asked.

"Damned if I know," Mitch said.

"Look, Steele," Ben said, his eyes no longer on the book. "I hear you've been spending time with that reporter Hamilton again instead of sending her to me, like I told you."

Mitch refused to allow himself to react, though he silently cursed Hurley Zeller for his big mouth and even bigger need to hurt Mitch. So Zeller would increase his chances of becoming sheriff if Ben became mayor? Not if Mitch could prevent it.

"Someone tried to poison Cara yesterday," he said mildly, "and it looks like it has something to do with my case. I'm not about to let a civilian get hurt if I can prevent it."

"So you protect her by shacking up with her?" Sarcasm dripped from Ben's voice.

Mitch felt his body go rigid. Stephanie rolled her eyes and left the room. Only Ben and he remained.

"Who told you that?" Mitch asked. Had he been seen at Cara's? Well, so what? He'd gone there to protect her. As far as anyone else knew, he could just as well have spent the night on the couch as he'd planned.

"Just be careful, Steele," Ben continued. "The woman

wants something from you—a story. And there's more than one way for a man to be bribed.''

"What the hell are you implying, Ben?" But Mitch knew. He was suggesting that more than one Steele was susceptible to taking kickbacks. And this from a man Mitch was all but certain knew a lot more about what had happened to his father. And was the most likely of anyone to have set him up, then made his murder appear a suicide.

If only Mitch could prove it.

"I'm not implying anything, Mitch." The sheriff's voice was softer now, though no less noxious. "I'm just saying you could compromise your case, and your career, too, if you're not careful."

"I'm being careful. Don't worry about it."

"So careful that you're not going to give her that." Ben made it a statement as he nodded toward the book, and Mitch figured he'd been given a warning.

Why did it seem so important to Ben that Mitch not share this bit of information with Cara? Not that he was certain he would, anyway. He had to weigh the pros and cons.

He leaned toward sharing this with Cara, though off the record for now. Nancy had probably intended to show the book to Cara. Cara was a fan of Shotgun Sally and might understand the significance of the notes. She could help with the case.

But he wouldn't lose sight of the fact that the book was evidence in a murder investigation. It should not be made public in the media, especially if it somehow pointed to, and could be used to convict, a suspect. Cara would have to honor his insistence that she not reveal its existence.

So far, she'd given him no major reason not to trust her.

Trust her? Heck, he was falling ass over beer bottle in love with her, if last night was any indication.

Not that he would act on it, other than to share pleasure with her. His life had no room for complications like a relationship. And right now he had to deal with his boss. Although Mitch knew Cara wasn't using her luscious, fiery little body to bribe him, he wasn't about to try to explain that to Ben.

"You know how much I wanted to be the lead on a big case like this, Ben," Mitch said. "I appreciate your trusting me to handle it." Mitch hated bootlicking, especially this man's. But he'd put up with a lot before now to dig out the truth. He would continue for as long as it took. No matter how much it galled him. "I'll do what I need to, to get the answers." In both matters. *All* matters.

"So you'll send your pretty little reporter to me to handle?"

Like hell he would. "If she needs handling."

"And you'll keep knowledge of that damned book from her?"

"Of course."

Mitch heard a sound from the doorway behind them. He turned.

Cara stood there, ashen. Her hazel eyes were so huge they'd nearly turned black, and she looked ready to spit fire. "What more, exactly, do you intend to hide from me, Mitch?"

More? What was she talking about? And he couldn't explain now. He shot her a pleading look that he immediately turned stony before the sheriff caught it. "How long have you been standing there?" he demanded. "And why are you there?"

"Because, unlike someone else I know, I live up to my promises. I had something to show you. Something important. But you can forget about it."

Ben responded first. "If it has something to do with a criminal case under investigation by this department, you'll hand it over, Ms. Hamilton, or I'll throw you in jail. Understand?''

"You ever hear of First Amendment rights, Sheriff? Or reporters going to jail rather than reveal sources they have to protect? Think of the bad publicity you'll get. And this at a time when rumors are flying that you want to run for mayor. *Did* you want that?'' She stalked into the room and looked up into the obviously furious Ben's face.

"Don't threaten me, young lady, or I'll take you up on—''

"Take it easy, both of you,'' Mitch interceded. He had to break this up.

He had to talk to Cara. Alone.

But she was jumping to conclusions based on eavesdropping on a conversation she had no business hearing.

"Now, Ms. Hamilton,'' he said, taking a step toward her to put Ben behind him. He kept his tone cool, as if she were any citizen he needed to handle professionally and not the woman he'd handled so passionately the night before. "You heard right. I've found something that might be an important piece of evidence in this case. I need to review it further before determining if it's something the media can report on.''

"Of course it can't—'' exploded Ben behind him.

But Mitch didn't stop. "That has nothing to do with whether you're obstructing justice by not turning over something else pertinent to the case. Are you?''

"If you think you'll take the fruit of my research without giving me anything in return, you can forget it, Mitchell Steele. And to hand it to another reporter—I saw the message on your desk that Beau's famous nephew, Jerry Jennings, called. Well, go ahead and cuddle up to him next time, Deputy.''

She pivoted and headed out the door. But before she got far, she turned back. "Oh, and by the way, Deputy

Steele, I just might have learned something from my sources that would clear your dad from those bribery charges a couple of years ago. Too bad we aren't sharing information, isn't it?''

And before Mitch could say anything more, Cara was gone.

Chapter Fourteen

Cara couldn't believe it.

Tears of fury flooded her eyes as she tried to start her car. She brushed them away.

Mitch Steele was no better than that damned Jerry Jennings. Worse, he was even conspiring with Jerry to rob her, once again, of the best story in her life.

She probably shouldn't have blurted anything out about clearing Mitch's father. After all, even if Juniper Holdings was affiliated with Ranger Corporation, that didn't mean it hadn't bribed Martin Steele, as claimed.

But the ties with Ranger…

She drove to her office. Of course, when she least wanted to talk to him, Beau was lying in wait.

"How'd you get Sheriff Wilson riled this time, Cara?"

"Why don't you ask Jerry?" she snapped.

"Jerry? What does my nephew—"

Resisting the urge to snap her boss's ugly red suspenders against his thick body—hard—Cara didn't wait to hear the rest. She slammed her office door closed behind her and slammed the case she had been carrying onto the floor beneath her desk.

Her office. Had it been only yesterday when Della had eaten that damned chocolate right here? So much had happened since then.

She looked at the place as if it belonged to a stranger. And a bunch of strangers had made it appear to be someone else's. The forensics gang had rolled through, taking whatever they wanted, dusting the rest with ugly black fingerprint powder. It even smelled different—like chemicals and throw up. She pulled from a drawer a small can of disinfectant she kept for those days when Beau ordered in pizzas with onions and extra garlic, and sprayed it into the air in a futile attempt to mask the odor.

Since the light on her phone was blinking, she checked her messages—three, according to the digital display. She drew in her breath at the first, when Mitch's voice blared into her domain. She quickly pressed erase. And then again and again. All three were from Mitch. And she was damned if she would listen to him, let alone return the calls.

Forcing Mitch from her mind, she began to straighten the things on top of her desk. Article drafts, printed pages of Internet research, memos from Beau—sure, a lot of stuff had been in her myriad piles, but those piles had been organized, darn it. Now she had to sort through every page to determine where it belonged.

After digging through the materials on the right side of her desk, she started on the left. That was when she found the yellow file folder with the neatly printed label: Shotgun Sally. It wasn't Cara's file. And that meant it was what Della had come here yesterday to give her.

Smiling for the first time that morning—since awakening with Mitch beside her—she began to read.

Della had copied pages from anthologies of Texas legends that referred to Sally, focusing on the story of her sister's murder. Reading them gave Cara chills. Sally's sister had been mistaken for her and had died, right near the ranch house on the property owned by the siblings' wealthy family.

Cara had asked where that property was. Della had apparently researched it and included a map of what today was Mustang County. She'd circled an area a few miles east of town, noting, "Shotgun Sally's ancestral land." She'd included some citations to book references, written by hand.

Interesting, Cara thought. She'd have to visit it. She thought she could picture it—not particularly pretty, fairly flat and with few trees. How could Sally have hidden? Her story suggested she'd holed up there while figuring out how to capture the true culprit in her sister's murder. Sure, Zachary, her lawman lover, had nabbed the drifter only hours after the killing, but Sally had insisted someone else was behind the murder. How else could the drifter have gotten so much cash?

She'd laid a trap for the real killer, right there on her family's ranch. Except he'd laid a trap for her first—on the same land. Zachary got snared first, but Sally saved him. Only then did he begin to believe her tale of conspiracy. And that had led to a beautiful relationship.

Sally and *her* lawman lover, and Cara and... Damn!

Impulsively Cara called Della's hospital room. "You caught me just in time," Della said. "They're releasing me."

"How do you feel?"

"Like a herd of steer stampeded on my stomach, but I'll get over it."

"I found the file you left on my desk," Cara said. "Thanks. I guess I didn't need to know where Sally lived, but I've always wondered." Not that she'd given it much thought, for Sally was such an integral part of Mustang Valley lore, Cara had considered the entire county Sally's domain. But Cara realized that her curiosity had been prodded since the story she was researching these days involved large tracts of land in Mustang County. Of course, the properties being scarfed up by Ranger Corporation and its subsidiaries were on the opposite side of town from Sally's—the western part of Mustang County.

"You're welcome," Della said. "We'll have to get together and toast Sally when I'm able to drink again."

"You got it," Cara said. "Drinks'll be on me."

The phone rang almost as soon as she'd hung up. Cara was glad she had caller ID; it was Mitch. She would answer and hang up on him, but then he'd know she was there. Instead, she let the call roll into her voice mail. Of course she checked the message right away, just in case it was someone else calling about something important. She gritted her teeth when she heard Mitch's remote voice asking her to call him. When the hounds of hell are on my tail, she thought.

After letting all her calls go into voice mail, she ignored two more messages from Mitch before she'd finished reorganizing her office. Didn't that dratted deputy ever give up?

When she came back from lunch, more messages were on her machine. And late that afternoon Beau buzzed her on the intercom to tell her Mitch was there to see her and that she was ordered to talk to him.

Give your commands to your nephew, Jerry, why don't you? Cara thought. Leaving Beau to entertain Mitch, she slipped out the back door.

She considered heading for her parents', since Mitch was unlikely to confront her there, but decided against it. She didn't want her folks to worry about her—any more than they would when the next bunch of rumors reached their ears.

Instead she headed for the Hit 'Em Again Saloon.

Too bad her closest friend Kelly McGovern, now Lansing, was still on her honeymoon. This popular dive belonged to her husband, Wade, so it was now part Kelly's, too. Cara would have loved to have belted down a couple of beers with Kelly, told her everything about her story and her research, and how Deputy Mitch Steele had screwed her—figuratively and literally. Well, maybe she'd keep some things to herself. Even though Kelly, in her own sometimes prissy, top-of-the-social-tree ways, had her own earthy side.

Tonight, wanting to get so high she'd fly, Cara didn't even bother trying to find an empty table in the overflowing lounge. She sat at the bar by herself and had a glass of wine. But she could hardly swallow it. Some sobbing lush she'd be.

"Can I get you another?" the bartender asked.

"Not tonight." Cara paid her tab, left a generous tip and headed out the door.

She drove home slowly. Not that she was drunk, but she certainly didn't want to be pulled over by some deputy sheriff who'd report the stop to Mitch.

She turned off Main Street onto a road that led toward her apartment complex. It was twilight. Why did it feel so much later? Maybe because so much had happened that day.

She'd woken up satiated, happy and in love. She was going to go to bed tonight alone and angry. And… Well, maybe she'd still be in love, though she'd get over it. But Mitch's perfidy hurt particularly badly because of how she felt about him.

Had he only slept with her to ensure her cooperation?

A flash from behind her startled her. Damn. A white Sheriff's Department car had blinked its lights. Was it Mitch? Had he followed her?

Why did the thought make her feel so warm and fuzzy inside despite how she wanted to hate him? It had to be the wine. As she pulled to the curb of the residential street, she just hoped she'd pass the Breathalyzer.

But the deputy who approached the driver's side window wasn't Mitch but that pig-shaped lout Hurley Zeller.

She pushed the button to roll down her window. "Is there a problem, Deputy Zeller?"

"Yeah. I thought that was you. I was just on my way to a crime scene and figured you'd want to know about it, if you don't already. It'll make a good news story."

There was something in the smug pleasure on this miserable, fat excuse-for-a-deputy's face that made Cara's blood chill. "What's going on?" she asked quietly.

"Officer down," he said with a smile. "Deputy Mitchell Steele, that is. Care to follow me there?"

CARA FOLLOWED on automatic—almost.

She wasn't surprised when Zeller's car headed toward the side of town where she only went when seeking a good, juicy story. It was always surprising to her that a relatively small town like Mustang Valley had an area that was the wrong side of the imaginary tracks, but it did.

Officer down.

Mitch.

Oh, Lord, how the thought scared her...as much as she wanted so desperately to hate him.

Zeller pulled into an alley. Cara followed. It opened into a lot behind a warehouse. An empty lot. Time for Cara to go.

Only, Zeller was faster. He jumped out of his car and pointed his Beretta at her.

She'd already reached into her purse—and pointed her camera at him. "Standoff," she shouted through her still-closed window.

"I don't think so." He came closer, the weapon still aimed toward her as she snapped one digital shot after another. "Hand over whatever you found that lets Steele's old man off the hook, and then you can go."

"You've come this far but you'll let me, a witness, live?"

"Sure. Now hand it over."

"Why?" Cara demanded. "Why do you care if Sheriff Martin Steele is cleared?" She wished her voice didn't shake so much. She wasn't an idiot. A gun was pointed at her head. And even though she was recording this with her small dictating machine hidden on her lap, she didn't have a death wish.

She didn't like the fact that Zeller's smile didn't falter as he replied. "Because if anyone digs too deep, they're just liable to find the truth."

"That you were the one who took the bribe, framed Martin and then murdered him and made it look like a suicide?" Not that Cara had figured it out before, but why else would Hurley be doing this?

"Could be. But no one's going to dredge that up again, once you aren't around to—"

"Drop it, Zeller," said another voice, slightly muffled outside the closed window but definitely recognizable. And definitely welcome.

Mitch stepped out from the shadows. He held a Beretta that looked just like Zeller's—both, undoubtedly, standard issue by the department. His was aimed right at his counterpart's head.

"What the hell are you doing here?" Zeller growled, not obeying.

"Drop it," Mitch repeated, pressing the barrel to Hurley's temple.

This time the other deputy obeyed.

"Cara called me while she followed you, you piece of filth."

She'd promised herself she'd call him only if the hounds of hell had been on her tail, and they had been.

"I kept telling her not to put herself in danger," Mitch

continued, "but she claimed this was the only way to flush you out. Now, why don't you tell me why you're so interested in evidence that would exonerate my father?"

"Shove it," Zeller cried. He ducked and lunged toward Mitch, who instead of firing hit him in the temple with the butt of the gun. Zeller went down without a word.

"I guess we'll have to find out later," Cara said with a shaky sigh.

"THIS DOESN'T CHANGE anything," Cara said a long while later.

Mitch hadn't had to argue with her about following him to the department. He'd cuffed Zeller, tossed him into the back of his car and dragged him in once they arrived.

Sheriff Ben Wilson had been outraged—at first. But he couldn't argue with Cara's photographs and tape recording of the whole thing.

Mitch had been furious with her earlier for putting herself in such danger for the sake of a story. "Not for a story," she'd told him in a soft voice that had reverberated inside her car. She had used the speaker feature of her new cell phone so Zeller wouldn't see it. "To find out the truth. And I know you want that."

He'd wanted to shake her afterward for not listening to him. And to hug her.

But their earlier argument in his office had gone too deep. And she'd refused to listen when he'd told her he'd been trying just to string Sheriff Wilson along. She didn't believe that the message on his desk from Jerry Jennings was the umpteenth that he'd refused to respond to, even though Beau Jennings's up-and-coming media-whiz nephew had tried over and over to get an interview with him about the Wilks murder.

He knew the pain Jerry had put her through years ago,

stealing her research and using it for his own gain. Mitch knew she believed he was similarly stabbing her in the back.

Well, he'd violated his own inviolate rule, and he regretted it now. He'd allowed someone to get close. Under his skin.

Caring for anyone had always been a mistake. He'd gotten through his uneasy teen years, then the loss of his parents and his only serious girlfriend, thinking his lesson had been learned. But he'd let down his guard just this once. And now he would pay.

"Let's listen to the tape again," Mitch said.

MITCH WASN'T SURPRISED that Hurley demanded a lawyer.

The first he'd asked for was Lindsey Wellington. *That* was a surprise, till Mitch thought it through. Lindsey had recently gotten a client off a murder rap.

Of course, that client happened to be innocent, framed by another lawyer in Lindsey's firm. And now Lindsey and her former client Bart Rawlins were about to be married.

It was with great pleasure that Mitch had informed Hurley that Lindsey declined to have anything to do with him.

"Donald Church, then," he'd demanded. Since Church was the only lawyer left of the town's former primo law firm, that wasn't a huge shock to Mitch, either.

The only surprise was that Church agreed.

Now they were in the Sheriff's Department interrogation room. It had always seemed too small before. Now, even though Mitch sat at the far end of its table from Zeller, it felt like the room had shrunk even more. Deputy Stephanie Greglets had asked to conduct the interrogation, and Ben Wilson had agreed. Mitch didn't see the sense of his reasoning. Sure, Ben and he were both too close to the situation to avoid the appearance of a conflict of interest. But so was Stephanie.

Hurley was Ben's protégé and wunderkind who'd let him down. And Mitch was the person in the room who wanted to ram Zeller's teeth down his throat till they sliced open his jugular.

The son of a bitch had taken from Mitch one of the people he'd valued most in his life: his father. And he'd threatened to kill someone else Mitch cared for, even if his feelings for her were out of line: Cara.

Lovely, brave, foolish Cara, who could have been killed because she'd insisted on trying to find out the truth. For her story. Or so Mitch tried to convince himself.

But he knew better, in his gut. She'd done it for *him,* too.

And Stephanie? Well, she'd been dealing with Hurley's inappropriate interest for a long time. That hardly made her impartial.

The inquiry had started a few minutes ago. A court reporter was present, and a tape recorder was running.

So far all they'd gotten from Hurley was his name, address, birth date and profession.

"Deputy Zeller," said Stephanie, "let's start with today. Ms. Cara Hamilton said you lured her to that warehouse parking lot by claiming Deputy Mitchell Steele had been injured there."

"That's argumentative," asserted Donald Church. Though Mitch had always considered the man, whose expensive clothes didn't keep him from looking chubby, a good guy, he was, after all, a lawyer. He was even taking notes on a yellow legal pad, with a gold pen that probably cost more than Mitch's salary for the day. "Deputy Zeller didn't *lure* Ms. Hamilton anywhere. And what is your question?"

Mitch caught tall, self-assured Stephanie's annoyed

look before she tried again. "Let me rephrase. Deputy Zeller, did you tell Ms. Hamilton that something had happened to Deputy Steele and ask her to follow you?"

"That's a compound question," Donald Church said.

Mitch glanced again at Stephanie. Was she too green to do this? He'd taught her better techniques in other interviews. But the contrition and confusion he expected to see as their eyes met was preceded by a flash of triumph. What was that about?

"I'll answer," Zeller said. He ignored his attorney's protests. "I know how these things go. Let me cut to the chase. Yeah, I've done some stuff I probably shouldn't have. See, as you known, I'm an ambitious guy, Deputy Greglets." He grinned at Stephanie, obviously forgetting that she'd tried to shake off his advances even when there was no indication he was anything more than an oversexed jerk.

Mitch couldn't interpret her return glance, but there was definite emotion in it. *Was* there really something between Zeller and Stephanie?

"I'm thinking of running for sheriff when Sheriff Wilson becomes mayor," Zeller continued. He grinned at Ben, whose expression remained stony. "I thought Cara Hamilton was being too nosy, and her bad-mouthing Sheriff Wilson could prevent him from being elected. So, could be I made a bad decision, but I thought I'd scare her a little." He shrugged and kept smiling.

"But when you were with Ms. Hamilton, you didn't tell her to stop investigating her stories," Stephanie said. "I've got the transcript of what she recorded right here. You demanded that she hand over something that she'd said would clear Sheriff Martin Steele's name." She again glanced toward Mitch, who was using every ounce of self-control he had to keep from taking over the questioning. Stephanie must have read that on his face since she looked away fast. As if trying to maintain control of the interview, she demanded, "Then Ms. Hamilton asked if *you* were the one who took the bribe, framed Sheriff Steele, killed him and made it look like a suicide, and your response was, 'Could be.' How does that fit into your story that you just wanted to scare Ms. Hamilton into backing off?"

"Don't answer," Donald Church insisted. The older man's fingers were pale from clutching his pen over his legal pad, but his face was red, a contrast with his starched white shirt.

Mitch had been silent long enough. He stood and waved Stephanie away when she joined him at the end of the table. "I know I'm not the most objective interrogator, but this is an informal session. I want to ask some questions."

"But—" Stephanie protested while leaping to her feet.

"My client is instructed to answer nothing," Church interjected at the same time. He'd also risen, as had Ben Wilson. Hurley Zeller, the subject of the inquiry, was the only one to remain seated, along with the court reporter.

"Who did you take the bribe from back then, Deputy Zeller?" Mitch asked.

Zeller said nothing, but his ugly, sardonic grin made it clear to Mitch that he was on the right track.

"Was it from Juniper Holdings, the outfit my father was accused of taking bribes from?"

No verbal response, but Zeller's eyes narrowed farther.

"What do you know about Juniper Holdings?"

"What do *you* know about them, Steele?" Zeller glanced at Stephanie, then toward Church.

"I'm asking the questions, Zeller. Here's a big one. Did you frame my father in the interests of furthering your ambition, as you called it, hoping somehow you'd become sheriff?"

"All I'll admit to is wanting to become sheriff after Ben." Zeller wasn't grinning anymore.

And Mitch had no intention of letting up on his barrage of questions. "There've been three recent murders in Mustang Valley. Two have been solved, but by outsiders. Did you sabotage the investigations to prevent this department from solving them?"

The look that Zeller shot his lawyer gave him his answer. Ben, too, for he took a few steps toward the man he'd treated like his son and successor. Mitch blocked him.

"You son of a—" Ben began. "I thought it was Steele sabotaging my department to make sure I was punished. I figured he thought I railroaded his dad so that I'd get the sheriff's job I was entitled to in the first place." He looked at Mitch. "Believe me, son, I thought all the accusations against your dad were the God's truth, including that he shot himself."

Mitch didn't try to take the chill out of his response. "Well, now we know, don't we, Ben?" At least he understood why his boss had always been so antagonistic, not that he'd cared. Mitch hadn't sabotaged any investigation, of course. But he had tried to prove the sheriff guilty of bribery and murder.

Keeping his anger in check, the way he did so well, he turned back to the worm who had, in fact, committed all of those offenses. "Okay, Zeller, let's continue. Did you date Nancy Wilks? And before you decline to answer or deny it, remember I have witnesses."

Zeller stood, his barrel chest heaving as he faced Mitch. He was so close Mitch could smell the reek of his cigars on his bulging khaki uniform. "Yeah, I dated her, but you're not going to pin her murder or anything else on me. Going out with her was a mistake. I thought she had some information, but she wasn't the one who..." He stopped, obviously realizing he'd said more than he'd intended. He darted a look toward Stephanie that suggested as much of an apology as that bastard was likely to give. Her return stare was switchblade sharp and looked designed to lop Hurley off at the knees. "I didn't kill her," he finished, taking his seat once more.

"I think this interrogation is over," said Donald Church, his eyes on his client.

"Yeah," Zeller said. "I'm not answering any more questions." He shot Mitch a furious glare, but the fear glinting in his eyes told Mitch the guy knew he was screwed. Mitch would never let up until all his allegations were proven—especially that Zeller had framed, then murdered, Mitch's father. And Mitch would learn Stephanie's real relationship with Hurley. Something there didn't ring true, and he'd get to the bottom of it.

The truth about Zeller wouldn't bring Martin Steele back to his son. It would probably not even bring Mitch's mother back from the refuge from this world that she'd sought by joining others of her background far from here.

But his efforts to learn the truth would finally have paid off, and that would make Mitch feel a hell of a lot better.

THE THING WAS, Mitch thought after making sure Zeller was settled securely in one of the Sheriff's Department's small and uncomfortable holding cells, so far it *was* only allegations.

Questions percolated in his mind as he helped Stephanie with paperwork relating to Zeller's incarceration. As they worked, they talked.

Stephanie admitted she'd given in to Hurley's relentless attempts at seduction. Mitch figured there was still more to it than that but had too many other things to dwell on to pursue her indiscretion further—for now.

A lot of apparently unrelated strings needed to be tied

into a cohesive knot. Somehow, much of what had gone on in Mustang Valley for the last couple of years had to be related.

He actually believed Zeller's claim he hadn't killed Nancy Wilks. The bullet wound in her forehead had come from a small-caliber weapon. Sure, Zeller could have a gun in addition to the department-issued Berettas, but he couldn't see the beefy deputy with something that didn't seem an extension of his already inflated opinion of himself.

By the time Mitch was ready to return to his desk, he had a headache. Too much. Why did Juniper Holdings bribe Zeller? Why did Zeller frame his dad? Maybe it had been his ambition, wanting to get Martin Steele out of his way. Or maybe he'd been concerned Martin would learn about the bribe.

But who killed Nancy Wilks? What was the Lambert & Church connection to the three murders? What was the Ranger Corporation connection?

Mitch didn't have the answers. But he knew someone else who was as interested as he was.

When he reached his desk, a light was blinking on his phone. Cara had left him a message: "Mitch, I'm still damned mad at you. But I've thought about it and realize I can't hold information back that may help your investigation just because you and I can't get along."

With a grin too big to originate only because a citizen had promised cooperation, Mitch placed a call to Cara's cell phone. His smile broadened when she answered on the first ring.

"Cara," he said, "it's Mitch. I'm returning your call. And I was just about to call you, too."

Chapter Fifteen

Cara agreed to meet Mitch once more in the coffee shop at the Lone Star Lodge. The dive was neutral territory, not too intimate, yet a place they were unlikely to be observed by anyone who mattered.

Like heck had Mitch been planning on calling her this time. Cara knew better. Yet his saying so had sent a thrill of relief and anticipation through her that she'd had to squelch.

How dare he try to reward her with so worthless a remark?

And how dare she sing inside as if he *had* rewarded her?

Though she was usually prompt, or even early, she purposely strolled into the restaurant five minutes late, her large purse slung over her shoulder. Mitch's patrol car was in the parking lot, so she knew he'd beaten her there.

She'd considered running home to change. Her dark blue slacks and loose knit top were not her most becoming outfit. But this meeting wasn't a game of seduction. It wasn't a game at all.

He sat at the same table where they'd talked cooperation in the first place. His crisp khaki uniform was in sharp contrast to the seedy surroundings. His Stetson rested on the booth beside him. Had the table been cleaned in the interim? She couldn't tell. The containers of condiments—ketchup, mustard, salt and pepper—all looked as if they could use a good scrubbing. Two greasy menus were stuck into the middle of them.

Mitch had coffee waiting. At least the cup looked clean. He stood as she approached. The brief smile on his face looked genuine, lighting up his handsome, angular features. But there was a wariness in his eyes, as if he expected her to shout or make a scene.

She wouldn't give him the satisfaction.

"Hi, Mitch," she said quietly as she slid onto the bench seat. Damn! Her heart was in her voice; it sounded sad and quivery, even to her. More strongly she said, "No matter how I feel about you or how you played games with me, I shouldn't have withheld this." She pulled out one of the documents she'd taken from the Ranger offices while in the guise of a heating and cooling repair person.

The paper that showed Juniper Holdings was one of Ranger's many clandestine subsidiaries.

"I'm not sure what it means," she said, handing him the page, "but it connects what happened to your father to Ranger Corporation. I don't understand Hurley Zeller's involvement, but the possibility that he killed your dad—Do you follow the connections? Sheriff Martin Steele's death was the first relating to Ranger. Then Andrew McGovern's, Jeb Rawlins's and now Nancy's. You've got to nail Ranger, Mitch. Stop all the killings."

"I intend to. With your help."

Shocked, Cara looked into Mitch's golden eyes. Was he mocking her? If so, she didn't read it there. He even looked a bit amused. Something else shone there—blatant desire. His warmth heated her instantly, as if he had ignited a pilot light in her soul. One she insisted remain a tiny, unfueled flame.

He continued. "I need to run by you what we learned

from Zeller this afternoon. Granted, it isn't much, but I figured we could brainstorm. Your insight's helped me before, Cara."

"The consummate loner, Deputy Mitch Steele, is actually asking me to brainstorm with him?"

"Yeah. Wild, isn't it?"

More than that, it was unnerving, as it thrust a sharp sliver of hope into her damaged heart, which Cara had thought was already healing.

She didn't want hope. She wanted distance. This man had taken her information for his own use. Had promised her nothing in return except what he chose to tell, which wasn't much. Had made it clear to the world how much he mistrusted her.

Had made it clear that their astonishingly thrilling love-making had been a pleasant bodily function to this man whose self-sufficiency could become as legendary as tales of Shotgun Sally.

The Sally legend had more than one ending. The sad one suggested that Sally had died in the ambush in which she'd saved Zachary Gale, her lawman lover.

The happy one said they'd both survived, vanquished her foes and lived happily ever after....

Don't even think about that, Hamilton. It wouldn't happen for Mitch and her.

She raised her chin. "You're right about one thing. Insight is my business. So, sure, I'll brainstorm with you as long as you promise I'll get the story—and mean it this time."

"I've always meant it, Cara." He leaned across the table. She intended to move back, but he took her hands, menu and all, and held them.

Glancing around to make sure no one was near them, Mitch related to her Hurley Zeller's interrogation that afternoon, his voice as low as if he spoke words of love.

Trying to maintain her nonchalance while being too conscious of their contact, Cara asked questions now and then, most of which he couldn't answer. She sought to weave threads from her own knowledge among the scant facts Mitch had gleaned from the interview as well as his own as-yet-unprovable speculations. And the side issue of Deputy Stephanie Greglets's apparent relationship with Zeller? Cara would have to mull that over. She didn't see the relevance. And yet, could she find some link between Stephanie and Ranger? Ranger seemed to have a tie with nearly everyone else in town.

"So we have Zeller accepting bribes from Juniper," she said, "framing your dad to make it look as if Juniper bribed him and then killing your dad." Mitch's grip loosened, but she wasn't about to let him go. "I'm so sorry, Mitch," she whispered.

"Yeah, me, too."

Taking a deep breath, she continued. "I've done some checking into Juniper. It's out of business now, but it was a subsidiary of another affiliate of Ranger's—Multistate Holdings. Multistate holds property that's already been developed. The biggest are a couple of theme parks in California and New York. The only site around here that Multistate owns of record is an office building in a Ft. Worth suburb. And guess which construction company built it?"

"O'Hallihan's?" Mitch sounded excited.

Cara nodded. "Not that it proves anything but an additional tie of Shem O'Hallihan's to a Ranger subsidiary." Regretfully, she pulled her hands from his. But he didn't need her comfort now. And he'd begun to stroke her palms with his fingertips. That tiny touch nearly drove her crazy with desire as she forced herself to concentrate on their conversation.

Quickly she recapped the murders and their apparent

ties to Ranger. "But I don't know about Nancy's murder. She worked for Lambert & Church, but that doesn't connect her enough to Ranger. She had something to show me, but we don't know what it was."

"Ah, but that was why I wanted to talk to you." The somberness of Mitch's face was replaced by a half grin. He lifted something from the seat beside him. "The real article is at the lab being tested, but here's a copy."

Cara took it from him and looked at it. "A book about Shotgun Sally?" Puzzlement swept through her. "I could see her wanting to show me this. But it shoots to smithereens my theory that whatever she wanted to show me caused her murder."

"Maybe, maybe not. That's the other thing I wanted to ask you to do. Look this over, including the notes inside, and see if there's any connection."

"Okay. Sure." Cara grinned.

They'd finished this conversation. It was time for them to go their separate ways.

"You'll keep in touch with me, Cara, and not wait till you're in trouble to call me? Better yet, stay out of trouble."

"Of course," she said, hoping it was true. "What are you going to do?"

"Pay another call on Shem O'Hallihan first. Make sure he's aware of Zeller's arrest and my knowledge of O'Hallihan's connection with Juniper Holdings and the bribes Zeller took. See O'Hallihan's reaction. And you?"

"First, I've got an article to write about Deputy Zeller," Cara said. "Then, I'm going to curl up with a good book." She grinned, indicating the pages about Shotgun Sally.

THERE WERE SOME strange things about the book Mitch had copied for Cara. After writing and e-mailing her article about Hurley Zeller, she had stayed up nearly all night reading it. Alone. Thinking about Mitch too much.

Pondering how the heck she was going to eject her lawman lover from being under her skin so deeply. From her heart...

Her conclusion: she simply would. That was all there was to it. He was using her now. Brainstorming.

They were using each other; she would get her story about Nancy's murder. He couldn't stand in the way by keeping so much off the record forever. And if he did, then she would have to defy him, no matter what.

One way or another they would go their separate ways.

It didn't take much effort to force herself to concentrate on the book. After all, the legends, full of Shotgun Sally's courage, common sense and integrity, were amazing. Cara was intrigued by everything about Sally.

The notes, in familiar handwriting, suggested that Nancy had been, too. They said things like, "This is great." "Must use this." "Visuals here."

Was Nancy involved with a potential movie about Shotgun Sally? But surely that wasn't what she had been killed over.

That was one of the oddities about what she read. The other was what appeared to be a discrepancy.

By ten in the morning, she was at her office putting together the article on dark-horse candidates for the local school board that she'd been researching for the edition later that week. She'd also worked on a follow-up on her article about Hurley Zeller's arrest that had appeared in that morning's edition, being careful not to include anything that Mitch could consider to be off the record. She sent both by e-mail to Beau for his review and then reached into her desk drawer, where she'd put the book pages for handy access.

Putting them on her desk, she made a phone call. This

time, she actually reached Della Santoro, rather than having to leave her usual message. Della had been recuperating well from eating the poisoned candy and had insisted on returning to work, although she was on a reduced schedule. "Hi, Della? It's Cara. Guess what. I have a surprise for you."

"Really? What?"

"If I told you," Cara said, "it wouldn't be a surprise. I'll drop by this afternoon to show you, okay?"

"Sure."

They scheduled a time, and then Della asked questions about Cara's latest excitement the day before—not surprising, since the article Cara had written about it was hard-hitting against Hurley Zeller, yet sketchy as to particulars.

"I can't go into it in detail now," Cara said, "because it's involved with a larger investigation by the Sheriff's Department. But Hurley Zeller's gotten caught up in some really nasty stuff."

"Nancy's murder?" Della sounded aghast.

"No, not that," Cara said, "except maybe in a remote way."

"What do you mean?"

"Can't talk about it." To change the subject, Cara said, "There's another thing I wanted to tell you about. You did all that research about where Shotgun Sally's family's land was probably located, and I really appreciate it. I went out and visited the area." With Sally on her mind, she'd gone there yesterday after meeting with Mitch instead of going straight home. "The thing is, I couldn't visualize it as both ranchland and the area where Sally hid out and dodged traps set for her by her nasty foe, that easterner who'd do anything to steal her family's land. It was too flat, not enough trees, that kind of thing. I suppose some trees could have been cut down in the century since then, but it still didn't feel right.''

"I gave you the printouts.'' Della sounded defensive.

"I know,'' Cara said placatingly, "and that seemed to be the right spot. But I've just come across some other information that suggests it wasn't on the eastern side of town but the western side. It's not that important, but I was curious.''

"Me, too,'' Della said. "If I didn't have a class to teach right now, I'd go take a look at the area you found, just to see.''

Cara pondered for a moment. Her current articles were complete. She had more research and writing to do that afternoon, but, hey, why not follow up while it was on her mind?

"Tell you what. I'll go take a look and report back to you when we meet this afternoon. I have to admit that my curiosity is stoked.''

"Mine, too,'' Della said. "See you later.''

There was another reason besides sheer curiosity that drove Cara to want to go see the property now. If she was right, it was the same area where Ranger Corporation had been buying up land. It was certainly near the Rawlins family property, where Cara's friend Lindsey now lived with her fiancé.

Cara dug in a file drawer and pulled out copies of the deeds she'd gotten from the County Recorder that had Ranger's name on them, plus the two remaining subsidiaries she knew about. Then she pulled a map of Mustang County from another drawer and made a copy. She sketched in where she understood the locations of the Ranger Corporation property to be, then the Rawlins ranchlands. Finally, she attempted, from the scant descriptions in the Shotgun Sally book, to overlay the area that seemed to have been in Sally's family way back when.

"Damned if it doesn't seem like the same place," she muttered aloud.

Not that she'd be able to tell any better in person, but she was certainly interested enough to go take a look.

OF COURSE, Cara thought as she neared the land in question, the area was vast. Plus, the description in the Sally book was not very detailed—just west, near the Brazos River, with juniper trees clustered into thick, green woods.

Juniper? As in Juniper Holdings? That could be coincidental, but Cara didn't believe much in coincidences.

Ranger Corporation was interested enough in juniper trees to name a covert, now defunct, subsidiary after them. And Ranger Corporation and its other affiliates still tried to buy up this land.

Why?

She wasn't certain where to go to view the area best, but there was one road off a major highway that led into it. The hills there rolled enough that, if she remembered correctly, there was a vista just off the road. That was where she headed.

Her cell phone rang. She glanced at the caller ID number.

"Hi, Mitch," she said, ignoring the rush of pleasure she felt at even so remote a contact as an electronic call.

"Hi." His voice was low and sexy and seductive. "What are you up to today? Getting into trouble?"

"Sure," she said lightly. "Right now, I'm trying to figure out the location where Shotgun Sally's family's land was, based on what's in that book. It's incredible, by the way. I really appreciate your sharing it with me."

"The original's evidence in a murder investigation," he reminded her. "And that's still off the record."

"I know." *Everything* was off the record to him. But this one she understood and had to agree with, even though it hurt. She wanted Nancy's murder solved, too. Fast. And that meant she had to share once more the fruit of her own musings. "By the way, Mitch, I sketched a map this morning that showed the property Ranger Corporation and its affiliates have bought with Sally's family's land superimposed on it, to the extent I could figure it out. It looks like the same property. I'm on my way there now to take a better look," she said.

"Now? Cara, didn't you get the message? I want you to stay far away from Ranger and its property till we get this all resolved, unless I'm with you."

Yeah, she'd gotten the message. But she'd chosen, in her mind, to tear it into tiny pieces. She didn't tell him she intended to ignore his orders again, though. Calmly, she said, "You sound as if there's something wrong, Mitch. Did you learn something else this morning?"

"Not really." She thought she heard an irritated sigh over the phone line. "O'Hallihan was out at a job site somewhere. I tried Roger Rosales instead, but he was tied up on a phone call when I first phoned his office, and then he ran out before his secretary told him I was on the line. But something just doesn't feel right."

"No kidding." As he talked, as Cara thought about Hurley Zeller and the book and the property, she realized she was getting the same sense of unease she felt the night she'd found Nancy Wilks's body. The news itch. Shotgun Sally's tattle bug stinging her right where it was most irritating—deep in her gut.

"Any interest in taking a look at the site with me, Mitch?" How foolish. It wasn't as if she needed protection, or even company, to take a gander at a major piece of property.

Still, having him there would feel awfully good.

"Sure, I'm interested. Thing is, with Zeller no longer

on duty, my responsibilities have multiplied. Tell you what. I'll meet you there in an hour.''

''Don't bother. I'll tell you all about it later.''

''No, Cara. Don't go there on your own.''

''Afraid I'll find something I won't share with you, Mitch?'' she taunted, then regretted it. ''You know that if I learn something vital to the investigation, *I,* at least, will pass it along to you. I'll call you later.''

''Cara—'' His tone sounded ominous, but she hung up. She was almost there, anyway.

She signaled and pulled off the highway onto a two-lane road that led toward the rear of the Rawlins ranchlands and other adjoining property. It was a pretty area, with stands of junipers on both sides of the road.

She hadn't gone far before a big, black SUV pulled out from behind a bunch of trees. She gasped in surprise, since she hadn't noticed it before.

She was even more surprised when it pulled up beside her. Roger Rosales was inside. He motioned her to pull over.

A frisson of unease loosened Cara's grip on the steering wheel for an instant. Her heartbeat quickened, a thunderous tattoo that reminded her of the night she found Nancy's body. She didn't like this.

Staying on the road, she grabbed for her cell phone and, half watching where she was going and half watching the phone, she pressed in Mitch's number.

But her reduced attention was a mistake.

Roaring in front of her, Roger's SUV swerved. Cara slammed on her brakes to avoid him, and her phone slid from her hand as her Toyota jounced off the road.

''Damn!'' she muttered.

Before she could back up onto the pavement, Roger had exited his vehicle. In moments he was standing beside her. ''I need to talk to you, Cara,'' he said, his voice muffled through her closed window.

''I don't think so,'' Cara called angrily, despite the way her skin turned cold with fear. What was he up to?

She knew in a moment.

Roger was aiming a gun right at her head.

Chapter Sixteen

Trying to ignore the continued cacophony of her heartbeat, Cara exited her car. The road was dappled with sunlight sneaking between the branches and leaves of the surrounding juniper trees.

"What's this about, Roger?" She didn't really have to ask. The guy *was* Ranger Corporation, at least in Mustang County. Ranger had been involved with three, maybe four, murders—so far—and she hadn't hidden the fact that she was looking for the truth, to make it public.

Would she be the next victim?

Mitch! she called out silently. He'd said he would meet her here. She'd pushed the button to make her cell phone call before Roger forced her off the road. Surely he knew by now that she was in trouble.

Would her lawman lover get here in time to help her? She couldn't count on it.

Shotgun Sally's lawman lover Zachary had walked right into a trap set for Sally. She'd had to save *him*.

Oh, Lord, if Mitch had to count on Cara to save him, he could be in big trouble.

"You've been meddling too much, Ms. Hamilton." Roger, in his white shirt, red necktie and herringbone sports jacket, remained pompously formal. Yet the pallor of his face and the way his gun hand shook indicated he was uncomfortable. Was that a good thing?

"It's my job to look into newsworthy stuff," she said as casually as she could with a wobbly weapon pointed at her. "Did you kill Nancy?"

"No!" The word came out as a shout, startling Cara. "I never meant... I called you and attacked you at the high school track, but I wouldn't really have shot you. And...look, this is wrong. Just get in your car and get the hell out of here."

Amazed, Cara started to do as he'd said, hoping it wasn't an excuse for him to shoot her in the back.

But before she got her door closed, another car sped onto the narrow road, then screeched to a stop right behind her Toyota, effectively blocking her, with Roger's car in front of her, from either going forward or backing up.

Mitch! Cara thought again—at first. Till she risked a look behind her.

The car—an aging BMW—was familiar. So was the person who got out of it. But it wasn't Mitch.

It was Della Santoro.

"Get out of here, Della," Cara yelled. "It's not safe!"

"For *you.*" Della, who wore a pantsuit with a long, flowing beige jacket, approached them, high heels teetering on the uneven pavement. Her oval face, even with her wire-rimmed glasses perched on her nose, didn't look so professorial with the contemptuous sneer she leveled on Cara. "Shoot her, Roger."

Cara froze, keeping one eye on Roger Rosales, whose gun hand continued to shake. But he didn't shoot her. Yet.

"What's this about, Della?" Cara's voice came out as an unsteady whisper. But she already knew, as all the questions she'd had suddenly developed answers.

This was a public road, even if it was a small one.

Would anyone drive by and see what was going on? Cara couldn't count on it, any more than she could be sure Mitch would be able to help her.

"It's about your meddling, you stupid reporter," Della hissed. She was close enough now to slam Cara's car door shut behind her. Her perfume smelled expensive. Had she dressed up to come here for this? Her dark hair was its usual perfection, pulled straight back from her face. "I tried to warn you off before. That truck I borrowed—"

"From Jackson Felmington?" Cara asked. That could explain why the car dealer had heard of her near "accident."

"Of course. He was terribly sympathetic when I told him I'd almost hit you. Even hinted I should try a little harder next time. He had the truck repaired and painted right away. But even after that, you kept on snooping. Asking questions and working with that damned deputy to solve Nancy's murder. And then, right in the paper, you tied her death to the others, and suggested Ranger Corporation's involvement. You could have ruined everything! I was concerned you'd realize I'd steered you wrong about the location of Shotgun Sally's family land. I even had to send poisoned candy to you and eat it myself to be sure you didn't suspect me of anything worse than ignorance."

"What is the 'everything' that I could have ruined?" Cara asked quietly, taking a step away from the vicious woman she'd considered, till moments ago, a friend. She deserved the truth before she died, for she was suddenly certain that if Roger didn't kill her, Della would. After all, the woman was mad enough to have poisoned herself.

Cara should have known before. Or at least part of it. The handwriting in the notes in Nancy's Shotgun Sally book had looked familiar. Cara had assumed it was Nancy's script. She'd received messages now and then from Nancy, on birthday cards, postcards and the like, but not recently.

She had, however, seen samples of Della's writing only a short time ago, on research materials about Shotgun Sally that Della had provided. And the notes stuck onto the book were in Della's handwriting, too.

But what had the notes meant? What was Della's involvement?

"Are you an employee of Ranger Corporation?" Cara asked.

"I'm a consultant. Their expert on local legends, especially Shotgun Sally." Her smile was smug.

Cara recalled what the notations on the Sally book had said. "Is Ranger filming a movie about Shotgun Sally?"

Della laughed. "No. Not yet, at least, though that might be a natural adjunct. Maybe I'll even get a role."

She was a good actress, Cara thought. Della had certainly fooled *her.*

"So tell me, Roger, why does Ranger need an expert on legends?" Cara didn't expect to get very far but had to try.

Roger hadn't moved except to wilt more in his sports coat, under the hot Texas sun and humid midday air. Della broke in before he could reply. "They intend to build the best theme park here that Texas has ever seen. Maybe the world."

"About Texas legends," Cara guessed.

"Exactly. And it was all my idea. I approached them with it a few years ago, and they loved it. A major theme park about legends, right on the property once owned by the most notorious local legend. But the land was held by a lot of different people. Things had to be set up right to get the project started, so Ranger relied on me to clear the path."

"By bribing Hurley Zeller to pave the way for Ranger's

entry to Mustang County," Cara surmised. "Martin
Steele, the sheriff then, was pretty straitlaced. He wouldn't
have let an interloping company coerce people into selling
their land if they didn't consider the price right. But Zeller
would have been happy to take money to salt the way to
his goal of becoming sheriff and blame Sheriff Steele for
it. Of course, there was one more person senior to him in
the way. You convinced him to be patient, make sure the
Sheriff's Department wasn't too quick to solve a few little
crimes like murder, and things would work out for him
in the end."

"You're the reporter," Della said. "But that story's
close enough to the truth." Without turning her back on
Cara, she edged closer to where Roger stood.

"Then you got Mayor Daniels involved, letting him
invest in what appeared to be a sure thing, right?"

"So far, you're on target," Della said. "Tell you what.
I'll explain the rest. Let you make notes in your head. It'll
all die with you, anyway." She gave a short laugh.

Cara saw Roger wince along with her. Did that mean
he might help her? Fat chance. She had to help herself.
But how?

First thing, she had to keep Della talking. "At least let
me die happy," she agreed.

"Sure," Della said with a careless shrug. "It was the
mayor's bright idea for Ranger to hire Lambert & Church
to do its local legal work. He figured Paul Lambert would
love the whole thing and Donald Church was too much
of a preening peacock to give a damn. Too bad that punk
kid Andrew McGovern got wind of how Ranger was trying to buy some of his girlfriend's land, then the mayor's
conflict of interest. Of course he threatened to go public
with it, so the fool Daniels had to kill him."

"Do you remember that I was once engaged to Andrew?" Cara said softly, soaking in her pain once more.

"Yes, but I figured his death was a good thing for my friend Cara, since he dumped you."

"We dumped each other mutually, but go on." Cara thought she saw a glint of sunlight on metal from the trees behind Della. She nonchalantly looked in that direction but found nothing. Mitch? Maybe. Or maybe she was she imagining. *Or are you there, Sally, with your famous Colt .45, ready to help me?* Sure, right beside her lawman lover, Zachary.

"Not much more to tell. Paul Lambert was charged with helping Ranger wrap up some of its land purchases and he got a bit overzealous in grabbing on to Rawlins land. Killing Jeb Rawlins and framing his nephew Bart didn't work. We're having to work around those properties for the moment at least, and I'm not happy about it. But your good friends, Kelly and Lindsey, won't hide out forever. In fact, when they come back for your funeral, they might meet with a sad accident of their own. Lindsey's dear friend Bart, too. That way we will get all the land we need. There's a lot of money in theme parks, you know."

Don't count on my funeral yet, you backstabbing bitch! But at least Kelly and Lindsey had left this woman's line of sight at the critical moment for each of them.

"What about Nancy?" Cara asked. As long as Della was talking, she wasn't shooting. Yet.

"I'm getting to her," Della said. "I'd shown Paul Lambert one of my favorite old volumes about Shotgun Sally, the one with all my notes about the theme park in it, and he'd asked to read it. I didn't get it back after he died and needed to retrieve it. Since she worked at Paul's firm, I asked Nancy a few subtle questions. She appeared to know about the theme park. I know Paul had drummed the concept of confidentiality into her. She told me so when she refused to answer much. But one day she asked *me* a few questions that told me she'd found the book. I went to her house that night, thought I'd get her to tell me where it was. When she let me in, she said you were on your way to pick it up. I had that gun with me, the one I lent to Roger today.''

She nodded in the direction behind her where Roger had been standing—and only then did Cara notice he was edging closer to the woods. Della didn't seem to have noticed.

''She refused to give me the book,'' Della continued. ''She didn't even notice I was wearing gloves. You know the rest.''

Cara did, and she wanted to nail Della for it. She'd murdered Nancy for nothing but speculation and an old book.

''And then,'' Della finished, ''I couldn't even find the damn book. But now that I know you've got it, I'll fix that. I assume you have it in your car?''

Cara didn't respond. No sense mentioning she only had a copy. She didn't want to make this any easier for Della than she had to. And there was more she needed to know. ''What about Deputy Greglets?'' she asked. ''How did she fit into the scheme with Hurley Zeller?''

''She didn't—except that dear Hurley talked too much in bed. Stephanie started asking far too many questions. Hurley was supposed to manage that by pillow talk or otherwise, but he got wind of my interest in Nancy Wilks and tried to get her into bed, too. Of all the ridiculous nitwits, he thought he could take control of everything. Of course, now that he's been caught, the situation with him has to be managed, too. Maybe we will enlist the curious Deputy Greglets after all, to handle him. She's bound to want her revenge.''

Cara suspected that Stephanie Greglets, who'd actually helped Mitch with the case now and then, had an agenda of her own that didn't involve getting in bed with Della and her cohorts, but she wasn't about to mention that now.

"What about Shem O'Hallihan?" Cara asked. "What's his involvement?"

Della shrugged. "Not much. We just figured he was a building contractor whose services and silence could be bought, thanks to your story about him. Isn't that ironic?" She didn't wait for Cara to answer. "Roger's already been in touch with him, and the guy's been cagey about agreeing to cooperate. But we'll get him on our side."

Heavens, what a fascinating, convoluted newspaper exposé all this would make! Shotgun Sally would have loved it. Right now Cara's usual news itch was a terrible and wonderful irritation. She fully intended to write a story explaining every incredible nuance of the story, Mitch's usual "off the record" notwithstanding. She would help to make sure Ranger got what it deserved, too.

But that meant she had to live. Of course she did! Could she get out of there now, somehow, with Roger, and the gun he held, slinking away? She had to try.

Good thing she was wearing an old pair of slacks today, and sneakers, too, instead of her sometimes slippery boots. With no prelude, she suddenly dropped low and ran behind her car.

"Roger, shoot her!" Della screamed.

Cara couldn't see him but heard no shot. But as she tried to tear her way into the woods, a shot resounded and the bullet hit the ground beside her, throwing up dirt.

Cara put up her hands and stood, turning slowly. Della aimed a gun at her, with her elegantly manicured hands encased in white gloves. The weapon looked bigger—and more lethal—than the one Roger had held.

"Don't try anything, bitch," Della spat. "You know,

there have been entirely too many bodies found around here. Yours is simply going to disappear.''

''I don't think so,'' Cara said with more bravado than she felt. ''You know what Shotgun Sally would have said?''

''No. Her situation was similar, of course, but history didn't say what her last words were.'' Della's scowl was ferocious. ''I'm the expert. I'd know if anyone did.''

''It was after her sister was murdered by the scum that wanted the family property…this property—'' Cara waved her arm about, designating the area around them ''—for his own ranch. The guy went so far as to set a trap to catch her so he could murder her, somewhere probably not far from here. Zachary fell into the trap instead. The villain shot at him, but Sally came to his rescue. That's when she was wounded. Maybe mortally, since there were two endings for her story. In one she died.''

''Like you will,'' Della sneered.

''In the other she lived,'' Cara went on. Would this work? She certainly hoped so. ''And you know how? I'll tell you,'' she said before Della could reply, ''Zachary turned things around. Came to *her* rescue. And you know what Sally said? 'What kept you, lawman?' She looked over Della's shoulder and grinned. ''Like now. It's over, Della.''

''You're not going to fool me with that one, bitch. Now, do you want it quick, in the brain like Nancy got it? Or do you want it slow, a little at a time?''

''Surely you can come up with better dialogue than that for my article,'' Cara said, wincing as she watched Della take aim right for her face.

''Drop it, Santoro,'' said the most wonderful, welcome voice Cara had ever heard. It *had* worked. She'd kept Della distracted enough for Mitch to sneak through the woods and get the drop on the madwoman who intended to kill her. The muzzle of his Beretta was against her temple, and his arm whipped around her throat.

Cara ducked as Della's gun went off. Pain shot through her. But she smiled at Deputy Mitchell Steele. "What kept you, lawman?" she whispered, as Shotgun Sally once had.

And then she fell to the ground.

Chapter Seventeen

"How could you do it, Beau?" Cara ignored the pain as she shifted position in her hospital bed. To avoid tugging on her IV, she clutched the day's *Gazette* in her right hand.

Featured on the front page was an article about the confrontation Cara had the day before with Della Santoro and Roger Rosales. The byline was Beau's.

He sat on a chair facing her, leaning over so his stomach bulged over his legs. Over his wrinkled white shirt, his red suspenders looked strained. *He* looked strained.

"That should have been my article." Cara kept her voice down with effort. This was, after all, a hospital. The sharply sanitary smells and pulsing sounds of the instrument measuring her heart rate proved it.

She knew she was being unreasonable. News didn't wait for someone to feel up to writing the story.

"You were unconscious, under sedation after your surgery," Beau reminded her. As if she'd forgotten. "If I'd waited, it'd have been today before you could have gotten to it. Maybe not even now." Peering over the glasses at the end of his nose, he eyed her dubiously.

"Maybe." But however unfair it was, Cara still didn't feel mollified.

"The local radio station picked it up," Beau said, standing. "From them, the wire services and Dallas/Ft.

Worth TV stations got it, and now it's being covered nationally. At least we didn't blow it completely, thanks to my article. But we're the ones who should have all the details. Especially because you're part of the story.''

Cara couldn't argue with that. She would have a hard time arguing about anything just then. She wasn't in the greatest condition. The bullet Della shot as Mitch took her into custody went wild, but it struck Cara in her right side. It hit nothing vital, at least, but it had hurt like crazy. Still did, though the pain had been dulled by medications here in the hospital. But she wanted to get out.

She wanted to get back to work. She *had* to get back to work. To get her mind off…things.

Who was she fooling? Every waking moment, however hazy her mind might be it focused on Mitch.

His failure to come and see her hurt more than the wound.

Not that she was surprised. He was a lone wolf who joined others only when necessary. His alliance with her no longer had a purpose. So, whatever they'd had together was over. If it had ever really begun.

"The problem with getting all the details, though," said Beau as he paced the room, "is that Deputy Steele."

You said it, Cara thought. But Beau's reasoning couldn't be the same as hers. "What do you mean?" she asked.

"I mentioned him in the article, of course, but I know he had a much larger role than simply showing up at the opportune time and saving the day. But anything else about him, he's said is off the record."

"I know how that goes." Cara shook her head. "He's been like that all along. But—"

"But only for me, he said." Beau continued as if he hadn't heard Cara. "While he was here last night, I came in to see how you were doing, and he—"

"He was here last night?" Cara sat up so fast that pain shot through her side. She ignored it. "When?"

"Around midnight. I came to see if you were conscious enough to give me more of the story, and since you weren't, I was glad to see Steele. At first. But then he told me that 'off the record' garbage. Until you could interview him.''

"He wants me to interview him?" Cara knew she must sound like a parrot, but her incredulity was overwhelming.

"That's what he said. You'd have thought, since you and he were cooperating, that he'd have talked to me, too.''

Cara smiled down at the sheet covering her lap. "You'd have thought so," she agreed. "You know, Beau—" she raised her head to look her boss in the eye "—I've a lot of insight into this story. And with what I can get from Deputy Steele—" maybe "—I'll have the firsthand exposé of the century here. Probably get interviewed myself by all the major media. All those murders tied together, including the former sheriff's, the culprits exposed. With a huge coup like that, I'll have the attention of people all over the country who'll be clamoring to get me to come work for them. And you remember your promise, don't you?"

He glared at her. For a moment it was a showdown. He was the first to look away. "All right, Cara," he said resignedly. "I'm not the only one around here who wants the inside scoop. If your story is as good as I suspect it will be, then you'll get your promotion. Editor in Chief."

LEANING HIS ELBOWS on his desk, Mitch rubbed his eyes with thumb and forefinger. He couldn't remember a more hectic time in his life. At least he now had an office to himself to work on it all—and to get his head straight. But it had all happened so fast.

Most important for the moment, he was supervising the case against Della Santoro, making sure evidence was collected and handled carefully for her prosecution. This was the most important case of his life.

But that wasn't all. Not only was the other most senior deputy, Hurley Zeller, in custody, but, embarrassed about everything that had happened under his watch, Sheriff Ben Wilson had tendered his resignation to the Mustang County Commissioners.

No sense in whipping the guy when he was down, so Mitch had made peace with him, more or less—apologizing for trying to nail him for sabotaging his own department's work, taking bribes, murder…and all that jazz. Ben had gruffly accepted it.

Mitch was now the acting sheriff. And with all the good publicity the arrest of Della Santoro had gained for the county and the department, he'd been told by more than one commissioner that his election as the next sheriff was in the bag.

For a guy like him, accustomed to doing things on his own, it would take some getting used to.

A day and a half had passed since all hell had broken loose. Since Cara had dutifully called to tell him she was disobeying his orders and, before he could head off the horror in front of his eyes, gotten herself shot. She was all right now. He'd kept track of her progress in the hospital, though he hadn't gone to see her since that first terrible night.

He'd left a door open a crack with her boss, Beauford Jennings, that he was willing to have Cara, and no one else, interview him for his perspective on what happened. But he hadn't heard from her.

The phone rang. He grabbed it. "Steele here."

"Sheriff, this is Deputy Greglets. The lab in Ft. Worth called with a report—" No big surprise. Deputy Stephanie Greglets related that the fingerprints on the book found at Nancy Wilks's included not only hers, but Della Santoro's, too.

"Thanks, Stephanie." Mitch hung up.

Stephanie had apologized abjectly for not keeping Mitch informed about her own clandestine investigation of Hurley Zeller. She hadn't told the sheriff, either, for ambition kept her from being a team player. Her seduction by Hurley had been an unfortunate slip, but she'd heard enough from him to be unsure who to trust. She'd only let some high-ranking officers in the Dallas Texas Rangers office in on what she was doing. Alone.

Since Mitch had been conducting his own surreptitious investigation, he'd had to forgive her.

Now she was behaving totally by the book, and Mitch felt sure he would have her loyalty. And she was, above all, a damn fine junior deputy.

The next call was from Jerry Jennings of the *Dallas News*. Grinning, Mitch declined to give a statement. "A local reporter, Ms. Cara Hamilton, has the exclusive on this one." He hung up.

Each time the phone rang like that he grabbed it, hoping it was Cara. Damn, he was like some fool schoolkid. He could just call her. He *would* call her, later. Not to say goodbye, since Mustang Valley was too small for that. They were bound to run into each other now and then. She'd probably want to interview him in the future about other cases, too, and—

It rang again. "Steele here."

"Mitchell?"

Oh, Lord. It wasn't the voice he'd been hoping for but another he'd craved, one he'd expected never to hear again. "Mother?"

Sunshine Steele had seen something on television network news, she told him, suggesting that her beloved husband Sheriff Martin Steele had been framed and murdered.

"It's true, Mother," Mitch said.

He heard her sigh.

"I knew it." And then she asked, "You're all right?"

"Fine. And you?" He knew she'd fled the pain and publicity by returning to where she'd grown up, near Oklahoma's border with Texas.

"Yes, but I'd like to come see you, for a visit. If it's all right with you."

"Sure. Just say when." His heart swelled in anticipation. Who would have thought a grown man would get so excited about the prospect of seeing his mother?

They talked awhile longer. She gave him a phone number where he could reach her, and they exchanged promises to call each other soon.

After he hung up, Mitch felt as if his grin would split his face clean in half.

He was still smiling when the phone rang yet again. He'd need a secretary, at this rate, if he wanted to get any work done. But hot damn, his mother had called. He answered once more, "Steele here."

"Hamilton here."

His smile froze. "Hi, Cara," he said softly. "How are you feeling?"

"Like I was shot. But I'll live. So how come you only came to see me in the hospital when I was drugged?"

"You're out of the hospital now?"

"Yes. The wound wasn't that bad, and I'm all patched up now." Mitch also suspected that the brave, stubborn woman had refused to stay down for long. "Beau said you'd promised me an interview," she continued. "On the record. Are you ready to make good on it?"

"Sure." He forced himself to sound casual. "This time I think I have more information than you do, so you won't be able to accuse me of stealing your research and using it."

"We'll see about that."

To his surprise, she insisted on meeting him in half an hour, at the same place where she'd been shot, outside town on the road to the Four Aces and Bar JR, the Rawlins family ranches.

There was a lot he had to do here, but nothing was more important than seeing Cara again. Making sure she wasn't lying, that she was fine.

And maybe then he'd see whether there was any hope for the ridiculous idea that had formed inside him.

He was a practiced loner. Never had any intention of getting close to another human being.

But Cara Hamilton had broken through that barrier, at least for a while. She'd made it clear, though, that they were partners for this case, and now it was solved. The fact that they'd made love was incidental to her.

And if he loved her…?

Well, tough. It looked as though he'd have to shore that damned barrier right back up again.

He'd start by seeing her, talking to her, making it clear to his pitiful self that alone was the only way to be.

"HI, SHERIFF," Cara said when Mitch got out of the white Sheriff's Department vehicle he parked behind hers on the dusty shoulder to the narrow road. As he strode toward her, she held herself in check, admiring every plane of his face, the way his dark hair blew slightly askew in the soft breeze. Handsome. Aloof. Sexy.

Lawman lover, sang something deep inside her. "Cool it," she whispered to herself.

Only, she didn't cool it. She threw herself into his arms and pulled his head down to plant a big kiss on his lips. He didn't let go of her easily. In fact, the kiss lengthened until she was breathless.

But then he released her completely and stepped back. That told her a lot. He didn't want her.

But when had Cara Hamilton been one to give up?

"That was to thank you for saving my life," she said brightly.

"You're welcome."

"Let's walk along the road, okay, while I interview you?" She didn't have to tell him what she had in mind just yet. And if it failed? She'd deal with it then.

The questions she asked were probably ones he'd anticipated. She took notes on a pad of paper as they walked, and recorded it, too.

She'd have the recording of his voice to listen to in the future, if nothing else...

Concentrate! she ordered herself.

"So when I called to tell you I was going to the property the book said was once Shotgun Sally's, what did you do?" she asked.

He'd dropped everything else and set out at once after her. He spoke calmly, yet she thought she sensed something emotional when he described that aborted cell phone call she'd made. Caller ID had told him who'd phoned him, but he'd heard only muffled voices, then silence.

"I wondered if you'd been killed right then." Was his voice shaking? She would have to listen to this part of the tape later.

He then told her how he'd driven along the highway a little past where the two-lane road cut off, then parked and hiked in, weapon drawn. That was when he'd found all hell had broken loose.

Della Santoro was holding a gun on Cara. And Roger Rosales was trying to flee the scene.

Mitch told her that Roger now was spilling all he knew in exchange for immunity from prosecution. Mitch had supported his plea, since he'd fled instead of threatening Cara further. And though he'd been in on the conspiracy from the beginning, he'd not killed anyone himself.

"I doubt Roger knows it," Cara said, "but I've spoken with some representatives of Ranger Corporation back east. I've promised to do what I can to get the media to ease up on blaming the entire company, if they'll continue work on the theme park. I'd love to have something like that here, focusing on local legends, and it would be great for Mustang County's economy."

"You bet," Mitch agreed. She basked in his admiring grin.

She asked a few more questions. By then, they'd gone

a ways down the road and reached the top of a hill. The vista from here was great, displaying rolling landscape punctuated by groves of junipers and vast ranchland.

"This was where Shotgun Sally lived," Cara told Mitch.

She'd called Lindsey and e-mailed Kelly, who would be home soon, and told them both about all that had gone on—especially her new insight about Shotgun Sally and the location of her family's property. She couldn't wait to share it all with them in person.

That would happen with Lindsey the very next day. They'd scheduled lunch and a long catch-up chat, though Cara had hardly been able to keep her friend from dashing to her side right away to make sure she really was all right.

Cara really missed Lindsey and Kelly. Once Kelly was back from her honeymoon, they'd all spend more time together, she'd see to it.

Just like Shotgun Sally had said, "Men folk, well, we need 'em, of course, but gal friends are the real treasure."

Speaking of Sally...

"I've read the copy of that book carefully now," she continued, "and I'm convinced of it. Of course, I don't have an expert like Della to authenticate the book now, but it contains all the Sally legends I grew up with." She looked up at Mitch, who stood by her side. "I really admire that woman."

"So I gather," he said. His head turned as if he were scanning the landscape. "Do you think this is the area where she hid out with...what was his name? Zachary?"

"Her lawman lover? Absolutely." At her words, Mitch's gaze turned to her, and she thought she saw desire there mirroring what she felt for him.

She smiled and grabbed his hand. "Do you know what the legends say Sally did right around here?"

"No," Mitch said. He didn't pull his hand away. That was a good sign.

"There are conflicting stories, of course, as with most

things describing Sally, but the one I like best was that she survived the ambush by the guy who was trying to steal her family land. By then she'd already saved Zachary, who'd turned around and saved her.''

Mitch nodded.

''Well, Zachary was a bit of a loner, and he seemed inclined to let Sally get back to her wild investigative reporting while he did his best to save Mustang County from the bad guys. She, on the other hand, had fallen hard for him. And she wasn't the shy type. So, right here, she took his hand and said, 'Okay, Zachary, it's like this. You and me are going to get hitched and live right here together forever. We got a deal?'''

Of course, there was another story where she'd held a shotgun on Zachary to get him to marry her, but Cara considered that one exaggerated—and wrong. The Sally *she* loved wouldn't have threatened her lawman lover. Making demands—well, that was another story.

''And Zachary said yes,'' she finished.

''No kidding?'' Mitch's smile was amused. And something more? Surely that wasn't hope she saw there. ''Did they get hitched and live right here forever?''

''That's what I think.'' She took Mitch's other hand and held on tight, since what she was about to do could be the most foolish—and most wonderful—thing she had ever done in her life. ''You know I like to imitate Sally wherever I can.''

She sucked in her breath at Mitch's nod. He looked more solemn now. Did he know what was coming? Was he going to try to let her down gently, tell her where to go?

Time to find out.

''So,'' Cara said, wishing her voice sounded more certain. ''Here goes. Okay, Mitch, it's like this. You and me are going to get hitched and live right here together forever. We got a deal?''

She watched his eyes. They gentled, even as their

golden highlights glinted in the sun. "How about if we live in town, since this area's going to become a memorial to your Sally?"

Cara laughed aloud. "Was that a yes?"

"That was a yes." He bent down and gave her the best, hottest and most promising kiss yet.

A while later, her hand snugly in Mitch's, Cara looked down at the land where Shotgun Sally once had lived. *Thank you,* she said silently. *For everything.*

Four people had died, and that could never be fixed. Even so, Cara felt that, like Sally, she had helped to mete out the Texas law of the West on her own terms.

As Mitch and she turned to walk back to their cars, Cara thought she heard something. The breeze stirring the junipers?

As she looked into the thicket, her eyes widened.

Hallucination? Who knew?

But there was a shadowy buckskin-clad woman with a newspaper under one arm and the other tucked into that of a tall man wearing a hat and a badge. They smiled at Cara, waved, then disappeared into the woods.

* * * * *

Look for Linda O. Johnston's next book,
NOT A MOMENT TOO SOON,
in November 2004,
from Silhouette Intimate Moments!

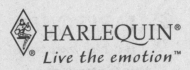

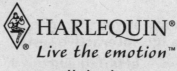

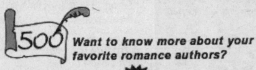